THE GOOD TOURIST AND THE LAUGHING CADAVER

Michael Gifkins is an Auckland writer whose short stories are collected in *After the Revolution and other stories*, *Summer is the Côte d'Azur* and *The Amphibians*. He was the Katherine Mansfield Fellow at Menton in the south of France while French frogmen were sinking the *Rainbow Warrior* in Auckland Harbour, an experience which he claims has provoked much of his travel and most of his fiction since.

Widely anthologised, his work has won a number of literary awards and he has held a Literary Fellowship at the University of Auckland and a Queen Elizabeth II Arts Council of New Zealand Scholarship in Letters. He works as a publishing consultant and literary agent in (he says) a shrinking world of increasingly fictional probability.

THE GOOD TOURIST AND THE LAUGHING CADAVER

Travel Stories from Australian
and New Zealand Writers

edited by Michael Gifkins

VINTAGE

Vintage New Zealand
Random House New Zealand Ltd
(An imprint of the Random House Group)

18 Poland Road
Glenfield
Auckland 10
NEW ZEALAND

Associated companies, branches and
representatives throughout the world.

First published 1993
© Introduction and this selection Michael Gifkins, 1993.
Copyright in the individual contributions in this collection
is acknowledged elsewhere in this book.

ISBN 1 86941 173 0

Printed in Australia
Cover photograph by Deborah Smith

To William Waterfield
at the Clos du Peyronnet
who travels by staying at home

CONTENTS

Introduction   ix

Shonagh Koea
The Woman Who Never Went Home   1

Lloyd Jones
Searching for Road Signs on an American Highway   8

Kate Grenville
Meeting the Folks   22

Fiona Farrell
OE   32

Barry Hill
Fires on the Beach   44

Frank Moorhouse
The Indian Bell Captain   60

Beverley Farmer
At the Airport   65

Michael Wilding
Kayf   75

Fay Zwicky
Stopover   95

Nick Hyde
Bang Bang   103

Owen Marshall
A View of Our Country   116

Elizabeth Jolley
The Libation   125

Anthony McCarten
The Bachelor   138

Peter Wells
The Good Tourist and the Laughing Cadaver   150

Debra Daley
A Bent Cucumber   163

Murray Bail
From Here to Timbuktu   175

Elizabeth Smither
In the Blue Mountains   182

Lily Brett
Chopin's Piano   193

Norman Bilbrough
Eel Dance   200

Tim Winton
Business   211

Biographical Notes   217

Acknowledgements   219

INTRODUCTION

AUSTRALIANS AND NEW ZEALANDERS are among the most travelled people of all time, with voyages of discovery rivalling in length and duration those of their colonising forebears and surpassing them in their frequency. But whereas twenty or even ten years ago travel was seen as a veritable rite of passage, a means of self-definition in relation to the world 'out there', today's traveller is more likely to be the impulse buyer of a cheap package deal from a beleaguered international carrier; and travel a form of leisure activity on a par with shopping, or with sport.

Some of the cultural icons of our present generation started out as travellers, but then neglected to come home. There is no doubt that until relatively recently, the opportunities for self-fulfilment and even fame were greater beyond antipodean shores, but it is possible too to feel an exile in one's own country, and that expatriation is, in essence, a way of giving form (to use Kate Jennings' phrase) to a state of mind. Something of the great divide implicit in swapping countries is to be found in Beverley Farmer's story, which captures the potential for heartbreak in the relentless perpetual motion of a traveller nominally at rest.

In a piece not collected here, Frank Moorhouse's 'Systematic Traveller' says: 'I think that at first I hoped that travel would chase away the overcast cloudiness of my own personal preoccupation. Instead, I found that I was deeper into preoccupation . . . Maybe in recollection — by story telling — the experience of travel comes alive.' There is no doubt that in the chronology of this collection, the early travellers — those who were going 'Home', and on sidetrips to discover the cultural heritage of Europe — found that the deep questions of self and of relationships (why am I here? what am I doing?) loomed larger in their travels than they ever would in Woollahra or Karori. But by externalising self-doubt into the fug of drug-induced awareness (and so by deliberately creating the condition of 'incapacitation and disorientation' that the Systematic Traveller sees as definitive of travel), it was the stragglers up the hippy trail of the early 1970s who were the vanguard of a newer generation of travellers. Europe was de-emphasised as the ultimate destination and geographical travel became a correlative for journeying in the head.

If the old imperialism had England at its centre, so America is the emotional coloniser of the world of present travel. There is an offshoot of travel writing which takes upon itself the task of damage-assessment and it is remarkable how many of the pieces submitted for this anthology (but not included) allowed a sense of outrage to overcome the story they had to tell.

'Travel broadens the mind' is an adage which must remain unproven. But the difference between the destination writers who do their travel pieces for the glossies and the writers of travel fiction whose work is included in this anthology is that given the continued shrinking of the global village, fiction writers can and do travel without ever leaving home. We might wonder where Owen Marshall gets his information, or doubt whether Anthony McCarten has ever travelled through Central Asia, but such questions do no more than assert the truth of that other adage, that 'travel is a state of mind'. Murray Bail's piece is reportage rather than fiction, but encapsulates deliciously the notion that our own countries are as strange and as distant to the inhabitants of far-flung destinations as theirs appear to us.

The stories in this anthology have been chosen with an eye to the kinds of travel experiences that are possible, and the different ways of writing about them. Some, like Anthony McCarten's, set out quite deliberately to play to the notion that travel involves great distances and exotic locations, peopled perhaps with 'Anthropophagi and men whose heads do grow beneath their shoulders'. For most of the other writers, their destinations seem equidistant from where they are seated at their desks. The true journey, perhaps, is in the writing. This is not to say that novelty, and difference, and movement, are not important and compelling components of writing about travel. Rather, it suggests to me that these things are even more important to the limitless world of fiction, in which travel may play a part.

I would like to have included travel writing from Maori and from Aboriginal writers, the original inhabitants of our two countries. That I was unable to unearth or to commission anything suitable (that is, dealing with overseas destinations) is perhaps worthy of a separate essay.

Beyond providing material for bedtime reading (and perhaps for dreaming), the present anthology has the twin purpose of introducing readers on both sides of the Tasman to writers with whom they may not be familiar. Now that passports are required for passage between our countries, the experience may prove to be a kind of travel in itself.

Michael Gifkins
Auckland, New Zealand

SHONAGH KOEA

THE WOMAN WHO NEVER
WENT HOME

THE MAN IN the chamois-leather shirt was sitting on a high bar-stool, whisky on the rocks in hand, on the evening of her second day at the hotel. He was looking out over the swimming pool with its cascades of bougainvillea.

The likeness was so extraordinary that she dropped her bag, and all the impedimenta women take to a tropical beach rolled out on to the floor.

The little dark-eyed maid who tended the foyer rushed forward to pick up the hairbrush, the lipstick that rolled under the receptionist's desk, the black bikini.

Was Madame tired? Had the sun been too much for Madame? Catherine waved her sunhat lazily at the maid and the porter and told them Madame was merely careless. Calm and clear as usual, her voice surprised her.

Halfway up the stairs she changed her mind and went slowly down again, taking now the left fork at the landing, the route that led to the mirrored Art Deco bar with its basket chairs, the lithe contemptuous barman and the man in chamois leather who looked almost exactly like the man she remembered so well, a man who had been dead for ten years.

The barman stood behind his counter from mid-afternoon each day, shuttered eyes removing from his tired gaze the droves of Japanese tourists who photographed each other in exactly duplicated attitudes with airs of terrified excitement, and the other travellers who arrived, en masse, by bus from the airport.

They all carried plastic carry-alls emblazoned with the names of tour companies. Go-Along Tours, Best Tours, Sunset Tours (for the aged) had all passed through in the last two days. They came to see life, Catherine supposed, though if they had looked round instead of at each other they would have seen only the contempt of the sinuous barman.

'Won't you be bored?' her friends had asked before she left home. 'Fancy staying in Noumea for three whole weeks all on your own. Whatever will you do?'

She told them she would look at things and they gave her up as ridiculous. At eighteen she had been a wild, shy, ridiculous creature and had not altered greatly in twenty years. She had merely become more practised at it and more accomplished at hiding her tendencies.

But here indeed was something to look at, and like an amputee who thoughtfully fingers the stump of a limb in unguarded moments she charted a course for the mirrored bar where the man in chamois sat so silently staring into his drink.

Almost on the parquet now, nearly at the bar entrance, her feet faltered on the last stair and she gave a scream, pointing to an ornamental fish-pool built into the wall. An enormous goldfish floated on its surface, eyes open, stomach distended, dead and trailing a line of glutinous slime from its mouth.

The lady who looked after the gift shop by the reception desk rushed up, forgetting for a moment her look of ceaseless allure. The fish did not fool those sharp French eyes that divined the needs of the customers so well — French perfume and handbags displayed on a velvet cloth and other, less presentable things underneath the counter. She briskly tapped the glass and the old trickster fish rolled lazily over, swam again.

The maid from the foyer, the porter and the lady from the gift shop all screamed with laughter. Madame was so droll.

If she had banged a drum her arrival in the bar could not have been more noticeable but the man in chamois still sat on the bar-stool, self-contained and uncomprehending, as she slipped onto the stool beside him.

He was not as tall as the other had been but he had the same beautiful hands that now cupped his drink. From the toes of his shabby shoes of Spanish leather to his hair which grew in the same careless way he was almost an exact duplicate except that his eyes were the wrong colour. She studied his reflection minutely.

He and the barman began to talk with the easy familiarity of long acquaintance. She could not understand a word of their rapid French, though his voice was soft and pleased her.

The barman turned sharply towards her and she ordered a glass of mineral water, his palpitating disdain now becoming almost a living thing like a black cat with golden eyes sitting on the counter.

There seemed an air of intimacy about them as they talked. Perhaps they spoke of the government or racehorses, she could not tell. When the flush of early evening customers arrived the barman had to go elsewhere, tossing a few words over his shoulder when he could.

The man in the leather shirt settled on the stool, melancholy and unmoving. He drank with no hurry but with a dedicated lack of satisfaction. As soon as one drink was finished the barman, with no bidding, brought another the same in a fresh glass.

The sudden tropical night was now deeply upon everything. It seemed the only world was that in the little bar. Dinner was looming up and people began to consult the menu.

'I'm having frog's legs.'

'Mummy, David says he's having frog's legs.'

'Alec, will you speak to David and tell him he's not having frog's legs.'

It was the time of school holidays and the hotel was riddled with bold, charmless offspring who bleated loudly about the pleasures of Bondi, Wellington or Hornby.

Presently the man rose and, speaking sharply but indulgently to the barman, who smiled for the first time, strode away through the geranium-scented night. The barman wrote on a pad and it was a moment before she realised the bill had been chalked up. He had not paid.

The street outside seemed deserted. Where the road forked three ways the street-lamps shone only on empty pavements, shuttered windows and the softness of flowers. He had gone completely and, suddenly bereft, she wandered back into the hotel with distant laughter from unknown doorways echoing in her ears.

Now at last the stairs could claim a triumph, for they claimed her completely this time, a full three flights. Alone, she dined in her room on an orange and a piece pulled from a French loaf and wondered where he came from. What was the reason for his air of past splendour?

Perplexed, she sat all the next day beside the swimming pool like a pensive mushroom, dressed in the strapless black bathing-suit purchased in Honolulu the previous year and screened from other bathers by the immense size of her Rarotonga sunhat of two years ago.

Before the rising scents of early evening had even slightly blemished the later afternoon she was waiting in the foyer, casually flicking over the pages of a magazine and wearing a diamond horseshoe round her neck for luck. Would he come again?

A dozen times she looked up the forking road and then set off to walk the maze of streets, hoping to see him emerge from a flowery gateway, but although she passed along many blocks there was never a sight of the magical one she sought.

After this futile excursion she saw him again, sitting on the same bar-stool with the familiar drink in his hand.

His eyes contained a sudden recognition or rebuff, she could not tell which so she bolted away, in her wild shy way, into the dining-room.

He lapsed once more into a sort of melancholy after he finished his talk of politics or women with the barman. With the same shouted exchange over the bill he disappeared abruptly into the night as the crowd thickened and she finished wasting some chicken and strawberries.

He would come again, she knew that now, and a sense of girlish skittishness came over her as though she had beaten death and destruction.

The following day she click-clacked into the bar as soon as it opened wearing a pair of French sandals with very high heels, a bikini made of black silk chrysanthemums and the large sunhat. Secrecy did not interest her. It was simply that she lacked the courage to carry out her quixotic plan and felt a need to boldly expose herself, thus becoming bold enough to act. Her shyness she carried with her, about the level of the third rib, and almost bent over to accommodate its swelling size.

The barman was alone and without preamble she began. The carefully rehearsed sentences, gleaned from her English-French dictionary the previous evening, fell easily from her lips.

The Monsieur who sat every evening on this very stool, she said, and with temerity actually perched herself upon it and sat there swinging her legs. This Monsieur was the exact image of someone who had been dead for ten years. The barman, tea-towel discarded now, looked at the rings she still wore from habit and placed his hand on his heart.

No, she said, it was another one, not her husband. Her grief, she told him, had become unresolved and she bore it with her always like a silver plate in her head. She had not cried when he died. She had gone on calmly cutting star shapes out of shortbread and had said, callously, 'Dead? Who? What a sad accident.'

All this she told the barman in her halting French and he listened quietly with his hand on his heart. It was surprisingly easy to tell him what she had told no other and she thought that the reason was her use of another language. The words were strangers to her.

Nothing was required from the Monsieur, she told the barman. The pleasure of looking at that face was sufficient. But Monsieur, for the sake of his face, must not owe money anywhere and Madame would secretly pay his bill. He must never know who did this.

With one hand still on his heart the barman took her money with the other, quickly. They arranged for the bar bill to be sent to her room each evening on a tray and thus their conspiracy began and flourished.

Warned by the recognition in his eyes, she widely skirted the bar area that evening and chose a shadowed seat behind a trellis for her observation of the man in chamois. His reflection was better value there because she could not only see it with a limpid clarity, it was mirrored in another glass. The price of anonymity in the shadows was a double image, a bargain.

An insomniac for years, she now fell at night into a gentle sleep which came upon her swiftly, as if she were a small falcon that rode on a prince's arm and had a velvet cover thrown over her head.

Waiting each day for evening, she spent her time on the beach observing crop-headed boys in military uniforms who watched sleek, exquisite girls. Even a deliberate seeker of evil could find no offence in their miniscule nakedness, she thought. Tourists lolled about in vile imitations of what they saw, the benedictions of the sand never covering the folds of flesh. But they were happy, Catherine told herself, and their happiness was new and topical. Her sudden content was an old illicit enchantment, remembered from days past.

Each evening, as he rose to leave, the barman showed the man in the leather shirt the clear page on the pad. At first the man laughed in a mocking way and looked round the room with a sneer that the face she knew so well never wore in the lifetime she recollected. His privacy remained inviolate and his suspicion was followed by puzzlement. Each evening he walked away through the double doors with his hand upon his face, perplexed. She supposed the barman had told him of the mysterious likeness.

The barman warmed a little towards her now but he volunteered no information about the man in leather and she was too proud to ask for any. As for the man himself, unruffled, self-contained, an enigma, he spoke to no one but a black and white dog which walked through the bar each evening and the sinuous barman who remained the custodian of all secrets and the broadcaster of none.

She used to look for him each evening, threading her way through the blocks of houses round the hotel, shrilled at by resident poodles and chihuahuas whose *Chien Méchant* notices advertised only their toy ferocity.

He was always sitting on the same bar-stool when she returned, appearing from the entrance she never found.

The daily bill grew inexorably smaller. He began to look round with a veiled curiosity.

Night after night his enveloping thoughtful gaze took in the plump Australian lady who favoured red and black spots, the old twins in pink cardigans, the sharp little blonde in a mauve velvet tracksuit, the myriad of travellers who came and went.

There were only three days left of her holiday, so filled with her own invented charming business, when she saw him glance at her shadowy reflection in a mirror. He had never before conquered the trellis wall behind the roses.

She was dressed in her favourite grey, with a silver rope belt twisted round her waist and silver sandals that tied in bows like wings at her ankles. One of the Australians had just said to her, 'You're lucky you're so thin.' Indifferent, she turned away and met the eyes that were the wrong colour in the mirror, staring him out with what she hoped was an unseeing vagueness.

A gypsy violinist in a black velvet bolero and sleeves of ruffled silk came the following evening and played sad endless tunes.

Her usual fruitless search of the streets was accomplished swiftly so that she could be back earlier than usual. It was, she knew, an absurd contradiction.

She sped along, with purpose now, hardly noticing the chic that made the smallest garden charming. The spills of miniature lettuces growing in terracotta pots beside secret, tiled doorways did not interest her, nor did her favourite garden, the one with the ornamental cast-iron wheelbarrow mounded with begonias and the scarlet blooms of impatiens.

He was at the bar, in residence as she called it grandly and wryly to herself, when she returned.

The melancholy climbing notes of the violin rose as the man in chamois walked towards her secret trellised perch among the roses.

'Madame,' he said, 'you remind me so vividly of someone I knew once in Singapore. In 1961.'

She had never been to Singapore, she told him. In 1961 she was aged eighteen, and under her narrow bed in an unpalatable boarding-house she kept a green cardboard suitcase filled with a few shreds of clothing and linen, purchased at sales, in preparation for a marriage as unpalatable as that boarding-house but more binding than its porridge.

He digested this piece of startling conversation for a moment, rocking back on his heels, and then he roared with laughter.

The other one had been exactly the same, she thought. She had always been able to make him laugh and that was how it had all begun.

LLOYD JONES

SEARCHING FOR ROAD SIGNS ON AN AMERICAN HIGHWAY

SOMETIMES THE BUS will pull off an exit ramp and locate a small hamlet among the trees and then, sometimes, we will see something we like.

Two days ago we wheeled into a town which made an immediate claim. Already we were quite a bit south of where we had left our children with their grandparents. The leaves hadn't yet turned and at midday people in this town of which I speak wandered about in shirt sleeves. A lovely sleepy quality hung about the square. Old men sat playing draughts. A large bookshop flopped onto the street with a long wooden verandah for idling. Its shingle read 'booksmith' and I liked the sound of that, of what it said about liking books and the careful mix of the very new with the old, and I felt pretty sure old bound copies of Emerson wouldn't be too far away from Susan Issacs and the *New York Times Book Review* 'bear in mind' list.

Holly nodded approvingly at what she saw out the window.

'Tim?' she said, and that time I caught it, a fountain, but this and that as various features came by.

'Tim,' she kept saying, stepping it up now as if we had things to mark off on an inventory spread on our laps. Things such as the noticeable absence of video stores; a front door left open back there, children on bikes, a kite wrapped in the pylons. I know this makes us sound as though we yearn for something out of Norman Rockwell, a place with the flag out on front lawns and air that is thick with homebaking. And yet we are not like that at all. No. All the same this place, Douglastown, was definitely shaping up to be our town. We were just about to, any moment then, I swear, jump off the bus and walk into a realtor's office when I saw a pickup pull into an Amco station. A deer was slumped in the back. I watched its killers, two unshaven men, get cigarettes from a machine and that was that. Sorry, but there was no way I was going to live in a place that could tolerate a shot deer oozing blood at a petrol stop. I wouldn't want my kids to get comfortable and familiar with such a thing. I don't think I could live with a boy cleaning his gun in his bedroom at night.

Holly was disappointed. Angry that a shot deer should come between this near picture-perfect town and us.

She closed her eyes and her head tilted back against the headrest. We didn't have much to say to each other and besides, it has been all said before.

I am too picky. No, make that 'far too picky'. She says I am too quick to judge. She hasn't said it but I know she is thinking, 'A shot deer, for godsakes!' Her eyes are closed as I said earlier, but her quiet fury is there, constrained by the even rise and fall of her chest. This is not an easy thing. It would be easier if we just threw a dart at a map of New York State.

A day later, then, and we arrived at Marion. The entire bus-load, including me and Holly, disembarked. Marion was not on our shopping list. It was just somewhere to stop and take a compass reading. We knew nothing about it and, although an asterisk on the map suggested additional information, we thought no more about it than as a place where we would take time out to stretch our legs.

Outside the bus depot an elderly man in blue overalls and long bony fingers stood in our way with a sign that read Pioneer Land.

'This way, ma'am,' he said, as if he had been expecting us.

'It's that asterisk thing,' Holly said, and I asked the old man, 'Are all these people headed out to Pioneer Land?'

'This here is Marion,' he said, and in his watery blue eyes I saw a quiet backwater still in shock from the recent arrival of Pioneer Land.

'Well, I don't know what else we're going to do here,' said Holly, and fifteen minutes later we were in a small minibus climbing the hills above Marion. The other passengers, mostly kids with their parents, talked excitedly of what they were going to do at Pioneer Land.

Holly, chewing gum to freshen her mouth, said she was going to shoot something. She thought she might shoot some rabbits.

9

Tin rabbits. And a small boy behind us who overheard, tapped Holly on the shoulder and said she could shoot buffalo if she wants. They have buffalo up there.

Well, we were above Marion now; and here, the hills had passed into corporate hands. Along the roadside a series of huge banners promoted the Pioneer Land activities. Roller-coaster rides. Wild river rafting. Shooting.

Where the bus pulled up we filed off to the sound of gun shots behind a tall iron fence. The bus driver took our tickets. 'Thank you, sir, ma'am . . .' Then another old-timer who, aside from his fur trapper's clothing, could pass for the twin brother of the barber back in Marion, pointed us in the right direction with the barrel of his gun. 'C'mon along, folks. Just head on up through the gates up yonder.' He said to Holly, 'You must be one of Ma Wilson's new gals.' Holly stopped the gum in her cheek.

'Excuse me,' she said, and the old trapper chuckled and brushed past.

'Jesus, Tim, did you hear what he said . . . Jesus . . .' But Holly's indignation lifted and spirited away the moment we entered Main Street, Little Falls.

The doors to a saloon swung open and a waiter with a cowboy hat and holster carried out a tray of Budweisers to a family seated at a café table. Further up the street a franchise senorita ladled beans and chopped bacon from a huge authentic-looking clay pot.

Outside the saloon a man seated high on a stage called down to Holly to ask if we were booked to head out West. 'Two minutes and we're outa here,' he said.

The people drinking Budweisers were arguing amongst themselves. A woman was saying that of all the things she wanted to do before she came to Pioneer Land the only thing she seriously had in mind to do was to be on that stagecoach. The way she said this it was clear that she was a little drunk, but equally, I could see she was not going anywhere. Her husband was leaning back in his chair with a Bud touching his lips and anyone could see there was nowhere else in the world he would rather be at that moment than in Little Falls. Across the street we met the still, lifeless gaze of elderly couples sipping on long pink drinks. They had brought their coupons up from Marion to get among the discounted margaritas — and I think that as much as anything on show made us want to get out of town.

'One minute,' called down the stage driver. Then he leant down to say that we were to get our tickets from the sheriff. A burly man who reminded me of Hoss in *Bonanza* asked whether Holly or I had a heart condition, or suffered from diabetes or any nervous disability.

Apparently where we were headed the land was still to be properly broken in.

'As many Indians as coyote,' he said, then he called up to the stage driver, a man he called Hank, and told him to fit me with 'a piece'.

A few minutes later, Hank shouted out something, then he flicked his whip over the backs of the horses and we creaked forward. The woman in the café gave a sad wave up to Holly. 'Bye for now.' And I noticed Holly eyeing the woman's untouched gherkin and potato chips.

Something about Hank, his deaf ears perhaps. Anyway he reminded me of the old fella back in Marion and the fur trapper who greeted us off the bus outside the gates. I wondered if they were all in this together and each with a memory of the other as the town's barber and plumber, and I could easily be persuaded that the fur trapper once worked for the US Postal Service. Nothing would surprise me.

Hank spat a neat spit ball out my side as we left Little Falls. He seemed happier to talk to his horses — Gertie and Rose-Beth. But soon he decided that he had something to say and back-heeled a small black box resting underneath the seat. He said, in the event of us running into Indians and, should anything happen to himself, then we were to open the little black box.

'I want to make that clear,' he said. 'Do not wander off on your own without first consulting the maps in the box.'

Weary from three days travelling in buses I don't think either of us gave too much thought to Indians or to the fact that we were headed out West.

Soon we came to a rise and behind us, blinking in the hard sunlight, were the flat roofs of Little Falls. Ahead of us lay an empty valley where the wind stirred dark trails through the tall, shimmering prairie grass. Hank lay on the reins and took a moment to rest the horses. It was a beautiful sight. Holly took a great mouthful of air.

'Look back to where we've come,' she said, and there was Little Falls and beyond, the tan and green plain of America lying belly-up in the Pacific — and by golly my face with more hair and wider-eyed pushed against the window of the airport bus as the territory suddenly changed from marble hotel foyers and Hispanics in grey uniforms with red sashes to boarded-up windows; underneath which, half-lit neon offered 'transient accommodation' at $8 a night or $32 for a week; deros leant in doorways sucking on bottles in brown paper bags; the graffiti were in Spanish and young Hispanic toughs in black trousers and kung fu slippers gathered around the pride of Detroit; here, the buildings were bedecked with fire escapes, and men in white singlets like still vultures perched high in the leafless window sills had grinned down at the line I had crossed which, at the time, I hadn't appreciated as a point of departure.

Holly was saying of the prairie: 'This is just so unexpected.'

I asked her now what it was that the man in Little Falls had said about Indians. And she looked at me as though I was being ridiculous.

'Will you please just look around you. Take it in,' she said, and she closed her eyes to inhale it.

Hank finished squinting at the empty prairie. He was uneasy about something. Hank was definitely uneasy. A few minutes later he felt around his clothing for a single cartridge which he got loaded into his shotgun. I felt I should be doing the same. My hand was on my holster but without so much as a glance my way Hank said it was already loaded.

'Shoot only when I say,' Hank said. 'Got that?'

'Yes, sir.'

'What was that?' asked Holly. 'Tim?' she said.

I said everything was okay. I said Hank was just being cautious.

'You people,' said Hank. 'You people think it's just a matter of finding a place with a pleasant view and building a homestead and getting some seed down before the first snow.' He said this, and sent a spit ball out Holly's side. Then he sang out to the horses,

Gertie and Rose-Beth, and we were on our way again, dropping down the hillside away from the lunch smells of Little Falls to where the wind smelt of a place uninhabited.

We promised Holly's parents that we would be back by the end of the week with news of a town which presumably has everything we are looking for, and I know Holly's father will be interested, very interested, to hear about the school district and the racial mix of the neighbourhood. For the last three days I have pictured him standing in the hall of his house with his fidgety hands in his trouser pockets and his chin in the air.

We left one town because our house was just two streets off the boundary of a reputable school district. At the same time Max and Helena were three years and eighteen months and talk of school districts did not feel to be of pressing importance. Holly felt the same way I did and I think her father's obsessive interest in this matter just drove us further out on a limb. It mattered, of course it did, but what I'm saying here is that Holly's father just wouldn't leave the subject alone. He said I couldn't possibly understand what he was on about because I hadn't grown up in this country. Holly, he felt, should have known better — and to underline his point Mr Franks would deliberately drive five or ten minutes out of his way so he could take us through the innercity slums to jab his thumb at the passing scenes of desolate public housing and kids playing in the rubble and within view of the crack dealers. Holly's father would start muttering behind the wheel. 'Say "hi" to Max and Helena's playmates.' And these mystified slum kids would stare back at Mr Franks. One or two of them might wave back, then Holly's mother would say something stern to Mr Franks and put a stop to it.

What could you say to this kind of stunt? I would pretend to be amused but too much tolerance on my part was sometimes taken to be patronising and then Mr Franks would be pushed to mentioning the war. Guadalcanal. Rabaul. The cruelty of the Japs. The names of his friends killed beside him and in virtually the same breath we would be back to the subject of where Holly and I lived, and if it came down to recognising that where we lived was a war zone then why the hell didn't I give up teaching remedial reading to blacks and save my own skin?

But this was the life, all right, and now down among the prairie grass we came upon the comforting sight of the rutted wheel tracks of Hank's previous journeys. It was warm and quiet and by now we had gotten used to Hank's silences. Hank held onto the reins in one hand and with his other drew a grassblade through his teeth. Whatever he had sniffed in the air back up on the ridge had failed to come to anything and some of Hank's ease had worn off on Holly. I could see her taking fresh stock of the prairie. The way her mouth drew a calculating line and, here and there, she was picturing a small cottage, a garden, and swings for Max and Helena. She rested back on her hands and threw her head back.

At some point, Holly decided Hank had had enough silence and she asked him what he had done before driving the stage.

'Mule skinner for a time. This and that,' he said. 'Scouted for Capt' Hurley of the Thirty-First . . .'

'Was that in Europe or Korea?' asked Holly, and Hank replied — 'Shiloh, and thereabouts,' which was when I checked with Hank as to the year we were in and without raising more than half an eyelid, he said, 'Eighteen hundred and sixty-four.'

'Oh I get it. I get it now,' Holly said happily.

Then she explained to Hank that she had meant the here and now, in Marion, what did he do before the Corporation set up Pioneer Land?

'Marion, ma'am?' — a little mystified — 'Little Falls is where I herald.'

Holly nodded her head with pleasure, as if to say she wasn't going to do or say anything to spoil the game.

'Okay then,' she said. 'Okay. Have it your own way. The year is eighteen hundred and sixty-four.' I can handle it, is what she meant. And behind Hank's back she winked at me.

'I don't see that it's something to argue about,' he grumbled, and he went back to drawing that blade of grass through his teeth.

A little further on, for the hell of it, Holly let go a wild Indian whoop which gave Hank a terrible start. He pulled on the reins and stalled Gertie and Rose-Beth. Next, he grabbed his shotgun and his eyes peeled back every strand of prairie grass. A long minute passed before he was satisfied and only then did Hank turn to deal with Holly. 'Of all the stupid stunts I've seen. I'd a thought even squatters'd more brains than that.'

The shotgun was stood back between his legs and gently Hank pulled on the reins.

'Gawn Gert. Rose-Beth. Gawn now,' he called.

Holly put her head on one side which is her wont whenever she wants to be exact about something. And after a pause she said to Hank — 'Is that what you think we are? Squatters?'

'All I know,' he said, 'is that you are leaving one place and going somewhere else. You're headed out West, right? The rest is your own business.'

'Squatters. Jesus,' she said. 'I don't think I like that. No sir.' She shook her head and tried to engage me behind Hank's back.

But I was not about to be drawn into an argument over our status with a make-believe stagecoach driver.

I closed my eyes and felt the sun spread over my face like warm fingertips and listened to the opinionated crows circling and wheeling overhead. At one point I heard a match struck followed by Hank's terse request to Holly that she not smoke which, so far, was the closest brush to revealing the corporate man underneath the skin of the stage driver.

Then, nothing. Until I heard what sounded like a stone landing in thick mud — a sort of 'plock' sound — followed by Holly's shriek.

The next thing . . . the next thing is this. An arrow struck Hank's chest. The quiver end shook like a nervous dog's prick. Then Hank slumped forward.

'Tim?' Holly said, and when I was slow responding she shouted — 'The reins! Get the reins!' This was something Holly could equally have done but I got the reins freed from Hank's hands and Gert and Rose-Beth plodded on without any sign of disturbance.

The noise was terrific. A dozen Indians on horseback were circling our coach, whooping and waving tomahawks. Holly shouted at Rose-Beth and Gert to go faster. Then she shouted at me, 'For chrissakes, Tim!' as a brave hauled alongside the coach and balancing skilfully on the mane of his horse, stepped lightly aboard the coach. He grabbed Holly by the hair. In his other hand a clasp knife. Holly said 'Tim?' Her eyes were hardboiled with panic, but her voice — good old Hol' — remained composed. 'Tim?' she said, her way of reminding me.

The gun. Well, I had to drop the reins and get the thing unholstered. Finally I got everything organised and levelled the short barrel. I pulled the trigger and there came that 'plock' sound again. A red mess oozed from the brave's forehead and he toppled off the stage. Holly made a grab for the shotgun. A couple of Indians were trying to unharness Gert and Rose-Beth, but the gun wouldn't work for her. She shook it and banged it against the stage.

It was hopeless. Gert and Rose-Beth, meanwhile, trotted after the Indians. 'Oh Jesus,' Holly said, and the next thing she tossed the shotgun overboard and without a word leapt from the coach. I showed about as much thought and blindly followed suit. Both of us got to our feet about the same time. I took a moment to brush some grass from my cords. I was about to ask Holly if she was all right. But she broke away from my hands and pushed ahead. 'Hey. Wait a moment,' I said. Then the both of us were pushing through the long grass which clutched and clawed at our faces and throats. I was running after my wife more than I was fleeing the Indians. I tried to call to her to slow down. But she didn't hear. She had only the one thing in mind. And worse than the prairie grass tearing at my face, a whole lot worse in fact, it occurred to me that Holly had not once looked back to check that I was following. She was running for her own life is what I'm getting at — her pointed shoulders driven with the one thing in mind.

Finally, we lost our footing, and I took to ground this prairie image of familial love — the bodies of Max, Helena, myself and Holly struck down by arrows — in a pile of unselfish limbs.

Above the prairie grass the war cries looped the air. Holly had her face pushed into the earth. For a moment I did actually wonder if I had been shot.

Holly reached out and took hold of my hand. She raised her face from the dirt and surprised me with a brilliant smile. She said — 'Tim, you shot that Indian. You got him in the head, I think.

He had me and you shot him.'

She said, 'He just cartwheeled off the coach.'

Then, after a brief pause, she recalled, 'When that arrow hit Hank he didn't say anything. It was like a rebuttal he just took quietly — like being turned away from a restaurant. He didn't say "peep".'

I was trying to remember whether or not I had taken aim. I preferred to think that I had shot blindly.

'Survival instinct. Snap judgment,' said Holly, and when I looked in to her eyes I was appalled to find the selfsame quality of calm I remember as having flooded Mr Franks' expression when told of our plans to move. He had patted my shoulder and nodded soberly and I was supposed to think that I had justified his faith in me, that sooner or later I would come around to his way of thinking. But what kind of doubts in Holly's mind, I wonder, could I have possibly acquitted by shooting an Indian brave?

'The black box,' she now remembered. 'Hank said . . .'

But I had turned my head away to search for crows in the deepening blue Montana skies. We were in New York State, of course, but by Montana you know what I mean.

I watched as Holly straightened at the knees and rose until the grass was up to her neck and I reached for the Indians' view of this bob of dark hair floating on a yellow sea. 'Tim,' she said. 'Why are you looking at me like that?'

Then she reported down to me. 'They've gone. The bastards have taken the horses.'

'What about Hank?'

'I can't tell. No,' she said, stretching. 'I can't see.'

We walked for some time in the direction of the hills closest but without coming across the wagon tracks. Once I actually thought I heard gunshots and told Holly to hold still. We waited. Nothing came of it and we carried on. Me in the lead and Holly trailing in my footsteps.

Perhaps this wasn't the time or place to have brought it up, and I said as much to Holly. 'You probably don't want to hear this,' I began.

'Yes,' she said.

'When you ran from the stage . . . You didn't once look back.'

'Excuse me?' she said, like she had no idea as to what I was on about.

'Well, Holly, for chrissakes, did you even pause to ask yourself whether I was okay? I could have been carrying an arrow in my leg. Anything. Anything!' I said.

'Tim,' she said, with a slow shake of her head, and I knew what that was supposed to convey. That shake of the head. The nonplussed look. But she definitely knew what I was on about. No question. She definitely knew.

'My God,' she said again, and after that we walked along in silence.

It must have been a good forty minutes before we reached higher ground. We still weren't talking much, other than to comment on the failing light which was cause for concern.

We came across an old log and Holly balanced on its highest end. She made binoculars of her hands and stared back in the direction we had come.

'There's Hank!' she said.

Holly stepped down and I took her place on the log. Sure enough, Hank and the Indians had returned to the stage. I could see Hank scanning the prairie, like Custer, his hands placed on his hips. One of the braves handed him the shotgun and Hank discharged it with the barrel pointed skyward. I wondered why the brave hadn't discharged it himself and whether it had to do with employee rules and Hank holding rank, and so forth. My hand rested on my empty holster. Had I not lost my own gun I would have responded in kind and this, of course, was what Hank and the Indians were waiting for. They let a minute pass, then one of the Indians reached under his saddle blanket for what appeared to be a mobile phone.

We watched as the Indians passed cigarettes amongst themselves. We were out of earshot of one another. It felt oddly confusing to admit that the danger had indeed passed — and yet not feel any the more secure.

I said to Holly, 'You think I'm being unreasonable?'

Holly lay her head to one side. 'You can ask what we should

have done,' she said, with special emphasis on the 'we'. 'You might even ask yourself why we gave up the city. You could ask yourself a lot of things.' She said this, and then she said she wasn't prepared to argue out here on the prairie where, she said, she wasn't sure whether I was complaining about events and behaviour pertaining to 1864 or the here and now. She wasn't prepared to say another word until we had gotten back to Marion and she had time to think, eat something, and have a good long drink.

In the distance Hank fired off another round.

'Hank,' I said, and we pushed on through the tall grass. Our direction was up — but anything more than that was lost to us.

It was noticeably colder now. Bath time back at Holly's parents' house. We had called every night to talk to Max and Helena. I wondered if we would be anywhere near a phone this evening. I thought about raising this with Holly — knowing it would upset her.

'Shush,' she said, and we listened to a familiar voice quite near.

'Gawn Gert. Gawn Rose-Beth.'

The tall grass suddenly gave on to the trail and climbing ahead we saw the sideways shift of the stage making slow work of it up the hillside.

Over our shoulder the skies melted to a bruising purple and a shooting star ran for the cover of Little Falls.

I don't know where the Indians had gotten to, but we were within sight of the rise when we heard the high whine of an engine and within surprisingly short time, a bright red four-wheel-drive rose over the hilltop.

The driver wore a Pioneer Land cap. The first thing he said to us was to ask for our tickets. He just wanted to make sure we were the ones with Hank when attacked by Indians and not 'tourists' out on a walk from Little Falls.

We climbed inside the vehicle and rested our feet on a carpet of squashed styrofoam coffee cups. There was an appealing smell of old jerseys and sandwich wrapping paper, which reminded me how close we had come to spending a night out on the prairie.

On a mobile phone the driver reported back to town that we had been located. He didn't have much else to say. He wasn't the slightest bit curious to learn how it had happened that we lost

Hank and the stagecoach. Holly went to thank him but he wasn't interested in that either. I had the feeling that he had been forced to drift into unpaid overtime.

He did say that we had missed the last bus back to Marion. He let that sink in and then when he felt the time was right he added that we could easily hitch a lift. Most of the Pioneer Land employees, he said, lived in Marion.

At the top of the hill there was the gladdening sight of Little Falls and in no time at all we were back on Main Street. The crowds of earlier in the afternoon had left. Outside the cafés, chairs sat upside down on tables. It was hard to believe that this town had a bright future starting over again tomorrow.

A blue van was departing the Pioneer Land gates, so we hurried to catch up and pull alongside. Once again Holly thanked the driver. This time he nodded, glanced at his watch and no sooner were we out the door than he reversed at high speed.

The driver of the blue van got out and hauled back the door — and there was Hank in collar and tie and a sports jacket, and with four or five Indians, all drinking from beer cans.

Hank had only the slightest nod for us. Then he said something to one of the Indians and a couple of beers were found for me and Holly.

On the tight bends the van crunched me, Holly and the Indians shoulder to shoulder. The Indian I had shot from the stagecoach was reading aloud from the *New York Post*. He was reading for Hank's benefit, I believe. 'Mets 2, Padres 4,' he said, and Hank said gloomily over his stiff grey moustache, 'That figures.' It was dark now, and every so often the top of the van brushed with an unseen lower bough leaning out from the roadside trees and all of us in the van ducked our heads for the time the branch scraped the ceiling. We couldn't help ourselves and there was no telling when the next stroke in the dark would arrive. One of the Indians asked Hank for the time. Then he leant forward and tapped the driver on the shoulder, 'Happy Hour at Lansing's.' After that, we took the corners at speed and the Indian I had sent reeling, in my own mind perhaps a dozen times, dropped a hand on to my knee to steady himself. We had left behind the corporate roadsigns pointing the way to Pioneer Land. We were nearly at

Marion now — we passed a gas station with a sign that read 'Happy Birthday, Carol' and a kid with one foot up on a skateboard waved — and then Hank turned around to ask the question which Holly and I had ourselves avoided ever since the run-in with the Indians on the prairie.

'Where to now for you folks?' he said.

KATE GRENVILLE

MEETING THE FOLKS

FRANÇOIS IS VERY handsome although he giggles too much.
His brown eyes bulge a little as he stares at me, and his fingers
tremble as he talks. He's a brilliant physicist and he's only twenty-
eight. He's spent the flirting years locked away in a dark room
with his molecules, but he's making up for lost time now.

Cautiously, I rehearse the letters home. Hi everybody, guess
what. I'm living with a good-looking Frenchman. The world's
at his feet. He taught at Stanford and his English is perfect. He's
every girl's dream come true.

When he asks me to meet his family my heart goes pitter-pat.

— You will meet my mother. I'm sure you'll like her.

He thinks, and adds:

— She has aristocratic blood. The château has been in her family
for hundreds of years.

A château! What will I wear?

— She can be a little difficult, he says.

He smiles his fixed smile.

— If she doesn't like people she can be a little harsh. She is very
highly strung. But she has a heart of gold.

I nod and try to look confident.

— I am the youngest son and the only one not married. I am
her baby, you know? And she hopes I do not marry just yet.

He stares at me and says rather loudly:

— But I do what I want. Not what she wants.

He continues to stare at me and I feel the daydreams jostling
in the wings. They make such a lovely couple. Two of the most
adorable kids you can imagine and very clever of course.

— Does your family speak English?

— Not my father. My mother, yes, but she prefers not to. She
thinks she does not speak very well so she prefers not.

I wish I'd been working at my French a bit harder.

The train takes a long while to get to the town near the château. Usually François talks about himself when we're alone together, or tells me about physics. Today, though, all the way down in the train he asks me about myself and my family.

— You have brothers and sisters?
— One of each.
— What does he do, your brother?
— He's a surveyor.
— And your sister?
— She's a teacher.
— Your father, what is his job?
— He's a doctor.
— Formidable! That will impress them.

He grins at me as if we've cooked up a good story.

— And your job, before you came to France, what was it again?
— I worked in films. A continuity-girl.
— Ah yes.

He stares at me consideringly.

— Perhaps it would be better not to mention that. In France, people who work in films are often . . . my mother might think . . . if she asks, of course don't hide it, but don't bring it up.

There's a long silence.

— We will have separate bedrooms in the château. My mother is a little old-fashioned. She would think you were . . . she would not approve. But you will like her, I'm sure. She is very cultured. She reads Proust all the time. You know, Marcel Proust the writer?

At the station an old man whom I take for a chauffeur greets us. This is François's father, and he seems to like my name.

— Villiers! Vous êtes Française?
— Non, je suis Australienne.
— Ah.

His welcoming smile fades and he drops my hand and turns to François. Without another glance at me they walk to the car talking, and I trail along behind. With perfunctory politeness I am ushered into the back seat, which smells powerfully of dog. I sit on a blanket covered with dog hairs and try not to think about fleas.

We stop at the village market for a little shopping and I wander among the smells of dead flesh and strong cheese. Whole pheasants hang by their feet from hooks, and hares with glassy eyes are lined up on marble slabs, their delicate mouths encrusted with blood. On one counter a whole pig lies in state, surrounded by small birds.

I stare at some unfamiliar-looking meat on the next counter and wonder what the smell is. The meat is very red, chopped in rough chunks like wood. The man behind the counter comes over to me.

— Vous voulez, Madame?

— Oh non, je regarde seulement.

He hears my accent and comes closer, spreading his red-stained hands on the counter.

— Vous aimez les chevaux?

He's grinning, showing rotten teeth.

— C'est du cheval?

— Bah oui, bien sûr, c'est du cheval. Très bon, très bon.

He's leering at me over the counter, picks up a lump of horse meat and shoves it almost into my face.

— Très bon, très bon.

I back away and he laughs.

It's a long drive to the château. François interrupts his conversation with his father long enough to say over his shoulder:

— There are no buses here, no buses at all. It is twenty kilometres to the château and the only way is by car.

He grins his fixed grin.

The château isn't actually a castle, but a big two-storeyed farmhouse set in misty fields.

A woman comes out of the house and throws her arms extravagantly around François — a rosy-cheeked old lady with a great bush of white hair, wearing down-at-heel slippers and a cardigan full of holes. I think this must be an old family retainer but it turns out to be Maman.

— Chéri, chéri!

She ruffles François's hair and kisses his face again and again. We're introduced. She shakes hands very fleetingly and says, looking at François,

— Mais tu m'as dit qu'elle est ... Australienne ou ... bah

. . . quelque chose . . .

— Mais oui, je suis Australienne.

She stares at me with hostility.

— Mais vous avez un nom francais!

The kitchen is a vast gloomy cavern with a stone floor. As I go in, huge dogs emerge out of the shadows in the corners. Some stand and bark at me but one cringes up, wagging its tail. It's a relief to have something to do so I pet it while a commotion of French happens around me and Maman tweaks at François's clothes, runs her hands over his chest and waist, exclaiming how much weight he's lost. She glances over at me petting the dog, comes over and shouts into my face as if I'm deaf,

— C'est sale, ce chien-là. Sale, comprenez? Dirty, dirty.

— Il me semble très gentil . . .

— Phoo! C'est sale.

She turns away. François puts his arm around her waist and asks her how it is she looks younger all the time, like a young girl. Later he takes me to show me the house.

— It's better if you don't pet that dog, he says with his eternal smile. Maman doesn't like that dog, it belongs to my brother.

We sit down and eat lunch. Each item is loudly criticised by Maman, who demands why the men have bought such rubbish. They've bought the worst meat in the country. Why are they so stupid? François grins at me, laughs, pats Maman's hand. Finally Papa protests mildly:

— Mais c'est mangeable, n'est-ce pas?

Maman takes out of her mouth the piece of slimy meat she's been chewing and throws it ostentatiously to one of the dogs under the table. Chin thrust forward, she stares across the table at Papa who munches on without further comment. François giggles and looks at me.

I'd been worried about which fork to use and all that. I'd never eaten with anyone of Aristocratic Blood before. However, as the meal progresses I see I needn't have worried. Papa reaches across the table for a piece of bread and butters it straight on the tablecloth. Maman watches him, then takes the whole loaf and rips a piece off. She chews it briefly, then takes it out of her mouth

— bah! — and flings it across the table where it lands beside my glass.

No one says anything to me so I sit and eat in silence. Maman's loud voice ricochets around the bare stone walls of the room in competition with the barking dogs, who are fighting over the scraps which everyone has tipped off their plates onto the floor.

After lunch I rehearse my best French and offer to help Maman wash up. She stares at me as if I'm speaking Swahili and says to François:

— Qu'est-ce qu'elle dit?

François translates. She shrugs impatiently and mutters something I can't catch, then looks at him and laughs. He laughs too, and glances quickly at me. I look out the window.

In the next room is a huge grand piano. François sits down at this and plays something very hard with great skill. Then he says:

— I will let you try to guess this next one. See if you can.

I listen hard.

— Satie, isn't it?

His face falls.

— You knew it already.

— No, I guessed.

— A lucky guess! We'll have to try again.

We hear Maman in the next room, apparently moving furniture.

— Maman never learnt to play, but she is very musical, François says. He starts playing again, but Maman yells to him, and grinning at me over his shoulder, he goes in to her. For the next fifteen minutes everyone within a range of about a mile must hear Maman telling François that there is no room for the Australian to stay here. She finishes by bellowing:

— Where is she going to sleep?

François murmurs that I can have his room and he will sleep in the spare room but Maman is enraged by this.

— Why should you sleep with the boxes, she yells. There aren't enough sheets and she'll use all the hot water.

I try to believe that Maman doesn't know I understand French.

Later, he and Maman and I walk down to the next farm to buy a chicken. I trail along behind while they walk ahead, arm-in-arm, discussing local scandals, and try to concentrate on how beautiful the countryside is. The road curves down between hedges and a twittering flight of birds sweeps through the pale sky. François turns back.

— This is a French oak, he says, pointing. You don't have these in Australia.

— No, we have other kinds of trees there.

At the farm I'm introduced by Maman simply as 'L'Australienne'. The farm women are very polite and ask me my name. Before I can answer, Maman says loudly that I don't speak French. She adds that François always brings foreigners here who don't speak French. Hoping to clear up this misconception, I tell them that in fact I do understand French, although I don't speak it terribly well. François's smile vanishes and he darts a distraught look at me. As we go in he whispers that I must not say anything to upset Maman.

Maman's voice fills this house as it fills her own. She talks on and on about the quality of meat while the farm women agree mildly. At one stage Maman glances at me and says very loudly:

— In Australia they eat nothing but sheep. Rien que mouton.

Her saliva lands on my face.

On the way back François lets Maman wander ahead and says to me in a low voice:

— It seems to be all right for a first meeting. You behaved very well.

Back at the house he brings out two chairs onto the terrace. Maman immediately appears from within and sits in one. There's a pause. François brings out another and the three of us sit admiring the misty fields, which are becoming less beautiful for me from moment to moment. François appears to be nodding off. Maman has a small smile on her face.

Finally he comes back to life and asks me if I'd like a cup of tea. I imagine a cosy pot for two in the kitchen and at last a few minutes alone together. But he bends over Maman and says:

— Maman, ma chérie, ma plus aimable Maman, mon amour, veux-tu du thé?

Maman sticks out her bottom lip.

— Non. Veux pas.

I'm pleased to hear this, but just as he's leaving for the kitchen she changes her mind, beaming at us like a sweet old dear. So tea is taken in the squalid formality of the dining room, where Maman issues a whole new series of complaints — about the tea, about the china François has chosen to use, about the brioche bought in the morning. Speaking very clearly, and loudly enough to rattle the cups in the next room, she asks:

— Are there many kangaroos in Australia?

— Yes, there are a great many, I say.

François watches me anxiously.

— They are grotesque animals, Maman asserts.

— Yes, they are rather odd.

— Monstrosities, she shrieks. The ugliest animals in the world! She stares at me. Being careful to get it right, I say:

— Yes, they are a little peculiar, but they are unique to Australia.

Across the table I see François lean back out of Maman's range of vision and shake his head and frown at me.

— And the Aborigines, Maman continues. They are not really human at all. They are monkeys. Grotesque. God was joking when he made them. And you, Mademoiselle, do you have any Aboriginal blood?

— No, Madame, not as far as I know.

Maman leans back picking her teeth with her fingernail. I think with relief that she's come to the end of what she knows about Australia.

— But the coral, she says at last magnanimously. The coral there is quite good. I have a coral necklace which is not too bad. It's a kind of rock which occurs underwater. It can be quite pretty.

— I think it's a kind of small animal, like insects, they build it gradually over the years . . .

She stares at me with contempt.

— It's a rock, she says and stands up. Well, François, are you going to clear this mess?

François and I go back to the terrace. Papa, who has been silent throughout tea, appears with a wheelbarrow and begins to trundle loads of gravel from a big heap onto the path. After each load he spreads it with a rake until it's perfectly even. Then he goes for another barrowload of gravel. He moves very slowly, looking dignified and aloof even when down on all fours on the path removing weeds. I ask François if he plans to spread gravel on all the paths.

— Oh yes, he always does this. By the time he finishes at the back, the gravel is washed away at the front again.

He shrugs and says:

— He does this now he is retired.

François decides to play some more Chopin. I sit at the end of the piano, an obediently admiring audience. Maman is constantly in and out of the room, measuring the sweater she is knitting him, asking what he wants for dinner, smoothing his hair, nagging about getting it cut. François protests:

— But Maman, doesn't it make me look distinguished?

She pretends to slap him and he catches her wrist and kisses her hand. She smiles down at him and they both glance over at me.

Dinner is no better than the other meals.

— Are you a good cook, Mademoiselle? Maman shouts, making mixing and eating gestures at me.

François winks across the table at me and says quickly:

— Oh yes, she's a superb cook. When we're married, she'll do all the cooking.

Maman stares first at me, then at François, who says:

— We plan to have a big family, Maman, so you'll have lots of grandchildren.

Even Papa is staring at François now, a mouthful of meat poised on his fork. François winks at me. Maman looks very old as she stares down at her plate. Suddenly she looks up and slaps him playfully.

— You love to tease!

But she glances anxiously at me. François smiles at the tablecloth in a non-committal way. She stares at his profile and there's a long silence until she turns to me.

— Do you still have your parents, Mademoiselle?

— Yes, they're both alive.

— Oh là!

She gives me a pantomine of astonishment before saying very clearly:

— They must be terribly old.

— Well, they are about your age, Madame.

She snorts and tears off a great chunk of bread, then hurls it clear across the table, where one of the dogs leaps up and catches it in his jaws.

After dinner everyone disappears and I stand in the middle of the piano room and wonder what to do. Maman has taken François off somewhere and Papa has vanished. Finally I sit down at the piano and start to play but within seconds François appears and puts his hands over mine on the keys.

— You will disturb Maman.

He disappears again without giving me any indication of what to do. When he next appears, nearly an hour later, I tell him I want to have a bath and go to bed and he leaps at the idea, taking me upstairs at once and demonstrating how to turn the taps on and off for the bath.

Later, in bed, I hear the rest of the family go to their rooms. The conjugal bedroom is directly below mine and I hear through the floorboards Maman continuing to exclaim and shout, though I can't hear the words. At last all is quiet. The door opens very slowly, and François tiptoes in. With a huge signalling for silence he comes to the bed and whispers:

— Get down on the floor.

I do so and he makes love, holding me down so I can't move. Each time I take a breath he puts his hand over my mouth.

— Shhh. Shhh.

One of my legs becomes cramped and I move it slowly. He holds me down even tighter.

— Sssssssh!

As soon as he finishes, he stands up, pulls his pyjamas back on and grins down at me.

— The bed is very noisy, he whispers. And Maman is right underneath.

I feel weak from the rigours of the day and my leg is still cramped. I lie and stare up at him but I can't be bothered to smile back. Suddenly he jumps on the bed and bounces up and down vigorously. The bed sets up a loud rhythmic rattle and squeak.

— Very noisy, he whispers. He lies still, seems to wait.

Underneath, Maman gives one short, wide-awake cough. We

hear it very clearly in the quiet. François stares at me with wide eyes and starts to laugh silently, covering his mouth with his hand, making the bed shake. When I stand up I see that he's crying with laughter and biting his fist to keep it in. I leave him there and spend a long time sitting in the bathroom staring at the floor. When I come back to the bedroom, François has gone and the house is silent.

OE

WHEN SHE WAS a child they used to have socials at the church to raise funds for the new roof and usually there would be a speaker and usually the speaker would talk about their Overseas Trip. With slides. Buckingham Palace a bland grey slab behind its railings. The Eiffel Tower, foreshortened, at a rakish Gallic angle. The Taj Mahal through one cluster of brown faces and the Pyramids through another. The parishioners sat in rows in the darkened hall and said oooh my word look at all those people and how did you get on for meals because you could get terrible tummy bugs in some of those places they were none too fussy. Then the lights were switched on and everyone had supper. Alison's father and mother usually went because her father was an elder and you had to show support and sometimes Alison and her brothers went too and it was usually very interesting.

Alison's father and mother had never been overseas. Not even to Australia. Not even during the war. Her father had flat feet and less than 20/20 vision so he was in the Home Guard. They had never even been to the North Island. They went to Queenstown for their honeymoon in 1950 and drove down to Milford on the bus. When the children came along they bought a crib out on the coast only twenty miles away which was nice and handy and Alison's father could pop into town to keep an eye on his plumbing business because drains blocked and pipes burst, holidays or no. The crib was an old shearers' hut by an estuary. Alison's mother's best friend from school, Tui Roper, had married a farmer called Ron Potter and they let them have the place cheap. The women sat on the step with their legs spread beneath cotton sundresses and drank tea while the men had a yarn round the back where Alison's father was building a dinghy, or cast for cod off the spit, or waded out at low tide on the mudflats for flounder.

Alison and her brothers liked the crib well enough when they were children, building forts in the macrocarpas, paddling in the warm waters of the estuary or on wet days playing endless games of Monopoly or reading old copies of the *National Geographic*: 'An Island Beauty Preserves The Ancient Traditions Of The Hula'; 'Persepolis's Scarred Columns Stand Sentinel Over The Desert'; 'Beneath The Fiery Banners Of Fall Basks The Quiet Charm Of A Quebec Village'. One summer Ron Potter took them in the pickup out to the headland where they filed through the dry scrub as night fell. The moon laid down a shining path to the east, all the way to South America, and wherever they stood they were at its beginning. 'Shhh,' said Ron switching off the torch. 'Listen.' There was an odd chuckling beneath their feet. 'Mutton birds,' he said. They came back here to this point every November all the way from Alaska and left again in April, regular as clockwork, flying along invisible paths thousands of feet above the earth and steering by the sun and the stars. It was a miracle of nature. Ron caught the odd one for Tui but they were a bit on the greasy side for him. Gave him heartburn.

Alison stood in the dark and listened: the slap of kelp and water on the rocks below and the chatter of the birds which flew year after year in that great circle and the wind pushing and shoving at the gorse and scrub and the clouds and the moon. The whole universe jittered about her. Everything moved. Everything shifted. Everything was alive.

The children marched in a row back to the truck and sang Livin' Doll all the way home, bouncing about on the tray as they juddered over the rutted track.

As they grew older such pleasures palled. The children became bored. They wanted to go to Caroline Bay or Alexandra, somewhere where there was a bit of action. Mum poured Tui another cup and said she couldn't see what the big attraction was: hordes of people drinking and carrying on when what you needed for a decent holiday was peace and quiet. Alison and her brothers sulked along the spit chucking stones at the gulls and squabbling over Five Hundred till the summer finally came when they were old enough to head off with their friends to carry on with the rest of the world.

One New Year's Eve at Mt Maunganui Alison met Steve. He was camped out by the beach in the van in which he had driven round the East Coast stopping at all the surfing beaches beginning at Waimarama and working his way north. It had been grouse. A summer-long search for the perfect right-hand curl. But the shocks went coming out of Waipiro and he'd had to work for a few weeks till he had the money for repairs, filling jugs and wiping down the bar at the Majestic. Over by the pool table a fight had broken out (all that drinking and carrying on . . .). Steve put his arm around her. 'Let's split,' he said. He had a week's pay in his back pocket. A seven-ouncer whistled overhead and thudded into the wall only inches from the Queen who was looking down at the carryings-on in the Majestic in bleached half-profile. They walked down the road to the shore where the van was parked amongst the marram grass. There was a mattress in the back. The shocks creaked beneath them all night.

The diff went on the road to Waipu and Alison helped push the van into the garage in a blistering southerly. Her friends Margie and Di had said she was mad as she stuffed her clothes into her backpack on New Year's Day and said she was off. 'But you don't even know this guy,' said Di. 'He's OK,' said Alison, T-shirts a grubby bundle, sneakers, a couple of pairs of jeans. Her back throbbed still where it had pressed over and over through the thin cotton wadding of the mattress against the ridges of the van floor the night before. 'And it'll be easier in the Bambina with just the two of you. Three's hopeless.' She tightened the straps. 'See you back at work then,' said Margie. She was a teller at the Lambton Quay branch. Di was in Customer Services. 'Sure,' said Alison. Over by the camping ground store the van gunned, blue smoke spurting. 'See you.' 'Hey!' called Margie as they bucked away past the ablution block. She was waving a white flag from the cabin door. 'You've forgotten your nightie!' 'Keep it!' called Alison. Steve had his hand on her thigh. The sun caught in every golden hair on his bare arm.

She did not return to Loans. They sold the van for parts in Waipu and went to Noosa where Steve met Rosa, a deceptively fragile blonde who had ridden the pipeline and wanted to show him Oahu. They waved goodbye from the steps of a Boeing 707 and Alison decided that she wasn't ready yet to go back to Lambton Quay. She withdrew all her savings, performance bonuses and all, and bought a ticket to Delhi. She remembered the Taj Mahal. It seemed as good a place as any. On the slides it had looked as though it were cast from molten wax, pure and white. The reality was legless blind insistence in every exquisite portal and the hyacinth stench of shit heavy on the air so she caught a bus out: the Polo Trekker, with Malcolm from Birmingham and Bron from Hawera and Chrissie and Geoff from Dubbo and Ken from Toronto. Up from the airless plains to Kashmir and on across Pakistan, skirting desert and seashore to Turkey, Greece, Yugoslavia, Austria, Germany, France. The world jolted past through dusty windows: waterless canyon, sulphurous river, azure sea, misty canal and poplar-lined road blinking away like a migraine, muting to grey as they moved north till they were in London and it was Euston Station, Pall Mall and all the squares on the Monopoly board together. Ken took photos of the gang at Persepolis, on a bridge at Isfahan, in a Yugoslavian cave, in a pub in the Vienna Woods. Alison took no slides. To see was enough.

In the cave near Porec she saw a salamander in a plastic aquarium. It was two inches long, with pale pink skin and tiny hands and feet and the label in German, French and English said it was a Human Fish/Der Menschliche-Fisch/Le Poisson-Humain which was found Locally in Underground Streams and bore an uncanny resemblance to the Human Foetus. The fish felt its way blindly up the sheer sides of the aquarium, hand over hand.

Ken stayed on with her in London. They shared a flat in Brixton, a single room above an Indian restaurant. The scent of fenugreek clung to their clothing and their hair and they walked to the baths on Deovil Street to wash. Ken got jobs relief teaching, Alison worked as an office temp. That way they were free to leave at a week's notice to hitch up to Stratford or round Scotland or over to France. They were standing on a corner near St Andrews when Ken said, 'Why don't you come to Canada?' A flock of sheep with long mournful faces huddled behind them in the rain. Alison said she'd think about it. Back in London the Christmas lights were down, the rubbish bags piled in black plastic hillocks in the streets. Ken was comfortable curved against her back as they slept, their rest broken by the burr and jangle of sitars from the Bengal downstairs. There seemed little reason to stay. She told the man from Immigration she was Ken's fiancée when he asked. Ken said it would make entry easier.

Toronto was white rectangles on a denim sky through which the taxi cut quickly and cleanly from the airport. They found an apartment in a semi-detached off Spadina near the Portuguese market. The elderly Hungarian Jew who lived next door shovelled the snow morosely from his portion of the sidewalk and said the street was no good no more. Too much noise, too much chatter. Twenty years before it had all been Europeans like himself: Hungarians, Germans, Poles. Then the Chinese came, digging up the tiny lawns and filling them with cabbages and onions. And now it was the Portuguese and the Italians and the vegetables had been replaced by flowerbeds: circles, squares and flounces to be filled when the weather warmed with petunias and pansies and African marigolds hardy enough to put down roots in the sour lake soil. The yard immediately across the road was more elaborate. The Da Silvas had poured concrete over the lot and decorated it with an intricate pattern of shells around an upturned bath in which they had placed a plaster statue of the Virgin. She simpered out at the new arrivals from her scalloped grotto clutching a bunch of plastic gladioli.

Ken found temporary work at Jervis Collegiate and Alison, cardless, got a job at the Acropolis. Mr Diamandopoulou, conspiratorial finger to nose, had said he help her and she help him so no fuss eh? It was a cold winter. The flat was small and dark and the toilet in the basement blocked regularly and cockroaches shimmered on the kitchen bench when you turned on the light, but it was cheap and they could save money to go to Mexico in the summer. Alison walked to the restaurant along streets slippery with ice and furrowed snow. Ken said this was nothing. Back in Myvatn Manitoba he remembered winters of 64 below. You got used to it. You even welcomed it because it shortened the trip into town. You could drive directly across the frozen lake.

They went cross-country skiing in Algonquin. Alison stood on a hillock and looked out on trees and river and rocky outcrop and thought I could move north or south or east or west. For ever. Behind stretched her tracks: a dark uneven braiding with Ken, touching, crossing and crisscrossing.

In the spring they bought a car, a rusted Chevrolet, and drove out west to visit Ken's folks. They went one morning to see the snakes emerge from their winter hibernation deep in caverns underground. The snakes, American garters, issued from cracks in a shallow depression beneath the wide shallow bowl of the prairie sky. Their striped skins were new and lustrous and they wove in mating round one another in their hundreds, a seething silent mass like kelp undulating in deep water. It was extraordinary. A miracle of nature.

That night Alison crept in beside Ken. They were in his old room, each in a single bed. His mother had not touched a thing, referred to it still as 'the boys' room'. The beds were two foot six inches wide, too narrow to share comfortably, but Alison wrapped her legs round Ken and said, 'I want a baby.' It was something to do with the snakes, their silent coupling in the spring sunshine. 'Are you sure?' said Ken. It would mean changes: a new apartment, permanent jobs, no summer trip to Mexico. 'You're quite sure?' It would mean permanence. Alison stroked his smooth skin. 'Oh yes,' she said. 'Oh yes yes yes.' They made love slowly and silently then because Ken's mother and father slept only inches away through the wall and as Alison knelt on the bed trying not to groan as Ken came from behind in a juddering thrust, she looked through the trembling blur of climax at the crossed pennants of the Myvatn Vikings and she felt sure. Oh yes yes yes. She was sure.

She was pregnant for three months then one afternoon as she spooned taramasalata onto the De Luxe Mezze Platter her stomach cramped and she had to ask Veta to cover for her while she took a cab home where the spotting became a flood, soaking sheets and blankets and she arrived in Ward 24 at St Mike's with Maria who told the nurses she had fallen off a stool to begin the bleeding but confided in Alison as they lay side by side, their hands punctured by needles and someone else's blood seeping into their own depleted veins, that really it was her husband who hit and kick and so, no baby, and it was hard eh, to be a woman. Across the ward Karen stretched her mouth to an O and applied a smear of Calypso Pink in readiness for visiting hour. On her black silk robe she had pinned her Weight Away! badge. She wore it everywhere she said. It was quite a conversation starter she said. You would never have guessed it but Karen used to weigh over 200 pounds. It had just slipped on with each of her four pregnancies till there she was: size twenty-two with a size zero self-image. Then her best girlfriend Tina out at Orangeville had seen the Weight Away! promotion on the TV and they'd gone along to a neighbourhood meeting and begun the No Weight Meal Plan that very same day and well, look, she said, peeling back black silk to reveal a smooth brown thigh. 'Pinch it,' she said. 'Go on.'

Alison extended a weak hand and took a pinch of Karen's flesh. 'See?' said Karen. 'Tight as a drum. And only six months ago that was flab and cellulite.' Basically, Karen said, when you had your body under control, you had your life under control.

Alison lay between sheets so crisp they might have been baked and thought she had never felt more out of control in her life. Her thighs hurt where they had been stretched uncomfortably for the D&C, her breasts tingled, her stomach cramped and between her legs the pad was an uncomfortable bloody wad. Her eyes filled with tears. They did that now over the slightest thing: over Johnboy's dilemmas on the TV, over the children in the ice cream ads, over magazine articles about plucky paraplegics or reunions of long lost sisters. 'Hormones,' said the nurse. 'It's usual. You'll be right in a day or so and everything will soon be back to normal.' Miscarriages were common, she said. Especially with the first baby. Maybe as high as 10%. Some people had multiple miscarriages: half a dozen or more and the reasons could be genetic or because of some infection or abnormality so that maybe it was a blessing as nature often knew best. Alison lay on her crisp sheets and thought about the little human fish swimming about in the dark waters of her womb and dying there, and her eyes filled with hormonally induced tears.

So Alison left the hospital and set about getting back to normal: back to Ken and the flat and the Acropolis and it was as though nothing had happened, as though the snakes and the swelling breasts and the salamander baby had been a kind of dream, an illusion. And one Saturday morning two weeks later she was standing in Loblaws trying to decide between Maple Walnut and Pecan Brittle. The freezer hummed and overhead through a crackle of product announcements Julie Andrews counted off her fav-ou-rite things and from the front of the store came a fuzz of chat and checkout bleep. Alison stood with a pottle in each hand and as she listened the sound amplified and she was aware suddenly of the aisles stretching away from her, long canyons rimmed with cans of baked beans and pineapple rings which were leaning, hemming her in. She couldn't breathe, her heart thudded. She was going to faint, to fall over, right there in the frozen goods section, she was going to scream and run mad, she was trapped and she was going to die. It was terrifying. In a frenzy of fear she abandoned Maple Walnut and Pecan Brittle and ran for the entrance, out of the light into the dark anonymity of Spadina where the night opened around her and she could gasp it in and become calm once more. There was fruit in the cupboard. They had that for dessert.

Next Saturday she tried again. It was a tentative experiment. Ken's brother was visiting. The football player. The Viking. And that meant steak and lots of it. She got as far as the supermarket meat counter before the noises grew and the shelves closed in and she had to run for home once more. She asked Ken if he'd mind, her voice carefully noncommittal, picking up the meat and veg on his way back from the LCBO and Ken said no trouble. And that set a pattern. Alison from then on avoided the supermarket, devising stratagems by which Ken could be persuaded to go instead or shopping herself at the Macs Milk a block away which was dearer but where the door was safely visible and the shelves stayed in their proper places. Meanwhile the panic spread, oozing out to fill the corners of clothing stores and cinemas and subway trains and buses and streets beyond what was absolutely known. At the hairdresser's she was overwhelmed before the cut was quite finished. She pretended a pressing appointment elsewhere.

Maurizio clipped on for a few minutes, annoyed at the interruption to his handiwork. She tipped him too much and escaped, her hair drying on the way home to an uneven bob which she straightened herself as best she could in the bathroom mirror. Even the apartment, so comfortably familiar, could become an alien place so that she lay on her side of the bed, Ken breathing evenly beside her, the fan whirring on the window ledge, and panic over her face like a warm pillow. She wanted desperately to run, to escape. But where could she run to?

Ken put his arms around her. 'What's the matter, Allie?' he said. It puzzled him: her sudden dependence, her timidity. 'If it's the baby, we can try again you know. It's not the end of the world.' He held her closely. Alison wriggled to be free. 'No,' she said. 'Not yet. There's nothing the matter.' How could she possibly explain that nowhere now was safe, that the world had inexplicably become a frightening place, full of invisible terrors.

At Christmas she rang home. 'Hullo dear,' said someone in a slow drawl Alison scarcely recognised. Had she got a crossed line? Was this really her mother? The strange voice, batted from earth to heaven and heaven to earth across thousands of empty miles, was saying that they were going to go out to the crib at New Year's and they were going to have dinner with the Potters: nothing fancy, just ham and salad ... Across the road the Da Silvas had added Bambi and Snow White and a Christ child in a manger to the display '... and we're going to launch the dinghy,' said her mother, 'after all these years ...' Happy Christmas winked the Da Silvas' front porch in red and green and blue and Alison was suddenly overwhelmed with homesickness. She wanted to see the dinghy bobbing about on the estuary, she wanted to walk out onto the mudflats at low tide, the clouds mirrored exactly on the slick surface beneath your feet so that it seemed for all the world as though you were walking upside down on the sky like a fly on the ceiling. 'Allie?' said her mother. 'Allie? Are you there?' Click click click went the phone. Alison could not speak. Her throat was a tight knot. 'Darn,' said her mother. 'This darn phone's gone dead.' Click click click. Alison thought of her standing by the phone table in the hall at Nuhaka Cres. and her eyes filled yet again with tears. The first snow of the season was falling on Bambi and Snow White. 'Alison,' said her mother, speaking very slowly and very clearly, 'I don't know if you can hear me but Happy Christmas darling. And love to Ken. I'll hang up now.' Click. The Christ child holds up his arms to the white flakes.

Alison flew out a week later. They had the money they'd been saving for Mexico and Ken agreed that it was a good idea: she'd had a rough year. Through a blur of Traveleeze which she had taken not so much for nausea as to quell the panic, Alison hugged him at the foot of the escalator to the departure lounge and heard him say, 'You are coming back though, Allie, aren't you? This is just a holiday?' 'Of course,' said Alison her arms round his neck. (But if she was so certain why had she packed the photograph of the two of them on the bridge at Isfahan?) They seemed to be speaking to one another from beneath deep water. She rose away from him into the crowd.

Alison's mother said she was looking peaky and those cities overseas weren't the best were they what with all the pollution and crime. Tui and Ron had had a trip last year and their bags were stolen in broad daylight from the bus right outside the Vatican and the Vienna Woods were dying from that acid rain and they'd carried extra money always to give the muggers because if you didn't hand something over straight away evidently they just shot you and there had been a programme on the TV about the Mafia and all the drugs and murders so it was no wonder she was feeling a bit run down.

'Toronto's not like that,' said Alison and her mother said that Tui and Ron had said they had had to keep their travellers' cheques in their socks for security over there.

Alison sat in the back of the Subaru as they jolted down the rutted track and watched a squall rumple the calm surface of the estuary. At night she lay on her old bunk bed reading and listening to her parents playing crib with the Potters in the kitchen. 'You all right?' said her mother, head round the door. 'Fine,' said Alison, flipping the page on 'Diakanke Girl Alone In The Bush Prepares For Her Initiation Into Womanhood'. 'Would you like some Milo?' said her mother. Alison wrapped her legs in her old chenille quilt. 'Yes thanks,' she said. The Milo came as always with a Shrewsbury biscuit. She sat on the bunk curled in the quilt and dunked the biscuit in hot milk while outside the waves washed up onto the shingle beyond the spit ... 'Tendamayo Women Extract Salt From The Earth', 'Life In Kenogami Centres Round Its Paper Mills' ... When she woke midway through the night she thought for a minute that the waves' crashing was the rush of cars on Spadina and found herself reaching for Ken.

In the morning she walked along the beach, she found the old fort amongst the macrocarpas, she sat in the sun on the back step, she swam out into the estuary, the water warm oil on her skin. At the end of the week her parents went back into town because drains still blocked and pipes burst, holiday or no, but Alison said she thought she would stay on for a bit, maybe another week or two. 'Good idea,' said her mother. A bit of peace and quiet would see her right. Alison stood on the step to wave as the Subaru, heavily laden, bumped away up the track and the silence settled round her. She made a cup of tea. She sat on the beach and watched wrybills and oystercatchers dipping and bobbing out on the flat. That night she sat up reading magazines and sometime late, she took the dinghy, rowed out into the bowl of the estuary and lay back looking up at the sky. The water lapped and sucked at the keel, and the stars overhead were glassy splinters wheeling about in their particular patterns, and she was a tiny speck clinging to the skin of a minute sphere which joined them, turning round the sun. Everything was in motion. And out here the sensation of the world sliding beneath her did not cause her to panic. It was in fact curiously comforting.

Days passed. Nights passed.

Ken wrote: So how are things back home? I guess you must be enjoying the summer. I'm fine, though some of the kids in my Grade Twelve chemistry class are driving me nuts ...

Alison wrote: I'm fine. It is very quiet here ...

Then she stopped. It seemed so little to say, so pointless to say it at all.

Ken wrote: Had a great day skiing today, out round the lake ...

Alison thought of him swinging easily down through the dark trees, the long stride of him, his trail a neat parallel parting in the snow.

Ken wrote: When are you coming back Allie?

She wrote back: Not yet.

Days passed. Nights passed.

Ken wrote: I miss you Allie. Do you want me to come down? Because I will if you want it ...

Alison thought of him, curled in their bed in the apartment, the Da Silvas' lights red, blue and green reflections on the ceiling.

One night she walked up to the headland, her torch scribbling light on dry gorse and scrub. She stood at the foot of the moonpath and looked out at it, its trail set across water to South America. Beneath her feet the muttonbirds chortled and muttered and groaned. It was cold, the wind chill off the sea. In a few weeks they'd be gone, setting off to the north as the winter drew in, following the invisible trail set between stars and moon and sun in the pursuit of food and warmth and shelter. Everything in nature was movement, everything in nature was change.

She thought of the baby wriggling in her belly in its dark and watery universe and its death there and she thought of Ken, turning to her in half sleep, his arm flung across her and drawing her to himself. Warm and alive.

It was time to leave.

It was time to pack her bag.

It was time to walk up the track to the road to catch the bus into town.

It was time to set the new pattern: the flight between two points, one to the north, the other to the south, finding warmth in both places.

In the morning she would rejoin the circle.

FIRES ON THE BEACH

FROM LISBON THEY went up the coast on a slow train, stopping at a village supposed to be relatively free of tourists. For part of the way they had a view of the sea — pale, glittering — but then they lost sight of it until they got off at the beautiful little railway siding. Sunflowers grew along the platform and pastel-coloured tiles adorned the ticket office, and there, through the miniature archway, was the sea again — still pale, but angry now with surf rolling in all the way from North America. After three winters in London it was a sight to behold. It was, above all, what they both wanted, and it only remained for them to get to the hotel and they would be launched, properly, on their holiday.

With barely a thought for Sally, Andrew scooped up the luggage and headed off, brusquely dismissing a porter, trusting that she would quickly follow on — which she did, the tangerine beach bag over her shoulder, impressing the porter with her abandon. Andrew laboured with the bags, sweating, already irritable, but under no circumstances would he resort to tipping. She followed on agreeably because she knew it was the only occasion he would have to carry everything at once: this year they had readily agreed on one thing — it would be best for them both to settle in one spot rather than feel compelled to see a whole new country.

The hotel was at the end of the beach. Andrew dumped the bags at the foot of the concrete steps and together they pushed open the frosted glass doors. Inside all was aluminium tubing and plastic. The people at reception were churlish — and slow. When they were finally shown to their room it turned out to be in the far wing at the end of cellular corridors, with its balcony looking inland. They waited until the boy left and threw themselves down on opposite sides of the rickety bed. The impossibility of advance booking! Yet, Andrew insisted, like the relatively young husband that he was, what else can one do but hope that a simple plan will work? She was not blaming him, Sally said, and they went downstairs to order coffee. In the lounge they sat in airport chairs set in a rectangular well, the centre of which was occupied by an enormous fish tank. The hotel had a reputation for excellent seafood. Green light from the tank seeped evenly towards each corner of the room. There was no window to the outdoors. A waiter came to ask if they wanted Irish coffee, and then, when they turned incredulously to each other, and each was faced with the other's lime green grief, they broke into laughter and ordered beer. Mishaps united them. They would stay the few days they had paid for in advance, then they would find somewhere else. At least they had reached the sea.

They spent the mornings reading, walking, swimming, before lunching sumptuously on seafood at one of the beach cafés (the hotel restaurant was not what it was cracked up to be). After lunch they made love, which was followed by a voluptuous siesta; then, late afternoon, they emerged hand in hand on the promenade, strolled to the village square, selected a quiet spot amongst the forest of chairs and tables. Each, then resumed their reading, each, in their own way, continuing the siesta which Andrew declared governed the life of the nation. He read *Books and Bookmen* because even when half asleep and on holiday he felt that one could not afford to be completely divorced from what the other publishing houses were up to. Sally read Irish Murdoch's *The Bell* because he had strongly recommended it. Of course they talked with each other as well: they still had a good deal to say to each other, especially considering they had been together for ten years (eight married, two as teenage lovers prior to that), and they did talk, quite animatedly about some things. But then the conversation would lapse and they contentedly returned to their reading, or observing the world about. Trust was still sufficient for one to be able to nudge the other and for them both to look — silently, while each assumed that the other was thinking and feeling at least roughly similar things. Together they managed to see a good deal of Asia, and most of Western Europe.

But here Andrew could not get over the locals, or rather, those villagers who did not depend for a living on selling trinkets and port wine. It was supposed to be a thriving fishing village. But there, out on the sand, were a solid proportion of the workforce. They lay on the sand between the dilapidated hulls of their boats which someone had dragged up from the water. In their black sweaters and shawls they sprawled — individually, in pairs, in cumbersome clumps, like schools of beached whales. Men, women, and children, men especially he noticed, seemed to spend the day with their heads down, faces into their black sleeves. One only saw their faces in the late afternoon, when they sat up, lit fires on the beach, and gathered in groups with their backs to the setting sun. On their way back to the hotel, Andrew could not resist going much closer to them than Sally thought necessary or polite.

He wanted to photograph them, to capture this unique feature of the shoreline, but as he approached children leapt away from the fires and pitched mussel shells at his telephoto lens. Their parents smiled: his lens would have brought up their rows of broken teeth wonderfully. 'You shouldn't,' Sally said, and he turned away from her in disgust. That cautionary tone of voice riled him as much as his own compulsion to set the most random of objects into some sort of order. He knew he took a good photograph: it was his way of making a little more sense of things. Were these the men who went off in the night fleet? Were these the same families they had seen at the daily fish auction? Sally did not show any interest in these things. And he did not want to encroach upon them unduly, there would have been something morbid in that. Yet what could be more morbid than a beach littered with the shrouded bodies of entire families? He felt intensely put out. She put his irritability down to their poor accommodation.

At last they could move out of what Andrew had come to call The Aquarium. Along the way they found a room right over their favourite café. It gave, in one direction, a view of the beach: the hulls, the bodies dormant, and of the sea which, when they went out on their balcony in the mornings, was a flat, wide silver blade all the way to the horizon, so dazzling that one almost overlooked the line of surf, that forever pounded in, running so hard that Andrew wondered whether a fisherman might occasionally be picked up from the beach and swept out. In the other direction they looked to the bluff, and the little white chapel which sat on the cliff top. It was altogether an excellent situation; they virtually looked out upon the best part of the village. Life seemed to flow beneath the awning of the café and they could have well sat there all evening, sipping their port, letting sounds signify reality.

Inevitably though, at dusk, they went down. They descended to the promenade, drawn by the smell of the sardines. For each evening, without fail, the promenade became an avenue of tiny barbecues. On the portable grills the sardines were roasted over charcoal. This was the surplus of the day's catch, and the smell of the fish — pungent, so rank of the sea — was such that one felt it in the palate whether it was being devoured — white, soft fleshed beneath the crust of burnt scales — or not. For Sally they were a little too strong. But he loved them. Each evening he insisted that they sit at one of the grills and eat until the sun was out of sight. 'Something to do,' he laughed — a most peculiar remark.

Each day she was perfecting her tan: a safe time on her neat, flat tummy, bronzing perfectly triangular shoulder blades, then on her back, an open invitation to the sun, cheeks and thighs glowing with the skin's osmosis and the best quality Swiss lotion. Lying an arm's length away, at an obtuse angle, he persisted with his reading, observing, from time to time, her easy transition from almond to honey, from bees' wax to maple syrup — she would stick at it for hours, occasionally rising to inspect the dark against the lighter patches, then resuming her position like a sleep-walker. When she sat up her eyes were blank from the marathon baking. Even when he said, into her perspiring face, 'Do you want a swim?' she would say, 'No,' and flop back comatose, fearless of sunstroke. He calculated that her mind would be completely vacant again by the time he hit the water.

The dip would save him.

Day after day the weather was perfect. Very soon they were both at their physical best. She was blonder than before; he was taut, pared down by the sun. Dressing for dinner, each admired the other as if they had only recently met — he her delicate, low-backed frocks, she his swank in the Indian cotton shirt. He threatened to wear her straw hat into the café, the lilac ribbon flowing. 'Don't you dare,' she protested, though she would have loved him to. It occurred to him that with someone else — God knows who though — he blooming well might have.

In the sun she could feel her body loosening from the London winters. She had decided that they should never stay away from real summers for that length of time again. The sun eased one into deeper mutualities. Lying nearby, he found it hard to credit that a village could be as white, and as quiet as this one. The hour before noon was utterly hollow. If it had not been for the heaving of the sea, he might have thought they were on an outcrop of coral, coral dried dreadfully by the sun, then left uninhabited for decades.

Sometimes she stretched and said, 'Oh, oh, I could live here forever.'

In the evening he vomited. Feverish, he lay on the bed in their charming room, shaking, cold, squirming with the contractions of the diarrhoea. She was very concerned and brought him numerous hot and cold drinks from the café below. He moaned about the cost. She reprimanded him for stinginess. In the course of the evening he began to improve. He sat up in bed with refreshments, wearing sunglasses against the glare of the bed lamp. She laughed, and then he did put on the floppy straw hat. She forgave him his irritability, and, acknowledging that sunstroke was a bugger and that he was really putting up with it quite well, said, 'You'll just have to be more careful.' Whereupon he threw the hat at her like a saucer. Next day he was properly better.

Agreeably — for she was, above all, an agreeable woman, seldom meaning to offend, a woman who had grown into the position of being a young wife with considerable ease — agreeably she was prepared to shorten their morning sessions in the sun. It was simply a matter of lunching earlier and siestaing with the resignation of the locals. So in the mornings she continued to turn her windowless face to the sun, while he read until they went in — with more time ahead of them to eat, and make love. She seemed, too, to be replete with the sexual attention he was, on holiday, able to pay her. Afterwards she slept with that animal indifference which would have gratified most husbands. But Andrew was not so sure, or rather, he could not bear to lie beside her on such shallow assumptions. Before she woke, when he could not sleep at all, he crept out of the room, down to the streets, walking through the deserted lanes of the village, taking the narrow ones as far as its outskirts, returning via the wider ones which ended at the sea, the lanes which seemed to telescope the sea and sky to a prism. He would return replenished in time to hear her splashing in the shower, in time for a quiet cigarette on the balcony while she dressed. 'Are you ready, dear?' he said, 'Of course,' and catapulted his cigarette towards the sea. And later, during dinner, he had occasion to go back to the room alone. He looked into his London contact book, into the diary, the snakes and ladders of weeks and months. They had been in the village for eight days. A week to go.

On the cliff top, beyond the chapel, there was a bull-fighting arena. It was a modest affair, and they discovered that in Portugal they did not kill the bulls. It was worth a visit. Of course Sally was still dubious. She loathed cruelty of any sort, and cattle, even bulls, were to her close cousins of the horses she had loved so dearly as a girl. Andrew persisted: it would be nothing like they had seen in Spain, not at all like they had been subjected to on Madrid television, where, eating in cheap cafés, they had the day's bull-fights replayed like the football — all while they tried to enjoy the hot sausages. No, it would be nothing like that, he laughed. They should go up to the arena while it was under the full moon and watch the gentle art of Portuguese bull-fighting.

And it was a highlight — of sorts — for him. It was a handsome, high-tiered arena, and they sat in good, middle-priced seats while the bulls came and went under the arc lights, the moon adding to the occasion. Young bulls, it seemed, that came down the race in fits and jerks of vigour, promising good entertainment. Sally sat tightly beside him, still anticipating the worst, shivering in her light dress. Their seat caught the wind from the sea. He put his arm about her and thought of the Roman women at the Colosseum, how they were open and wet at the sight of blood. Sally said, 'They're not going to, are they?' and hid her face in his neck. 'Of course not. How many times do I have to tell you.' He had snapped again. He tried to compensate with an extra hug. She pulled away. The bull continued to charge about, the gaily dressed young men in hot pursuit, then in rapid retreat when the bull turned and they had to tumble over the rail, their laughter revealing that the escape from the thundering hooves was just a little too easy, a little too safe. It was a very antique, courtly affair, with nothing any longer at risk. At one stage a bull dared to stand completely still in the arena, brazenly benign — moonstruck. And even when he was jabbed and poked, the run that he made towards the toreadors was desultory. It was as if the courtship of bulls had gone on for too long for everybody's good. The little arena stood on a splendid cliff top, only a dash from the raging sea, yet everything happening in it was tame: all events seemed to be held in abeyance.

Yet it was not until the following day that Sally said, finally, what he knew to be preoccupying her, what she had been grooming herself to say, what she always brought them around to on holidays, when she considered they had reached a certain state of mind. She had the knack of waiting for the peaceful moment. They were eating breakfast on the balcony. He was poised over his eggs. The surf had not yet sprung up. She spoke with eyes wide — blue with the morning.

'Andy, are we going to make a baby — one day?'

She spoke with such loving, unavoidable sweetness.

'Yes, of course, yes.'

'Are we really?' She was looking up under his gaze.

'Yes,' he said, smiling, and drawing the word out. He could be immensely patient, soft. He could say just about anything to forestall the next question.

He explained that clearly it partly depended on the reshuffle in the marketing division, whether it happened or not. Then they had to decide whether he was willing to be posted abroad, and whether they really wanted to start a family in the U.K., or wait until they might be well set up in the U.S. He went on to reassure her that she was not really starting late (she was 27): loads of women had perfectly healthy children well into their thirties, the risks, statistically, empirically, factually speaking, were not that great, not really.

Sally heard him out before asking, 'Don't you wish we had a love child?'

'Can I just finish my breakfast before we go on?'

'Bugger.'

'Sal, please don't spoil the morning. What difference does it make if we wait another eighteen months, another two years even? Why should we rush into it now and spoil all the other options?'

'Options. Options.'

'Sal . . .' he said. He finished off the hard, cold egg. He swirled his cheeks full of coffee, discarded the toast. This was giving her plenty of time to be reasonable and now he was going to stand up. He was on the way to the beach, since she was not going to be sensible. He threw down the napkin as she said, 'I know, I know that. I'm being silly,' and he smiled, thinking that the pale blue of the morning was back between them, when she added, 'I know that we've got a whole lifetime ahead of us.'

Together they went down to the beach and lay on the sand. The sun was ruthless. He was forced to let drop his small volume of verse and shut his eyes. The heat, biting his back as if it were shell grit, drove away the light and seemed to wedge solid shadow at the back of his eyes. There was little point in looking up at things. He was indifferent to everything. He longed for something to happen — anything.

Something did. The next day there was what might be called an incident.

It was towards the end of the morning and they had been reading, nodding off, even swimming together, in a fairly amicable way, his seizure of the previous day having insinuated itself, somehow, elsewhere — perhaps into the hulls of the forsaken boats, into the bodies of the fishermen, into the azure sky. He had, at any rate, settled for a morning's decent reading, from time to time lifting his head to look out to sea. The breeze off the water was immensely refreshing. He kept taking lungfuls of it, quite unaware of how much he would need them.

There were people in the water — splashing in the shore break rather than swimming, throwing their arms up and down in tune with the surf, shrieking when the water billowed over their heads: simpletons at play, the epilepsy of the faint-hearted and incompetent. Andrew had always been an able, much praised swimmer. His eyes swept beyond the shore breaks towards the line of proper waves, those which reared into glassy walls before rushing down their invisible race to the beach. Beyond that line a man was swimming, and absent-mindedly, with half a thought to joining him, Andrew was looking. The man was waving.

God only knew who to.

But he kept waving.

Andrew returned to his book.

Sally sat up and said: 'I think that man out there is in trouble.'

'Hell, I think you're right.'

It was ridiculous, the way one had no choice about such things. Andrew ran down the sand at a graceful trot, as if he might have been running up the beach for an ice-cream rather than down to the surf which he waded through with quick high knees, pushing himself through and under the early waves, before striking out in the heavy water. When he took his first strokes he felt his heart beating. All of a sudden he wondered whether he was fit enough to pull it off.

A good fifty yards' dash it was to the drowning man. Between waves he dipped and disappeared from Andrew's view. Once reached, he was gurgling, and calling out in Portuguese. As soon as he drew close enough, he heaved and scratched in an effort to sit on Andrew's head.

'Turn around,' Andrew said.

The man lunged.

Andrew punched the man firmly in the ear. Then, very quickly, he turned him about, and lassoed the man's chest with his right arm, rolling the thrashing body on to his hip. That was the way you did it. Now you side-stroked, if you could, back through the foam, doing your level best to keep the patient's face in the air. The man was still yelling in Portuguese.

'Save your bloody breath will you,' Andrew tightened his grip.

A breaker swamped them.

'Keep still you mad wog.'

The next wave was a high roller which did not break but gave them a spurt towards the beach. Andrew began to do his side-stroke like a champion. The man stiffened, but lay still. They made progress.

In fact they made such rapid progress that they were in chest-deep water before Andrew realised; he was side-stroking determinedly when the Portuguese broke loose and stood up, waving and calling to the bathers in the shore break. Within seconds they were surrounded by people. Men, women and children, the children coming up to pull on the belt of the man's bathers, touch his arm, walk in his wake, gathered around to hear the man's story of a life almost lost, and, presumably, regained. It was impossible for Andrew to tell as all this took place in Portuguese, and, before he could say anything, the man had left the water and was holding court on the sand.

'Did you see that? Did you bloody well see that?' Andrew flopped beside Sally.

'You can still swim,' she said, admiringly.

'No, no — did you see that chap just walk off like that, like a bloody peacock?'

'He's happy to be alive,' she said.

'He didn't even say thanks!' Andrew spluttered.

'Perhaps he doesn't speak English.'

'You must be joking ... look at him. Anybody would think he'd pulled me out.'

Sally laughed.

'What the hell is so funny?'

'Come on, come and lie down and get your breath.'

'Look, if someone hadn't gone to get that rat he would have swallowed the Bay of Biscay.'

'See, you're making poetry out of it already. Sit down, Andy, for God's sake.'

He did, eventually, lie flat out beside her, waiting for his chest to stop thumping. He had his face in the crook of an arm, could feel his eyeballs, of all things, pulsing with fury at the man's cockstrutting exit along the beach. He lay there for a long time in a rage. Rage at his outburst. Rage at his pettiness, and a seething pulsating rage at her equanimity, her calm, her dogged refusal to acknowledge that he had put himself at risk. Yes, that was it — her absolute insistence on taking for granted everything he did, would do.

Three days to go.

He professed, unashamedly, a weariness with the village. The need to exercise on an open stretch. While she slept he would explore the other side of the cliff, look at the chapel, perhaps take a few photographs from the cable car. 'We could do all that together,' she said. 'I want to go for a hard run,' he replied, and, fortunately, she did not take offence. After all, they had been married long enough for that sort of thing to be said without threat of desertion.

At 1.30 in the afternoon he trundled into the air on the cable car. The cabin was filled with cream-trousered, middle-aged men, and young mothers, their children so excited by the ride that their ice-creams melted over the edge of their cones, running unlicked to their fingers. One woman seemed to be unescorted, a pretty creature in a green silk scarf. She was French, most likely. He could feel her in pursuit of his eye. But as was a married man's unwitting wont, Andrew spent his time in the sky looking elsewhere; he looked back and down to the village, observing the patterns in the bleached hives, the dark clumps on the beach, the expanse of sand beyond the village, a coastline which the midday sun had drained of colour. Andrew let it all slide back beneath him as the cabin crawled in the air. He did not look at the woman until they reached the top.

Passengers went off in the direction of the little chapel, to the look-out point, or inland towards the bull-fighting arena. The French woman went towards the only hotel on the cliff top, a large, pine verandah affair which occupied dry ground beneath some bedraggled palms. Andrew thought he might have a drink there on the way back.

He went to the edge of the cliff.

A path went steeply down to the beach. It was a long, very exposed beach, and it was deserted, wonderfully deserted. As soon as he reached it he ran. He took off his shirt as he began to run. He ran to the first headland. The next. The beach was still deserted. He ran on and on. With the surf beating its way in beside him, raging, he ran until he had to stop, bend, drop into the soft, powdery sand before him. And there he rested, splayed upon the warmth. And then, so quickly, urgently did his loins burrow into the sand, the sea heaving and rising from its depths to meet him, that he pulled back and sat up.

He ran straight into the sea.

It was icy, so different from the water at the village beach. And the surf was stronger. Waves beat him back. He attacked again, head down, legs as pistons, lunging beneath the assaults of white. Finally his feet left bottom. Soon he was swimming in the skimming troughs of large waves, making progress, striking out with his real strength, jubilant in the knowledge that he would ride the waves all the way back to her, that he would land to tell her that he had to go, that he had gone, gone long ago, that they had been together long enough, too long, that not even solid, sound things should have to last forever.

Beyond the break he paused. He trod water. It was sensible to deliver the news gently. It was sensible to transmit this still, pellucid water. Treading water: the sea beneath his feet emerald, the water around him as pure as the sky.

He floated on his back — whistled, spurted, breathed deeply as he floated. A world up-turned. Sun beat upon the silver rivulets on his chest and loins as he lolled — a firm, fine piece of free floating timber.

He would tell her nothing but the truth.

Truth lives in water. He duck-dived. Came to the surface with a howl. Roaring, swimming like a sea lion, he forgot her then completely. Already he had accomplished the deed.

After a time he looked back towards the beach. An amusing surprise: he was a mile, at least, off shore. The surf tow had swept him, silently, effortlessly, a good way out. He would have a pleasant job of it getting back in, bridging the chasm between himself and the dry land. But he set out, more or less at once, still roaring within himself — swimming with strong, steady strokes, making simple clean work of the task, exhilarated, in a way, by the mild risk which had been so immediately granted him. He put his face down and pressed forward with pleasure.

He was carried further out.

He had, of course, a great deal of worthwhile experience in the sea. He knew that it was often pointless, once one was caught in a decent sweep, to struggle against the flow. Best to go with it until it petered out somewhere further off shore, then swim in to the nearest land. That was the sensible thing to do if one was in real difficulty, and if one wasn't there was no harm in testing the strength of the current before giving up.

So he swam seriously, concentrating on a regular rhythm, pulling evenly with each arm, touching each thigh with his thumb, the better to ensure that accuracy of his bearing. He had lined up a dune just down from the chapel — that was how far along the beach the current had taken him — and he was heading for that. But when he paused to look up he was already in line with the cross. And when he stopped the next time, it was clear that he had made no progress towards the shore but was being carried around the cliff to the village beach.

'Ahoy,' he thought. 'A free ride home.'

He could see the cable car inching its way up the rock face. A perfect profile, one that fishermen must have each dawn. He felt immensely privileged.

He let himself drift.

Such deep, crystal water, the sun pouring into the halls of light below him. His feet circled in the upper reaches of cathedrals.

He trod water. It was cold, but he kept his arms moving as well.

Only a matter of exercising patience and commonsense.

Around the point he went. He was, in steady succession, in line with the cable car, the ticket office for the cable car, the village square, the three hotels south of the square, the body of the village, dumb white in the glare, the tents of the fair, the long rectangle, parallel with the shore, of the fishing market, which was, he could see, shut tight and deserted of the people who manned the boats. Boats, in fact, were anchored off the point, in the direction of which he appeared to be travelling. If he continued in the way that he was going — drifting was a much easier business than he had thought — he would actually come to those boats and be able to climb aboard and dry himself in the sun. If he drifted as far as those boats he would be able to lie on their salty decks until sunset, then set off with the fleet for the evening's work, returning at dawn with a good supply of mackerel which could be eaten at breakfast. If he drifted as far as the boats he would at least be able to get warm again.

He thrashed about with his arms. Swam a while with the current. Then, well before reaching the boats, he stopped. No, he had not stopped so much as eddied to a perpetual pause in roughly the same vicinity — he could tell from the stationary landmarks. Directly opposite the outskirts of the village his current seemed to have exhausted itself against an outgoing drift from the beach. He splashed, shouted, waved towards the shore, then rolled on his back once more. His own Sargasso. He floated and thought.

If he put all his efforts into swimming in against the current from here, he ran a risk of being too exhausted by the time he reached the breakers. If he set out for the boats he risked the complications of another cross current. Whereas if he stayed, the tide, surely, would turn. He would get in pretty much under its own steam. It was only a matter of keeping warm. And hoping to Christ against sharks.

'Ship ahoy, sailor boy
Don't you get too springy
The admiral's daughter
Lays down by the water,
She wants to ride your dinghy.'

Towards the cable car he projected his voice. It drowned in the spray of the first breakers. Defiantly, he performed several duck dives and thought: 'Yes, this is keeping calm. I am being fairly brave.'

He could see the shore so well. Lit by the late afternoon sun, it was as clearly defined as a stage set. The stripes on the umbrellas in the village square stood up pink and yellow, the awnings of the cafés had already been rolled down for the evening, people bicycled and walked along the promenade in uniform fits and starts, and, for some inexplicable reason, a light went on in a second storey, then went off again, as if signalling a boat on the horizon. And he could see the people still on the beach, the bathers standing, looking, to all intents and purposes, towards him, one of them, God knew how, actually engaged in conversation with one of the fisherman. Andrew waved.

The fisherman stood up from his hunched position on the sand. He joined another — their black figures leaning together. Others joined them, who gathered near one of the beached hulls. They crouched, as if in conference, and then he saw, between them, the dart of orange. The flame of the fire lit their feet. And not long afterwards he could smell, yes, he could smell the tang of burning skin, as the flavour of the sardines settled on the still water right under his nose.

Every detail of life was going on without him.

Where was she?

The day ended.

In the dark, in the cold dark that fell on him so quickly, he could see everything happening on the beach. Beyond the fires, lights went on. Rooms above every café were lit. Waiters bustled beneath the awnings. The well-dressed emerged on the promenade. He fancied he could see the couple who had sat with them the night before, the turn of the man's shoulder. The wife's gesture. It was not so far away in there after all. He could see everything going on — regardless.

What was she doing?

As he waited for the tide to turn he consoled himself in the cold dark that was not thinking of her in ways which were in any way pathetic. He kept his body moving. He did not romanticise. His mind did not fill with images of her beauty, he did not yearn for her warmth at his back at night; not even then, in the cold dark, did he yearn for that, the marital addiction. Nor did he pause to think of her constancy, the gentleness of her womanhood which had budded since knowing her. No, what he thought of was her getting ready for dinner.

She was in their room. She had showered. She had put on the cotton frock and was luxuriating before the mirror, dabs of Ma Griffe already at her throat as she hummed to herself, because, yes, for once, he was late, he was the one that would keep them from dinner, make them late to the table. She was humming because just for once he had nothing to be irritable about. She sang with girlish relief.

Andrew's burst of laughter left him breathless.

Then, out in the dark water, the tide turned. His legs felt the shift of the current. Press in now — or never.

In the cold inkiness he swam breast-stroke, biding his time, watching carefully for the first line of breakers. The waves would come upon him suddenly. He had to watch for the quick fluorescence of the surf, listen for the roar of the first valley he would slide into. He took it easily, sure now that when he went down into the first trough that he would be loose enough to roll with the swirl of the bottom, firm enough with his chest barrel full of air to come up again with the next toss, with the sea's endlessly renewable force. It was simply a matter of going with its incessant, inexorable energy.

He rolled.

There is no such thing as a simple reversal of forces. He went a distance along the bottom.

Up from the first wave, he could again see the shore: lights in the village, the square bustling, and the sand, when he reached it, bone dry. Even as he lay there — grey fleshed, chilled, breath rasping back to normal, he could see the fishermen up ahead of him, each one of them huddled about their fires. They were settled, well and truly, about their fires. And later, as he made his way up the beach to her, he was taking very deep breaths — and still no one was noticing him.

FRANK MOORHOUSE

THE INDIAN BELL CAPTAIN

PROBABLY THROUGH AN American aid program, most of the
Western hotels in India now have bell captains. As a world
traveller and cultural delegate, this dismayed me. I have warred
with bell captains in many US cities and believe it is the traveller's
job to re-train bell captains. On my last trip I experimented to
see how much it would take in tips to make an American bell
captain grin, but had to leave the experiment unconcluded.

India, however, is a different question.

My first understanding of the Indian bell captain question came
in Hyderabad. I wanted to post two cards to Australia and tried
to buy stamps at Reception, but they directed me to the 'bell
captain'.

Bell captains in India smile at you, unlike US bell captains who,
having an optical defect, cannot see you. As George Kaufman said
on the death of the head bell captain at the Algonquin in New
York, 'I don't know how God did it.'

'What do you mean?' asked Dorothy Parker.

'How did God catch his eye?'

Catching the eye of the bell captain in the US requires
gymnastics. I found that I have to manoeuvre myself into the field
of vision of the bell captain without getting behind his desk and
without taking his head in my hands. Sometimes I found myself
leaning over the bell captain's desk, an elbow nonchalantly on the
counter, chin in hand, leaning so far as to have one foot off the
ground.

Perhaps to lie on the bell captain's desk might have been another
way.

But the Indian bell captain, I found, was a different problem
entirely. It was how to keep the bell captain's eyes off me.

If I tried to do anything, tie a shoe lace, the bell captain would
be there.

And unlike the US bell captain, he did not put his hand into your pocket, take out the wallet, remove the tip, and put it back.

If the Indian bell captain thinks he is not going to get a tip, he looks hungry, dispirited. On the way out of the room without a tip he is likely to stumble with fatigue, lean weakly in the doorway, cough pitiably, spit blood into a handkerchief. He might even fall and have to be helped up, saying, 'It is nothing, I will rest for one moment.'

Foreign Affairs advise me to tip about 2 rupees for service (about 20 cents), but other Australians told me that this could be got down by haggling. Australians, of course, resent tipping because they never know how much to tip.

I found that if I over-tipped bell captains in the US I got service but it was service with contempt because the bell captain knew that he had me beaten.

If you over-tip an Indian bell captain he will move into your room.

He will send in the sweepers, the valet, they will spray for mosquitoes, polish the drinking glasses, take the telephone to pieces and clean it, replace the sheets while you're still in the bed, gesturing with a hand, 'No — to leave the bed is not necessary, please remain,' and as two assistants gently lift you the bed will be made under you.

But it was the problem of the postage stamps which caused my only doubts and suspicions about the bell captains.

There were stories from other travellers about the postage stamp racket. And letters in the Indian newspapers said that anyone who handled mail was likely to remove the uncancelled stamps and throw the mail away (and this presumably included bell captains). As one letter in the *Hindu* said, 'The outgoing foreign mail was not infrequently tampered with for collection of the stamps affixed thereto resulting in the mails never reaching their intended destination. And, nothing used to be heard of them or their fate.'

To forestall this temptation in the Indian bell captain, I intended to buy the stamps and post them personally.

The bell captain was young, perhaps still in training.

'Where to, sir?'

'Australia.'

'Ah — back in Australia you are a cricketer perhaps?'

'No.'

'Would I be asking a personal question if I enquired of you why it is that you do not play cricket?'

'I was no good at it.'

'Surely not, sir, you have the build of a cricketer, a very fine cricketer perhaps.'

'Thank you — stamps — do you have stamps?'

'Sir — which is the finest cricket team in the whole world?'

That was easy, 'India — definitely India,' I replied.

'No sir, you say that to flatter me, to flatter India. The answer, sir, is the West Indies.'

'Thank you. How much is it airmail to Australia?'

'Unfortunately I have no 1-rupee stamps but we will solve it.'

He went to his stamp folder and produced eighteen 20-paise stamps, 'We will make do, never mind. We will get the mails through.'

'But they will not fit on the card — nine stamps will not fit,' I said, 'there is no room.'

'Not to worry — they will fit — you see. If it is fine by you, sir, I will not lick these stamps, for reason of hygiene.'

'It is all right, I will put on the stamps.'

But I knew they wouldn't fit.

'No, sir, it is my duty to place the stamps.'

Hah, I thought, I will not move until the stamps *have* been placed.

I would stay anyhow just to see how they could possibly be fitted onto the postcard. The Lord's Prayer can be written on the back of a postage stamp, my knowledge of Hindi can be written on the back of a postage stamp, but I could not see how this postcard of Hyderabad's Rotary Park could fit onto the backs of nine 20-paise stamps without losing either the address or the message.

The bell captain separated the eighteen stamps individually and laid them out on the glass top of his desk.

He took from a locked cupboard, a jar of clag with a huge brush.

He began to paint the backs of the stamps liberally with glue; the glue overlapped the stamps onto the glass top.

He smiled at me, 'This will prevent theft of the stamps from the postcards between here and the destination.'

The bell captain then had trouble getting the individual stamps off the glass top of the counter because the glue was making them very wet. He smiled again, 'Small problem.'

He slid them along the glass counter and off the edge where they stuck. He then used a fingernail to lift them off. He smiled at me, 'Please, easily done.'

The stamps had picked up a little grime in their journey across the glass top, but you could still see that they were stamps.

The bell captain then had trouble getting the stamps off his gluey fingers. While he held the card he also gave the stamps a second coat of glue. And so with the other eight stamps. As I had calculated the stamps did not fit. I looked away to ease the bell captain's embarrassment. When I looked back the stamps were all in place, pasted over the address.

'The stamps are in place but you will see that we have lost the address,' the bell captain said, still smiling, 'but I will rectify that.'

He went on with the second card, slopping the stamps generously with glue and fixing them on the card. The first card had been placed down on the glass top in the swamp of glue and the ink was running. Both cards looked as if they had been left out in the rain. The bell captain finished the second card and found that the first card had adhered to the glass counter.

The glue, however, was still fluid enough to allow it to be slid off the counter. The bell captain wiped off the excess glue with his sleeve, blurring the message and wiping off two of the stamps, which stuck to his sleeve. 'Oh dear,' he said, looking at me with a resigned smile.

He peeled them off his sleeve and fixed them back on the card after giving them a good slopping with glue.

At this point a clerk came to the bell captain with the autographs of the Australian cricket team. The bell captain became interested in the autographs and placed both the cards down in the swamp of glue on the glass top of his desk.

I rescued the two cards before they became permanently stuck to the glass top. I took them to another table and tried to reprint the addresses, but found the cards too soggy to take ink. I leaned back, wiped away the perspiration from my brow and muttered a mantra.

The bell captain came running over, 'Sir, I will do the mailing of the cards.'

I said no, it was all right, and I took the cards to the lift with the bell captain following, hurt, 'Sir, it is my duty.'

'But I have to let the cards dry so that I can reprint the addresses.'

'No sir, I will do that for you. That was my plan. You tell me the address and I will print it.'

He took out a ball-point pen.

'No, it is OK,' I said, tipping him, 'please — thank you.'

'I will not accept the tip, sir, until I have completed the task.'

I reached my room, gently eased the bell captain and the others out of my room and closed the door. I could hear them outside, discussing the matter among themselves with mutual recrimination.

I placed the two sodden cards on the air-conditioning outlet and they dried within the hour, although they curled. They were heavier, too, from the coating of glue and probably required additional postage. I printed the address in minute script around the stamps on the remaining space. I had no confidence in their arrival.

Later in the bar (for a holy person the bar is a holy place) I asked an Indian friend, 'Why did the bell captain use the glue? Was it for hygiene, because he didn't want to lick the stamps, or was it to make it harder for someone to steal the stamps? Did it make them removable so that if I had left them with him he could have peeled them off? Which was it?'

My Indian friend said that none of these was the answer — the bell captain used glue because the stamps had been stolen from other mail and consequently had no glue.

'Why did he handle the glue so badly?' I asked.

My Indian friend quoted from the novel *The Serpent and the Rope* by Indian writer Raja Rao. In the novel the Indian character allows his French wife to pack the luggage into the car and to drive the car, saying, 'How incompetent we Indians felt before *things*.'

BEVERLEY FARMER

AT THE AIRPORT

HER SON CLATTERS into the airport building, impatient to go. She gloats over him, his wheaten hair, his eyes the same colour of dark honey that his father's are, his sturdy long body and legs. He is eight and she will not see him again for three months. Again he is going with his father, who used to be her husband, to spend the winter, the Greek summer, in his grandparents' village. He will write to her.

Dear Mum haw ar you good you shod come one day it is relly fun we have watafites and jamp off the hen house. Grand Dad is all ways snoring i can not go to sleep! Zzzz i wish we cod stay here. love from me and Dad and Grand Mum and Grand Dad and the rest off the famaly X X X X X X X X X X PAUL

He will send photographs of himself with his grandparents, who were fond of their foreign daughter-in-law. She will see him grinning into the sun in villages and on beaches that she will never go to again. As time passes they are becoming like the house she keeps dreaming of, which has never existed, she is sure, yet which she recognises when she goes there.

She will miss him. He will not really miss her. They no longer live together and haven't for four years. He stays at her flat on weekends and school holidays. For all this, her ex-husband blames her. Her mother, who is dead, blamed her. Her son, more than anyone else, blames her.

Her ex-husband, flustered and tired, waits in line to check in his luggage. The girl he lives with now fills in his immigration cards for him. To give the couple time alone, her son and she go to the cafeteria. On the way they buy a doll for a new baby cousin in Greece whose godfather her son is going to be. She herself will never see this baby girl. Photographs will show him taking a wet and oily naked baby from the bearded priest, just as six years ago he was taken, splashing and furious. She buys a coffee, and a trifle for him. She asks for a taste. He gives her spoon for spoon of it, sandy, soaked with wine.

'I thought you liked trifle?' She is disappointed.

'Oh yes, I do.'

'But you've given me half?'

'Well, you like it too. Don't you?'

His smile is sad. He is sorry for her, because he is going and she is not.

They are stopping over in Bangkok. She remembers her son at two on his father's shoulders at a rainy temple in Bangkok, a flounced and gilded temple full of a statue of Buddha. A cat lapped a puddle in which grey pigeons and the gold robes of monks were reflected, fluttering. He climbed down to stroke the crouched cat.

She remembers him that year on the shoulders of an uncle emerging from the dark vault of a mulberry grove into the noon heat. He munched, stained with juice. His hands made crimson prints on his uncle's bald dome. They washed each other at a tap in the yard. His white hair trickled. Seeing her, he opened his arms and leaped into hers. He was glossy, cold-skinned. '*Moura*,' he said. Mulberries.

That year he was baptised in the font of the village church. He was given his Greek name, his grandfather's: Pavlo. And Greek nationality.

After drinks at the bar and hasty kisses and farewells they are gone. She is left with Vanessa, who lives with them now but has never gone with them, not yet. She and Vanessa go back together to sit in the bar beside a window through which they can see all the plane. It is late taking off. She is sipping Riesling and Vanessa vermouth. They are not alike in any way. Even the man each of them has loved in her time is not the same man. She looks in the pane at the sleek eyes and hair of this younger woman warmly nestled, looking out. No sadness is showing. She sees herself, looking no less calm. Their glances, meeting, jump away.

The plane taxies and turns. They stand to watch it hurl itself up. Then they take polite leave of each other.

She pays her parking fee at the gate and drives on to the freeway. Planes in the foggy air blink their lights and rise and sink. There is a dim full moon. It will shrink and fill again three times before his father brings him back. He must, he has made promises. No self-pity, she thinks, having worked hard to keep her composure, the outward sign of dignity, intact. It is her crust, her shell. Her carapace. Loss and the fear of loss assail her.

'Daddy wants us to go and live in Greece now,' she remembers him saying a while ago. 'But you can come too.'

'I couldn't go and live in Greece, Paulie.'

'You used to.'

'Ages ago. I don't belong there now.'

'Why not?'

'I just don't.'

'*I* do.'

'Yes, I know.'

'I'm Greek.'

'Half-Greek.'

'No. I'm Greek.'

'Well, I'm not.'

'You can speak Greek.'

'That's not enough.' She hugged him. 'You belong here too.'

'There's better, Mum.'

'Why?'

'Well, *there's* a family.'

In the next two months she is patient. She goes to her job in a coffee shop and then to classes. She hands in work on time. She sleeps late. She walks along the winter beaches. On the grey sand she finds mussel shells, feathers, dulled glass. She sees a yacht trail close in to shore. Its heavy sails move cloud-coloured, the late sun in them. Out past the shore water shadowed by this or that drift of wind, a red ship hangs in mid air.

She remembers their summer beaches. She dwells on the time when he was four, only four, and they were in Greece for the last time together. She blew up his yellow floaties on his arms, took his hand and swam with him in tow far out into the deep water where a yacht was anchored. Puffing, they clung to a buoy rope that threw bubbles of water in a chain on the surface of the sea. Scared and proud, they waved to his father and the rest of the family, those dots on the sand, aunts and uncles and cousins. The yacht tilted creaking above them. On the sea, as if in thick glass, its mast wobbled among clouds. They glided back hand in hand. Used to waters where sharks might be, she had never dared swim out so far before. Here there were none. They passed, mother and son, above mauve skeins of jellyfish suspended where the water darkened, but not one touched them. Bubbles had clustered, she saw, on the fine silver hairs of his back, on his brown legs and arms and on hers.

She often dreams of this swim now. It was a month after it, back home in the early spring, that she left home. Her son was asleep. When he woke he thought Mummy was playing hidey. He laughed, looking in wardrobes. Then his father told him. 'Your Mummy's sick in hospital,' he said. Her son told her all this later. 'Well, what I should say?' his father shouted at her. 'You walk out, you want I say that?'

She found a flat in South Melbourne, two hours' drive from their town, and a job in a hotel. 'I thought you'd be a good mother,' was what her mother said. 'You were at first.'

Her son's black kitten, black but for the circles of gold round his eyes, sits and nibbles one paw. He has been entrusted to her while her son is away. He is used to her now. He falls asleep on her lamb's fleece stretched on his back. When he wakes the bell at his throat will tell her so. At night she sits and studies. A cowled white lamp peers over her shoulder at the shadow of her hand writing. The kitten wakes — chink — and gazes. He eats crouching, his sharp little shoulders almost bald. She lets him out during the day, but is anxious. At night he must use the litter box. He prowls in it and flips the granules over the carpet obsessively. Nothing must happen to him while he is at her place. Growth, of course, must. He is becoming a stolid cat. Will her son still love him? Will her son come back?

On her balcony she listens to a slow sonata, a hollow clarinet, watching a sunset douse its cold flames in the bay. The bridge has its gold lights on. The moon, when it rises, is nearly full again. The moon she sees tonight shone a few hours ago over her son. Does he ever think of her? Remember me, she says. Miss me. I miss you.

The pot of basil they gave her for her balcony before they left is still there, but black and dry. Basil dies in winter. Her balcony faces the sea wind. The lane opposite is always full of dark rainwater. The sunset shows in it. Night fills it with lamps.

'It's breaking your mother's heart,' a neighbour reproved her when she first left. It was true, in a way. Her mother's little clockwork voice was always on the phone.

'I've talked to a lawyer,' it piped. 'Act fast, she says. The longer you delay the more weight it gives to the status quo.'

'Delay — what?'

'You have to *apply* for interim custody. You can't wait till the divorce.'

'Oh, Mum, no, I can't contest custody.'

'What do you mean? He's not going to hand you the child on a platter. He'll fight you for him.'

'He talked about that before I left. Even if I won he wouldn't let me get away with it. He'd kidnap him and go home. He would.'

'There are laws —'

'Constantly being broken. You know that.'

'Well, try, at least. What's got into you?'

'That'd turn him completely against me.'

'So *what*?'

'Mum, as things are, he lets me see Paul. And he lets *you* see Paul. He's sorry for us.'

'Why should anyone be sorry for you? You've brought it on yourself. Where did I go wrong? A real mother would go to hell and back to keep her child!'

She writes to Paul about his kitten and the football and the village. She knows it amazes him that she knows the village. He forgets that she went there before he was born and then twice with him when he was little. With an incredulous grin he looks at slides of her in the village with his family, when he comes to visit, as if she was there by some magic. She knows how he feels.

She takes out the old projector and looks at the slides again. She gets photographs from him in the mail and studies them. She gets a letter.

Dear Mum haw ar you i am very well evry day we go to the beche, evry after noon the weves have gron hiarh and hiarh and moore hiarh and hiarh. i went very deep on tuesday. how is my cat. there is a kitten here its names psipsina. i was bitten by a wosp on the neck twis i was pritending i was drackula. any way love from me and evry body X X X X X X X X PAUL

He used to ask her why. Why don't you love my Dad? Why did you leave us? (Why didn't you wake me? Take me?) Won't you ever come back? Why not? Will you always be my mother?

He would understand one day, she used to answer: it was a long story. She doesn't ever want to show him wounds or admit to the rage and spite that caused them. Nor, she thinks, does his father. They both cringe under their son's accusing gaze. They have stopped accusing each other, and now make what amends they can. They trust each other to behave well. It was not always so.

What matters after all is that there came, in their anger and terror and despair, a point of silence one night in which she went to her sleeping child, kissed his cheek, picked up her suitcase. Left. This is what counts. Might it have been otherwise? Yes. No. Whatever happened before it belongs to one life, which is over. What comes after is another. In dreams, what is meshes with what was and what might have been; as in dreams she goes to a remembered house which does not exist. What might have been cannot be.

Since Vanessa moved in, he has stopped asking questions.

She brought him to stay at her new flat and took him to the zoo. Politely they gazed at the animals, especially the sandy, sleepy lions. He rode on the train and on a white pony. On the spiral slide he made her go up with him the first time and clung to her as they spun down; then he went up alone again and again while she waited to catch him at the bottom. They had hamburgers and milk shakes. Then he had to go to the toilet. The Men's, he insisted. She promised to wait but after a while she called out that she was just going to the Women's: wait, she said. When she came out he was not there. She stood in the smelly shade until a man looked in and told her there was no little boy inside. She rushed over to the lions, then to the slide, the ponies, the train, the toilets again. A microphone blared. Reception! she thought and hurtled along crowded paths. There he was, red-faced. He turned his back.

'A lady brought him in. He said his Mummy went home!' the woman at Reception accused. 'Of course I said Mummies don't do that, but he was that positive! "Why ever would she?" I said and he said, "I don't know." '

'I was only in the toilet,' she explained.

'You were not!'

'I was. I called out.'

'You did *not*!'

'Darling, I *did*! You just didn't hear.'

'No, you never! You did not call out! Oh, why didn't you?'

She tried to hug him and wipe his eyes. Sobbing, he pushed her. But he walked beside her out into the sun.

'Remember our long swim?' she asked as they watched lions.

'In Greece?'

'Yes. Remember?'

'No,' he muttered.

One afternoon the cat doesn't come back in. She wanders, calling, along streets filled with cars and darkness. The lamps twitch on. The pairs of gold eyes that she stalks and chases all belong to strange cats. His cat must be lost. The wind tugs and hurls cold sea-spray. She blunders through puddles.

At home in the lamplight she can't concentrate on work. She can't finish her letter to her son. A child is wailing in the flat next door. Mamma. Ma-ama. Every half hour she goes to the door and calls the cat.

Once as her son stepped out of her car after a visit with her, he saw his kitten playing on the road. He called, but the kitten lifted his tail and danced away. 'If I catch him I'll kill him!' Her son's face was dark red. 'He knows he's not allowed out! I'll kill him!'

'Oh, Paulie,' she said.

'I will. I mean it. I'll flush him down the toilet!'

'He'll come back,' she said.

He just looked at her.

Before she goes to bed she opens the door a last time and calls out. Suddenly the cat is there, flattened against the wall in the wind, thin and black as his shadow. He struts in and prowls, purring, and folds himself on the lamb's fleece.

After the divorce, when her ex-husband took her son home to Greece, her mother would not be consoled. Paul was gone, her only grandchild. He was as good as gone before that. But now his father would never bring him back.

'Mum, he will.'

'What makes you think so?'

'He just will.' Compassion, she thought. Respect for the tacit bargain: you keep him, but *here*. Even mercy, for the defeated opponent. 'His business, for one thing.'

'Why did you have to go and marry a Greek?'

'Oh, come on. You always liked him.'

'Can't you work something out?'

'No.'

'I can't get over it. How could you do it?'

'I had to.'

'It wasn't that bad.'

'It *was*. I was spending days staring at one corner in one room. The sun never came in. Everything was grey. Shadows moved, that was all. Nothing mattered, not even the child, and he was so persistent. When footsteps came near me, I banged my head on the window frame until it bled or they went away.'

'You should have seen a doctor.'

'A doctor! When my *life* —'

'A doctor, yes. Depression can be treated, you know.'

'I've come alive since I left.'

' "I, I, I." When you realise how selfish you've been all along, and how *weak*, when you finally think of the *child* —'

'It's best for him not to be fought over.'

'You *hope*. Oh, the easy way out, as per usual. You're a callous and self-centred woman. I'm ashamed you're my daughter.'

'You make better chips than Vanessa,' her son told her on a visit a few months ago.

'That's good. Who's Vanessa?'

'A lady. She lives at our place. She's got this dog. Its name's Roly. Guess why.'

'Short for Roland?'

'No. Because it's always rolling! Mum, if my Dad marries Vanessa, will Roly be in my family?'

'I suppose. Vanessa. She's not Greek, is she?'

'No. She comes from Sydney.'

'Has she been to Greece, do you know?'

'Yes. She loves it. She'd like to live there, she says. Could she take Roly?'

'I don't know. Maybe. Is he friendly?'

'Oh, yes. You make the best chips I've ever aten.'

'Eaten.'

'Eaten.'

They did come back from Greece that first time, and the next. Her son loved her mother just the same after the divorce, and she spoiled him. Now, two years since her death, he often mentions Granma, his voice hushed and sorrowful. He remembers her best cooking dinners when they visited, ladling gravy, hovering over a sizzled chicken. He knows he will die one day. He buries dead birds and crickets, and saves moths from his cat.

One morning in September she has a good dream. She is at the house she is always dreaming of. It has a deep verandah of sagging boards that looks on to muddy grass and bare trees. A window burns with light. As the sun sets she strolls in and opens a door of gold wood that she has never opened in any previous dream. She knows the moment before she looks that her son will be in there. He is asleep, his cat at his feet. He wakes and looks up, smiling.

She lies awake breathless with joy in her rented bed. She wishes she could tell her mother this dream. Some time, she hopes, her mother will be behind a door, in one of the bright rooms in this house.

Dear Mum haw ar you we ar coming back 15 september. its at 4 oclock in the morning. pleas meet us at the air port. i wont you to. X X X X X X X X X PAUL

She rings the number Vanessa has given her, but is told that Vanessa is up in Sydney because her mother is sick. So Vanessa won't be at the airport. On the night she wakes to the alarm with a sour headache at three, crams the cat into his basket and drives through the dark under all the faint lamps of the city. The airport building, full of light, is crowded already. Voices boom, echoing. The plane has landed. After an hour passengers start bursting through the door with luggage trolleys. Her eyes are crusted, dazed. They will keep watering. Her ex-husband and her son push through last of all. Her ex-husband looks smaller, gaunt and grey. But her son! So big, so brown! She is full of exclamations and this delights him. He thinks she is crying, though she says no. They all talk at once and wish aloud for coffee, but there is nowhere open, so they go out to the car-park. She has forgotten where she left her car. In the cold wind and half-light they all wander over the painted asphalt, looking. Her son sees it first. He wraps himself in his sullen cat. The sun comes up, a gong on the rim of the sky.

'Glad you're back?' She hugs Paulie.

'Yes, if you are.'

'I am. I'm very glad.' To her ex-husband she says in Greek, 'There are times when —' She can't speak. 'Life —' she tries again.

'Oh, life. Life. Well, yes.' He smiles wanly.

The trees toss and swill the gold light. Their eyes glitter with it.

MICHAEL WILDING

KAYF

WONDERFUL WAS THE contrast between the steamer and that villa on the Mahmudiyah canal! Startling the sudden change from presto to adagio life! In thirteen days we had passed from the clammy grey fog, that atmosphere of industry which kept us at anchor off the Isle of Wight, through the loveliest air of the Inland Sea, whose sparkling blue and purple haze spread charms even on N. Africa's beldame features, and now we are sitting silent and still, listening to the monotonous melody of the East — the soft night-breeze wandering through the starlit skies and tufted trees, with a voice of melancholy meaning.

And this is the Arab's Kayf. The savouring of animal existence; the passive enjoyment of mere sense; the pleasant languor, the dreamy tranquillity, the airy castle-building, which in Asia stand in lieu of the vigorous, intensive, passionate life of Europe. It is the result of a lively, impressible, excitable nature, and exquisite sensibility of nerve; it argues a facility for voluptuousness unknown to northern regions, where happiness is placed in the exertion of mental and physical powers; where Ernst ist das Leben; where niggard earth commands ceaseless sweat of face, and damp chill air demands perpetual excitement, exercise, or change, or adventure, or dissipation, for want of something better. In the East, man wants but rest and shade: upon the banks of a bubbling stream, or under the cool shelter of a perfumed tree, he is perfectly happy, smoking a pipe, or sipping a cup of coffee, or drinking a glass of sherbert, but above all things deranging body and mind as little as possible; the trouble of conversations, the displeasures of memory, and the vanity of thought being the most unpleasant interruptions to his Kayf. No wonder that 'Kayf' is a word untranslatable in our mother-tongue. In a coarser sense 'Kayf' is applied to all manner of intoxication. Sonnini is not wrong when he says, 'the Arabs give the name of Kayf to the voluptuous relaxation, the delicious stupor, produced by the smoking of hemp.'
— Richard Burton, 1855

North Africa. Somewhere warm, somewhere to get stoned away from cold weather and cold wars, somewhere to relax. The need to relax producing its own tensions, of course, the desire to relax, the will to relax, maybe not a need, put like that Marcus would have hesitated about need, he felt guilty about having needs, needing to relax being no need. But it would be nice, and to obliterate all those anxieties about unnecessary needs the sooner he could score the better, and how do you score in a strange place where you know no one, don't know how legal or illegal it is anyway, is this the sort of hotel you can ask the desk clerk, what about asking the taxi driver on the way from the airport, is that insanity or practical common sense?

And outside the palm trees along the boulevard and then the railway line and then the beach, and first thing in the morning boys playing football on it, just like *L'Etranger*, the long stretching beach, the boys playing football and doing headstands and cartwheels, the port at one end and the old town above it, the new tourist hotels stretching along to the other end of the beach, cargo ships and hydrofoil ferries coming into dock.

They went out of the hotel in search of somewhere to eat breakfast, first one direction, then back and towards the port and the old town. A figure in black homed in on them.

'Good morning, how you like it here?'

Black jeans, black T-shirt, walking along with them but a couple of paces ahead and to one side, like a fighter plane escorting an alien invader of airspace.

'You from England, London, I have a brother in London, I like to practise my English.'

They walked along.

'I'm not a guide,' he assured them.

'What's this?' said Lydia. 'What have we got ourselves into?'

Marcus shrugged. 'I don't know.'

'Is he police?'

'I don't know.'

They walked along the boulevard, past the souvenir shops and the cafés. There didn't seem to be anything that they wanted to eat, people either drinking tea or coffee, or grilling meat. Marcus scrutinised them as he passed. One old man with a smiling, wizened face held a pipe in one hand and shook a round tobacco tin. The knowing smile suggested kif. Was shaking the tin a selling gesture, how would you know, and what if it wasn't?

'These places too expensive,' Mustapha said, he'd already given them his name, elicited theirs, the shops draped with blankets, rugs, windows full of brassware, leatherware, the smell of freshly tanned leather thick and yellow and sweet across the pavements.

'What do we do?' said Lydia.

Marcus shrugged, smiled, his smile tighter, less persuasive, harder to maintain now, the facial muscles tired, unconvinced. He didn't know what you did, he just drifted along, looking for some likely eating place, dope place.

'If it isn't him it'll be somebody else,' he said.

Mustapha walked ahead, keeping up a brisk pace.

'These were the cannon used against the Spanish,' he told them.

They were in the socco, the tiny narrow streets and alleys, the archways, children helping weave, taking threads down the length of the alley, this criss-cross of threads, and the cross-legged tailors weaving, sewing, people calling from the shops, 'Buy something from me,' 'Don't trust the black man he gets a commission from all the shops.'

At least if that's what it was about, the financial basis was clear, Marcus figured. They wouldn't need to work out a tip for having been shown round where they didn't want to be shown.

They came up to the casbah, a coach load of tourists watching the snake charmers. Marcus took one look at the swaying, hooded snakes, metallic grey, scaly dragon tails, that was enough. They walked to the walls to look across at the sea, the houses along the cliff. But what he wanted was something to eat, something to drink, something to smoke.

They went back down through the narrow alleys, the people with things to sell calling out from doorways, the others looking at them, this silent looking, the familiar passive watchfulness, blank doorways opening and closing directly onto the narrow pathways.

'Tell him we want to get something to eat,' said Lydia.

'You try,' said Marcus, surrendering to the flow of it, not knowing where or why they were wandering through this ancient alien city, so other, it was all so impermeably other, familiar from movies and books, but familiar only in its otherness.

'Here is the house of the lady who had seven husbands,' said Mustapha. 'You thirsty? We'll have some mint tea, I'll take you to my relatives.'

And on they wound.

They came into a shop that opened into room after room, draped with carpets, blankets, djellabas, kaftans, shirts, handbags, cases, little stuffed model camels. They sat down and drank mint tea and looked at all these things. Marcus tried on a djellaba and a fez.

'Now you look like an official guide,' they said, there seemed to be two or maybe three people showing them things. 'You buy one of these and you'll have no trouble, everyone will know you've bought something and they won't ask you any more, you wear a djellaba and you don't look like a tourist.'

Marcus doubted it.

'You're not wearing a djellaba,' Lydia said.

'Some days I do,' the man said, 'but today . . .'

A sad smile, no meaning.

Marcus found some hookahs and waterpipes in a corner and gazed at them with longing.

'You want one of those?'

'They're very nice,' said Marcus. 'What I'd rather have is something to smoke in them.'

'No, we don't smoke,' said the man in the shop.

'But people do?'

'People do?'

'People do smoke? Here? In the town?'

'Oh yes, people do, they smoke in the cafés, no problems, sometimes the police come along and they confiscate their kif and their pipes. So they go and buy another pipe.'

Marcus saw an endless vista of smoky, dark cafés, sniffing around hopefully for the familiar smell, for somebody selling, surrendering pipe after pipe to the invading police. There had to be a better way.

'Where do you get it? In the cafés?'

'In the cafés, yes,' the man said. And then he caught the drift of Marcus's laboured conversation. 'Ah,' he said, 'you want some? We don't have any, I don't smoke. But I'll send the boy.'

'Sure,' said Marcus.

Then he sat around trying on djellabas and sipping mint tea while Mustapha went off to score.

'He won't be long. You smoked before, no?'

'Yes,' said Marcus.

'You like it?'

'Yes, he likes it,' said Lydia.

'Ah,' said the man, 'I smoke a lot. But not while I'm working. Good stuff.'

'Good stuff,' agreed Marcus.

Mustapha came back without success.

'No good stuff in the casbah,' he said. 'We take a car ride. I take you to my place, smoke some good stuff, you know it's good there.'

It seemed fair enough. The terror of the unknown but a better price and a better quality out of the tourist area. Marcus bought his djellaba, maybe it would be insurance against the wrong sort of car ride, when was he ever going to wear a djellaba? It seemed a lot of money for a djellaba, for anything that he wasn't really likely to wear but if the dope was cheap and you added the cost of it onto the dope and treated it as the necessary way to score, then you could write off the cost that way.

Back through the narrow alleys, finally they passed a cake shop near the medina and stopped to stave off their hunger and then Mustapha hailed a taxi and they were going through the newer town, the colonial development, the new housing blocks. The Spanish mosque. The new mosque. The American school.

They stopped at a café, an open street, looking across at new housing blocks. The juke box or cassette player was playing modern black American music, commercialised energy, electronic precision. They ordered mint tea again and sat out at a table on the street.

'You wait here,' Mustapha said. 'Five minutes, ten minutes.'

When he came back they went inside. There were two rooms, the one with the counter, the other a bare room at one side. They sat there, out of sight of the shopkeeper, who brought them an ashtray and then went away. Mustapha produced a block of blond hash.

'You have an American cigarette?'

'No,' said Marcus, 'I'll get some . . .'

'No, I have one,' said Mustapha, breaking one open. Milder than the local tobacco, he explained. He crumbled a piece off the block of hash, crumbs lay on the Laminex table top, he broke big crumbs of hash into the joint, Marcus watched transfixed, stoned already, imagine being able to use that much hash in one joint, what a life, happiness began to spread around him, Mustapha passed him the joint, lit it for him, and then the café was a sandy ochre, a soft capsule of warm, vibrating well-being, now they had arrived, now they could relax. He passed the joint to Mustapha.

He shook his head. 'No, I don't smoke, makes me too paranoid, you know.'

'Go on,' said Lydia.

He took a couple of tokes to be sociable. Then he produced the rest of the block from his sock.

'Two-twenty dirhams, twenty pounds. How much would this cost where you come from?'

'Don't tell him,' said Lydia.

Marcus beamed. He had been trying to work it out, was it three times as cheap here, ten times as cheap, the bare white café room waved in the viscous gentle air, the whole breathing movement of the earth passed through it, nothing still, nothing solid, no fixed straight lines, but a gentle waving in the soft susurrus of the perceived day.

'What about the stuff you eat?' said Marcus. Dawamesc back in the Parisian 1840s, but the word, or their pronunciation, meant nothing to Mustapha.

'Like a sweet,' Marcus tried.

'Ah, majouna, you want to try some majouna?'

'Can you get it?'

'Yes, I can get it. Not now. But tonight. You want some?'

'Sure,' they said.

'You want me to get you some?'

'Yes,' said Lydia.

'You tell me your hotel room and I will come.'

The paranoia there, wavering, but there didn't seem any great reason not to since he'd already elicited the name of the hotel, so if it was a police set-up they already knew enough.

'You'll be there tonight, seven o'clock, seven thirty? I'll bring it then.'

They agreed.

'We go now?'

And that was good, he'd made the deal, no more hanging around, as long as he would find them a taxi and they could get back to the hotel and have a relaxing smoke . . .

'If anybody asks,' he said, 'say you don't smoke. Don't trust anybody. Roll it in your hotel room and then smoke on the beach.'

'But not in the hotel room?'

'Yes, that's what I'm telling you, it's all right in the hotel, you smoke in your room, no one bothers, if anyone asks, say you don't smoke. You don't look like you smoke, that's why I didn't ask you before. You'll be all right.'

They walked down from the café, down the dusty road to the market below, they waited there for a cab, rectangular buildings, women in kaftans, their faces covered to the eyes, men in djellabas, others in western clothes, the rest just a blur, a warm golden glow.

They went out later in the afternoon, somewhat uncertainly down the stairs, past the burnished brass trays and pots, smiling at the smiling desk-clerk, out into the bright light and the shadow of the palm trees. Marcus had never possessed such a store of hash, the future days were assured, the weight of anxiety slipped away into retreat, for a few days it was driven off by the soft yellow golden blocks.

'Hello, how are you?'

A figure in a black T-shirt and black jeans slid across from somewhere and was walking along with them.

Marcus nodded.

'Casbah, Bedouin markets, medina.'

'We've already been,' said Marcus.

They kept walking and he kept pace with them, smiling.

'This you first time here?'

Marcus agreed.

'Where you from? London?'

'Tell him we already have a friend,' said Lydia.

'You tell him.'

'We already have a friend who's showed us round.'

'You have? That's good. You want to get high?'

'I already am,' said Marcus.

'Ah,' the boy in black smiled, 'have a good time.'

He dropped back and curved round to wherever he'd appeared from.

The palm trees swayed a bit.

'You needn't have worried about scoring,' said Lydia.

He thought about the djellaba. Maybe he should have put it on. Then they mightn't have been approached. But then they mightn't have found out how easy in fact it was to score. And even with the hefty stash for the future, it was good to know you only had to walk along the boulevard to score again.

'Chocolat, hashisch,' a voice called out to them.

The weights lifted from Marcus's already lightened shoulders. Even if he made a pig of himself and smoked it all he could always get more. Without having to buy another djellaba. After a while they turned round and walked back along the boulevard to the hotel. They waved to the boy in black. He waved. They smiled at the smiling desk-clerk who smiled back. They climbed the stairs past the burnished brass, looked into the lounge in which they never saw anyone sitting, and then they were back in the room and Marcus could set about making a pig of himself.

They ate dinner in the hotel. It seemed easier than going out.

'If someone comes for us, we're in the restaurant,' they told the desk-clerk.

But when Mustapha did arrive with his brother the waiter clearly didn't like it. There was a place for street hustlers and a place for tourists. A chill came over his genial manner. Mustapha and his brother rode it through. The familiar discriminations, the assessments and judgments and dismissals that permeate everything.

They hadn't got the majouna.

'Tomorrow. Tomorrow we will come for you and you come out to our place. You must meet our mother. You must have a meal with us.'

They were both in black, black jeans, black T-shirts, Mustapha had a casual black jacket.

Marcus ordered beers, suffering the icy chill of the waiter; once he'd gone the warmth returned, the table melted a little softer, flowed round, congealed against the outer influences.

'My brother is a law student,' said Mustapha.

'That way I can help my family and make money,' he said.

'What does your father do?' Lydia asked.

'He's a customs officer,' Mustapha said.

Lydia made an involuntary noise reserved for police, customs officers.

'No,' said the law student, 'he's a good man, a good father.'

'That's good,' said Lydia, she liked the idea of good men, good fathers, affectionate families.

'He is a good father. You know, like the movie. You know the movie.'

Marcus shook his head. Good fathers were rather out of fashion in the movies he ever saw.

'*The Goodfather*, you must know the movie, our father is like the good father, he looks after his family, anybody in trouble he looks after them.'

'*The Goodfather*,' said Mustapha, 'you know, Marlon Brando.'

'Ah, yes,' said Marcus.

The law student raved on. That was his ideal of the good man, the good father. 'I want to be a big shot. Lots of money. New York. You know.'

'I know,' said Marcus.

'I become a lawyer then I make lots of money and I can help my family. That's what I believe in.'

'God?' said Lydia.

'No,' said the law student. 'I believe in money. That's my god.'

Mustapha looked down at his beer, moved his head from side to side. He wasn't so sure. God still had a place.

'Our mother is very Muslim. You must meet her. She is very Muslim. Very religious.'

Marcus ordered mint tea and the waiter spilled it over him. Hot mint tea.

'Ouch,' said Marcus.

The waiter gestured apologies.

'It's all right,' said Marcus. 'I'll just change my jeans.'

He dripped off to the hotel lobby and up the stairs to their room. He took off his jeans and his thighs were mildly pink from the hot tea. He rolled a smoke quickly and smoked it slowly, looking through the window at the palm trees along the boulevard, hearing the talking and laughter from the restaurant below. As long as everyone was happy he needn't exactly rush back, he could enjoy a smoke, maybe roll a second one and smoke that while he dried out. The flags hung from the lamp standards along the boulevard, a different colour in the street lighting than in daylight. You could make a mistake describing the flag if you only saw it at night.

He went back down. The waiter smiled.

'We have hot showers here.'

'We thought you must be drying yourself,' said the law student. 'Drying your throat.'

Marcus smiled happily. Within the protective cocoon of the m'hashished all was calm. His gums were feeling a bit tender and his lips a bit burnt. He'd looked at the little waterpipes in shop windows but he found it easier rolling joints. Even just rolling them became a pleasurable sensation, delaying the next consumption. And he liked the packets of rolling papers, different sizes, different textures from what he'd been used to. Some people wanted to be big shots, others became connoisseurs of rolling papers.

Mustapha came for them in the morning and they walked up through the colonial town.

'He's a good man,' someone called out as they went past; yesterday's hustler in black smiling at them.

But when they came into the main street a little boy of ten or twelve walked alongside them, 'Don't trust him, he gets a commission from all the shops.'

Mustapha gave the same short chuckle as he gave to the words of recommendation. The little boy bounced up and down and started a running argument with Mustapha, but in the end he dropped back as they carried on along the pavement. They stopped to get tea at one of the pavement cafés, buying cake at the patisserie beside it. Already stoned, and the hunger for sweet things doing its urging. At the next table a group of aging gays talked and surveyed the scene. They all looked like Christopher Isherwood or William Burroughs. Mustapha gave his short, barking chuckle.

As soon as they'd eaten Mustapha hurried them on to a cab rank. They drove out to the suburbs. Blocks of apartments, four, five storeys high, the streets unpaved, rutted sand, climbing up and down the undulations of the land, children and youths playing, hanging around, watching them. The room had couches all round it, some blankets folded in one corner, and a large brass tray, table-sized. Mustapha put on a record, Jimi Hendrix, winding in through the archway from the next room. His brother had answered the door — 'the lawyer', said Mustapha with his short laugh — and then disappeared, either studying or in pursuit of the majouna, verb tense uncertain, explanations ambiguously merging what had been being done with what was going to be done.

'I had some mushrooms last night,' Mustapha said. 'I bought some from some German students.'

'Good?'

'Good, yes,' he said.

They'd talked about drugs the previous day, how hashish made him too paranoid, how he'd had some acid from Italy. Lydia had recommended mushrooms, gentler than acid.

'Where's your mother?' Lydia asked.

'She's in the kitchen. Cooking.'

'Does she need any help?'

Again the short, barking laugh. 'No, she's all right, she likes to cook.'

'Are you sure?'

'Of course.'

Then the lawyer came through with food, chips, egg, minced steak. They had expected couscous, tagine. Was this served for them because they were foreigners, tourists, the food they were expected to expect; or was this what they normally ate? Marcus and Mustapha talked about drugs, music.

'Funny,' said Mustapha, 'you are the only person who ever mentions J.J. Cale.'

He put on J.J. Cale. It wasn't just sales talk, the pretence of shared tastes. So across the world you could find people with shared tastes: hashish, Hendrix, J.J. Cale, mushrooms. It added to his relaxation.

The mother didn't join them.

'No, she'll eat later.'

'You mean she cooked this specially for us?' said Lydia.

Mustapha chuckled. 'Of course.'

'So she's been slaving away.'

'Not slaving,' said Mustapha. 'She likes to cook for people.'

Lydia doubted it.

The lawyer produced the majouna, a block about the size of a tin of pipe tobacco. 'We found someone who knows how to make it,' he said. 'Since we are not sure, we found someone who knows.'

'You smoked kif too?' asked Mustapha.

'No. I'd like to.'

'You want some? Forty-five dirhams a bush.'

'What's a bush?'

'That's how they sell it.'

And off went the law student again. He came back with a pipe so they could smoke some there. And then that lighter, speedier stone. The world lit up brighter from the soft, burnished golden somnolence of hashish.

'You tried opium?'

'I tried it once,' said Marcus. 'I rather liked it.'

'Don't get opium here,' said Mustapha. 'If anyone tries to sell you opium tell them you know what they have here. Hashish and kif. Here there's no opium.'

He went out of the room and came back with a screwed-up piece of paper. He opened it out and showed them some shiny, hard black substance.

'Know what it is?'

'No,' said Marcus, sniffing it, feeling it.

'That's what they sell you as opium.'

'But it isn't,' said Lydia.

'No,' he laughed.

'What is it?'

He screwed up his face, what was it? 'They burn it for the smell.'
'Incense.'

'Yes, incense.' He chuckled and rolled it back into its paper and
stuffed it into his pocket. He wore tight black jeans, tight T-shirt,
but somehow he managed to stash things away into pockets and
socks without any revealing indication that he was carrying
anything.

'Does your mother mind you smoking?' Lydia asked.

'No, she doesn't mind.'

'Does she know you smoke?'

'Yes, no problem.'

'What about drinking?'

'No, she doesn't know we drink. She wouldn't like that.'

'Does your father smoke?'

'No, not any more. He made the pilgrimage to Mecca, you
know, and then you give up things and you don't go back to what
you give up.'

Lydia wanted to eat the majouna then, but Marcus wouldn't.

'Let's go back to the hotel and find out how trippy it is. I don't
want to be blundering around out of my head somewhere I don't
know where I am.'

'It takes an hour to work,' said Lydia.

'Maybe. Maybe not. I'd rather wait till we get back.'

He could see it coming on in the medina and utter craziness
and paranoia taking hold, he didn't want to perceive what the
people in the medina thought about western tourists, imperialists,
infidels, he felt he probably knew, probably agreed with them,
he could see himself fractured into warring parts in the bright sun.

They shook hands, they said goodbye to the mother, she came
out from the kitchen and they said goodbye, they drifted off along
the undulating sandy road, the blocks of apartments standing out
with the clear, rectangular, flat look, walls of pastel pinks and
greens and whites, and then Mustapha put them into a cab and
told the driver where to take them, now they were organised for
a while, now they had taken in provisions and needn't venture
out again, no more arrangements, no more anxieties, no more
doubts.

They ate the majouna which was sweet like a spiced fudge.

'If you want to get higher,' the law student had said, 'you just eat more.'

'To make it work better,' Mustapha said, 'drink some hot tea.'

So they drank mint tea and walked across the road from the hotel to the beach.

'Chocolat, hashisch?'

'No thank you,' they said.

They walked across the sand to the sea, watching the sand shimmering, the sea resonating. A string of three camels loped across to them.

'You want a ride? You have a ride?'

But they declined. It seemed very high up on the camel's hump, a height out of the dimensions of the heights they were on, no more material, no more precarious, but they felt better with their feet on the ground, indeed Marcus felt better lying perfectly flat on the ground, certainly he had no wish to move or to climb onto something moving. The world's moving was movement enough. He smoked a couple of joints he'd rolled in the hotel. Lydia's eyes glistened, she walked down to the sea to walk in the ripples of the waves. Pale, white English tourists stretched out on towels determinedly getting the sun despite the wind that blew across the sand's surface. 'They are like eggs, the English,' Mustapha had remarked. Marcus watched them frying on the beach.

They walked arm in arm along the sand, Lydia and Marcus, they walked round in a circle, they couldn't find the spot to be, out of the afternoon wind, and the long vistas of stretching beach were luring but long, as they began to walk along it they realised how long it would take to get to the end, so they veered back, describing this erratic circle. They went back to the hotel, leaving the sand to the boys playing football and the frying eggs, chewed some more majouna in the hotel room and looked out at the palm trees, the passers-by in their djellabas, Berber women in their layers of clothing, towelling, and the hustlers walking up and down the street. The palm trees framed by the window were the imprinted image. To see the passers-by you had to stand at the window. But the palm trees were in sight both when you stood at the window and when you lay back on the bed.

They spent a lot of time lying on the bed because they got the usual stomach bug. But though their bowels turned to water, they survived on mint tea and kif and hashish. In a way it suited Marcus, he was quite happy lying down stoned all day, if he had been well he would have felt obliged to go out, wander around, explore, consume, consume. He had enough to consume.

He sat shakily on the hotel's terrace beside the boulevard when he felt strong enough to venture out again, sipping mint tea, picking at a croissant. A boy in black went by and waved. He smiled back cautiously.

'Mustapha's friend,' the boy said, and Marcus remembered bumping into the two of them one day on the street.

Five minutes later Mustapha was there. 'Good morning, how are you?'

'We've been sick, but we're going south tomorrow.'

'You going south, you need some more hash? It's better to buy it here, down there it's more expensive, down there it's harder to get, not like here.'

'Really?'

'Oh yes. Don't trust anybody down south.'

So they went out to the café again, Mustapha's brisk walk, the cab ride, and then the wait. 'Don't trust anybody down south,' Mustapha warned again.

Marcus chuckled, interpreting it as local pride, sales talk maybe.

'No, seriously,' said Mustapha. 'If anybody asks, you don't smoke. Don't give any information.'

Then he went off leaving Marcus at the table in the bare room. The man came through from the counter.

'Your first time here? You like it? What hotel you stay at?'

Marcus mumbled. Mustapha's warning hanging there, something about the south, going there, arriving from there, as if he was between hotels or something, something anyway so that there was no answer.

The man went back into the other room, came back with an ashtray.

'You smoke?'

'No,' said Marcus.

The man looked at him strangely, 'I leave it,' he said, leaving the ashtray anyway, as if there was some language problem and Marcus wasn't understanding.

Marcus sipped at a soft drink and listened to the music till Mustapha returned.

They took the train south. They struggled along the corridors with their bags and every compartment was occupied; or if there were spare seats the other occupants denied that they were vacant. When they'd reached the end of the train and there were still no seats they sat on the folding seats in the corridor. Five hours on a folding seat in the corridor. But it wasn't as bad as that. When they were clear of the station someone stuck his head out of a compartment and said there were two seats there perhaps. Perhaps if the people who had been there before came back they would have to surrender them; but perhaps the people had now left the train. And so they sat in the compartment, anxious it might only be a temporary seating, but no one came back and the anxiety seeped away.

He was a student, the one who had offered them seats. He had been studying abroad.

'How did you like it?' Lydia asked.

'The courses are good,' he said, 'but my professor, I think he is a racist. It makes it very difficult. And for my essay on colonialism, he gives me a C because I take a Marxist position.'

'Uh-huh,' said Marcus. No surprises here.

'I think,' said the student, 'there is a kind of double imperialism. First, all our raw materials and products are taken. And second, we have to buy these expensive imports. So we pay both times, both ways we are exploited. I think the people in the rich countries must now share some of their wealth.'

Marcus tried to explain that the people in the rich countries were also exploited, that there was an internal imperialism, the colonised classes were exploited like the colonised nations. Not all the people in the rich countries were rich.

The student shook his head doubtfully. 'But the rich countries, they still have all this wealth which they use to maintain the system here. They pour in aid and it all goes to keep a government that the people do not want in power.'

But Marcus held back, it was not a conversation he wanted; he would have liked it, yes, but knew enough, feared enough, not to pursue it.

'Do you believe in God?' the student asked.

'Yes,' said Lydia.

'And you?'

Marcus nodded.

'And you?' Lydia asked.

'I think,' he said, 'we all come from one source, all the people on the earth.'

'From God,' said Lydia.

The student nodded.

The man in the corner, about fifty, who had pointed out natural salt panning as the train went past, pottery kilns, all the things they passed, which the student translated for them, said something.

'Does he believe in God?' Lydia asked.

The student spoke to him and the man grinned and touched his forehead, the brow over the third eye.

'He says you can see the hollow where he prays, where his head touches the ground.'

The man rolled his trouser legs up to the knees.

'The skin is hardened where he kneels to pray.'

He said something else and the student translated.

'He does not speak English but his son and daughter do. But he speaks Esperanto. He is in communication with forty-five countries. He has Esperanto correspondents in all these countries. He attends the Esperanto conferences in these countries as a delegate.'

The vision of world unity through communication, there on that crowded train: the man with callouses on his knees from praying who spoke the international language that no one else shared; the woman and child who said nothing; the student — 'The only philosophers I think who say anything are Hegel and Marx. The rest, I don't think they say anything to me'; Lydia — 'We all come from one source, we are all children of God'; and Marcus, locked in the inexpressible, the things that mattered not to be talked about; and another silent young man who smiled and shared cigarettes but kept out of the conversation; so much silence.

But the Esperanto speaker was also a poet. He was committed to reviving and maintaining the traditional folk poetry. The student of Marx translated for them tentatively, was there half a smile on his lips, and yet a respect for the project. 'I had wondered, when I was translating, some of the things he said are hard to translate. I had wondered, yes. But now he explains, he weaves into his conversation this traditional poetry.'

Which could not be translated, which remained for Marcus and Lydia with the silent ones. Yet the vision of it, that old and now fading vision of international community, faintly comic as all good and true things now seemed faintly comic, vegetarianism, prayer, pacifism, so that Esperanto was in that category of mild craziness, but outside their own familiar crazinesses and now they had to reconceive their position; for it hung there along with the project for the revival of traditional folk poetry, a vision that Marcus could share but also a fading one for him, how long since he had called up that vision and sat before it, how long since he had surrendered any such hold on that possibility and had accepted unawares the élite specialisation of the marginal man of letters?

He could not hear the revived folk poetry. But it was enough, for this moment, to know that it was there, that it was part of this holy man's commitment, that these things could still be believed in and practised with love.

'The true criticism is to create something better,' the student translated, 'the other criticism is —' The gesture of the hand flipped away from the body, and a dismissive sound, a word that Marcus did not catch describing the literary studies he practised, well we all have to practise something, even if we fail to catch the dismissive word for it. 'There is also a cultural imperialism,' he could have begun, 'both internal and colonial.' But he sat silent, listening, this way he heard things and did not talk himself into trouble saying things other people heard. He accepted the holy man's verdict, offered no defence. Who knew what the silent young man was thinking or hearing, who knew what anyone was, always there was this possibility not to be repressed of the inauthentic; even the highest moments in the cocoon of ecstasy had that possibility, that nothing was free from the possibility of the permeation.

'And imperialism is maintained internally and externally by the mechanisms of the police state, of provocateurs and informers, this is what the money poured in as aid goes to maintain.' But it was enough just to think that, not to say it. To maintain it there as a memento. Et in Arcadia ego.

Then further south by road, long bus journeys through stretching brown fields, buildings of earth and stone rising out of the bare brown land, hedges of prickly pear the only vegetation, the land being ploughed with donkeys and camels. And at the bus-stops meat grilling at roadside stalls, boys selling bread and hardboiled eggs. Plains, hills, high snow-capped mountains inland, police at the intersections outside the major cities.

Marcus sat drinking mint tea outside a café. It was a tourist resort, there purely for tourists, the old town the other side of the port, quite separate. Huge expensive hotels, big bank buildings, hotels still being built, and older cheap hotels, too.

'How many camels for your wife?'

Two boys at the next table smiling at them. The usual hustle. But they didn't seem to be trying to hustle anything. Down there no one had come up hustling dope. Marcus was glad he had taken Mustapha's advice and bought another deal. This was a sanitised, hygienised, tourist resort, tourists walking up and down the pavements looking displaced, sleepwalking. Marcus sat there stoned, watching them.

'G.I.s,' one of the boys said as three tall, shapeless gangly figures went by. 'American ship.'

'Here?' Marcus said.

'Yes, came in last night.'

He pulled a face. Just a face. The fatal involuntary reflex.

'English people don't like Americans,' the boy said.

'Not much,' Marcus said. He was about to say, 'Who does?' But didn't. 'Don't trust anybody down south,' Mustapha had said. And now he was down south about to launch into a discussion of American ships.

'See you,' he said to the boys, and paid the bill.

He walked with Lydia through the dusty, sandy park.

'What I hate worst of everything,' he said, 'is having to do that, having to cut off as soon as any conversation might be political.'

'You're getting better at it,' Lydia said.

They had been practising for a while now. They had come to this country as a relief from their practising. But it was no less difficult here.

'So the only conversations you can have are the empty, boring ones. And anyone who looks like they might be interesting, you can't afford to talk to. Anyone who looks like they might agree with you you have to suspect at once of being a provocateur. It makes it very hard to go on.'

Off the beach the submarine was moored, the black outline breaking the water's surface, Leviathan rising. The aircraft skimmed in over the sand to the tourist airport, the runways ready for any military contingency. Inland the guerillas encroached on the desert boundaries. At the airport when they flew back all the baggage was deposited on the runway beside the aircraft. Passengers had to identify their own bags before they were loaded onboard. It was all around them, the inexorable process. Marcus smoked as much hashish as he could absorb before they left. The days of the imperialist decadence were numbered, who knew how long it would last?

FAY ZWICKY

STOPOVER

FIRST THERE WERE the premonitions. Capricious, unreasonable, deepset, each ringed with tiny sulphurous bubbles of panic. The lurking possibilities of a future before which she wavered and shrank. The heat seized her, pressed like some great grey fist, giving her the excuse she so urgently needed to hate everything about the place. The eyes, for instance. Those melancholy sepia jellies set in expressionless faces, the daguerreotypes of new wars. Hundreds of them. Waiting. A sea of silent grey-green phantoms, each with his hands dangling between his knees in the great open vaulted airport at Honolulu. They kept coming in groups of two, three and more, forming in long silent lines, serious and unexpressive. Two smooth powdered stewardesses in tomato red uniforms chattered, oblivious to the slowly growing files. One licked an icecream cone from time to time, her tongue flicking in and out like a lizard's. The children wanted one too but the shop was too far away. When Mark became shrilly insistent she turned to him sharply. 'For God's sake shut up! We haven't got time for icecreams now. The plane's coming soon.' And so the family sat close. A small knot of colour in a grey-green sea.

It was an old habit of hers to regret war. Was it anything more than a self-indulgent reflex? 'Give me a superficial impression,' she'd asked the night before in the stopover room suspended above flat Waikiki water, two or three off-season heads corking the surf below. 'And try and make it stick.' I am terrified, she reflected, terrified of this country. This madness so quickly absorbed into rituals of assassination, violence, penance, grief. And, finally, blankness. She looked at her children sleeping in white sheets, exhausted by the long flight from Sydney and wished they had never come.

'What do you think will happen to them? To us? I feel so unreal here. What's going to happen?'

'Now what sort of question is that?' he'd replied, irritated. 'They'll live through it. Europe did. And so will we, if that's what you mean.' He'd never felt obliged to wrestle too hard with her questions. The answers didn't greatly matter at such times so long as the tone was kind and serious.

And the bloodstains. Those clearly discernible streaks on the turquoise wall and dull yellow sofa near the window of their hotel room. Excessive and out of character, but still visible. At first she could scarcely believe what she saw, kept staring at them as if by the constancy and intensity of her gaze she might deny their existence. She had begun then to feel the ground shift under her, scarcely trusting her senses. A woman travelling with her husband and two young children simply isn't given a room with blood-stains on the wall. Fresh white towels, yes. Shining porcelain. Toy soap cakes in pink, blue, green. But those gothic suggestions matched more daring lives. They were, after all, quiet people in search of a night's sleep.

Driving from the airport to the hotel the plaintive chill of a Joan Baez song drifted through the taxi radio:

The dove has fallen and torn her wing.
No longer songs of love will she sing.
I am not here to sing songs of love.
I am here to kill the dove.

'Aloha to paradise!' The disc-jockey's frenetic whoop between swelling ukeleles cut the pure thread of sound.

'Doesn't "Aloha" mean "welcome"?' she had asked the slumped bull neck of the driver.

'Can mean anything, lady. "Welcome", "Thank you", "Goodbye" — now days mostly "goodbye".'

'Ah, yes.'

Passing the Ala Moana shopping complex, warm, heavy smells of food and flowers filtered into the air-conditioned car. Donut stands. Bloated orchids. Vegetables of an almost grotesque perfection. The delicate furlings of cabbage leaves aligned with curling ginger roots, creeping marrows, water chestnuts like small spiked clubs, and white swollen turnips. The vast coarsened cornucopia of a diseased luxuriance. Japanese-looking families hunched over plates of fish and beans. A Hawaiian youth with a sagging stomach stepped out in front of their slowly cruising taxi wearing a T-shirt which said, 'Visit Saigon, Fun Capital of the World!' Missing him, the driver sighed.

'These kids don't care.'

'Oh?'

'Die here. Die there. What difference? People can't choose.'

'Can't you secede?' Her husband looked away with an impatient movement. One of the children was clamouring for a T-shirt with words on it like that boy.

'With food in the belly like we got and a twenty percent discount to the military, are you kidding?'

'What would happen if you tried?'

'Trouble, lady. More trouble. We can't afford no more trouble. You interested in the surf reports?' Without waiting for an answer he leaned forward sharply to swell the disc-jockey's yelp. 'Waikiki three feet. Kailua breaking at two to three feet. Pokai Bay five feet, fair weather ahead . . .'

'You got surf where you live?'

'Not bad. Some good beaches on the east coast,' said her husband.

'You letting coloured folk in yet?' The expected came casually. Or so it seemed.

'A lot come in all the time.' They both bristled. What was wanting in his answer? It was the truth, wasn't it?

'You just don't want everyone to know about it, eh?'

'Could say so.'

The driver spat neatly between two blue rubbish bins on the kerb. They looked very shiny and new. On each was written, 'Mahalo'. 'Thank you'. So, 'Welcome'. 'Goodbye'. 'Hello'. 'Thank you'. This was America already.

The night passed uneasily. Sirens wailed in the streets. The lifts purred up and down, leaving remote voices on their floor. Muffled in the air-conditioned room, her husband and children slept. Disturbed by vague pains in her chest she got up several times to listen to their breathing, opened the window once or twice to hear the far murmur of the surf. The bathroom mirrors reflected more aspects of herself than she wanted to see and, after swallowing a glass of water, she quickly turned off the light. Stood very still in the dark. Further down, car lights swept through the palms clustered about the hotel, passing over walls and windows. Crowded, erratically placed neon signs reddened the sky near the trees but beyond these she could see nothing. On one of the balconies of the darkened rooms in the next block, a seagull came to forage. Soon after their arrival, at the children's urging, she had thrown a few cracker crumbs out on their own balcony but so far no bird had come.

On the way to the airport next morning to catch the plane to San Francisco she was glad the driver had not spoken, welcomed the mind-numbing ukelele. The children were mostly quiet, their chatter rising in little spurts of interest in the passing sights. The native village. The huge pineapple on top of the Dole factory.

'Are we in plenty of time?'

'Of course. We've got an hour yet.'

The drive seemed longer than it had the day before, but she accepted his calm, even though breakfast had made her slightly nauseated. The restaurant had been crowded. Men and women in hectic colours hung about the door waiting for an empty table. The waitress had been courteous but rushed. And Jill had knocked over her glass of milk just as they were getting ready to leave and had demanded another. With a slight sigh of exasperation the waitress had returned to wipe the table as another family moved swiftly in their direction.

And now they waited with the soldiers. The children had moved away a little and were making a game of picking their way over all the bags and attaché cases. She felt very proud of them. Mark was whispering something to Jill who nodded vigorously. How fresh they are, she thought, how spirited and attractive! Mark's auburn head was close to Jill's little blonde plaits and she was suddenly filled with a great and weakening tenderness for them. Why don't these men respond? Americans were supposed to like children, weren't they? She said as much to her husband. He looked up for a moment from his map of San Francisco. 'Perhaps they've been through too much to care. They haven't won a war, don't forget. It spoils a national mood pretty quickly.'

She was still put out by those unresponsive silent men. No. Solemn boys described them better. She took it almost as a slighting of herself.

'Seven years ago they would have been offering them sweets.'

'A lot's happened in seven years. Maybe they've learned something about being hated after all. It's taken them years to learn that nobody likes to receive charity.' He had memories of occupied Europe to draw on. She had nothing. She felt snubbed, yet knew what he meant. But she persisted with some petulance. 'What's that got to do with our kids? Surely they could crack a smile?' Sounding a little strident, so he returned to his map.

'Why should you care if they smile or not anyway?'

How much of her own anxiety had he detected in the wish? Did she, in fact, want reassurance, love (if it must be named) for herself through her children? It seemed very likely, but because it put her in an ingratiating defensive position she dismissed the idea, trying to focus her thoughts on San Francisco. To look ahead as he did. Why was she always turning back to the unwieldy past, trying to handle the slippery events of a present that always got away. He, on the other hand, seemed able to scoop up the essentials of a situation no matter how varied its components. Hovering over them uncertainly, she found their shapes too hazy and irregular to either seize or digest. She was, she often thought, a slow learner. One of the slowest.

'Excuse me, is anyone sitting here?' An English voice. She looked up, pleased. A resonant deep-toned voice. Since childhood she had been drawn to people by their voices before anything else. A tall stooped man in a lightweight grey suit wearing dark glasses and holding a small black briefcase was motioning towards the empty seat beside her. 'No, please do,' she said. Her husband glanced briefly at the man and continued to read. The newcomer put his case on the floor between his shoes. As he sat down he looked around at the silent soldiers.

'It seems we're to have company on this flight.' An accent of sorts? A certain old-fashioned courtliness, or was this overdoing the charm stuff?

'Some company. They haven't said a word ever since we've been here. Almost an hour. Not even to each other.'

'They've probably seen things they'd rather not talk about.'

Another snub. Well, she'd asked for that. Hesitating a moment, she tried to erase the mistake, surprised by the urgency of her need to correct it. 'Yes, how stupid of me. They're only boys after all. Young enough to be my own sons, some of them.' Then, to help herself over the hurdles of such despised platitudes: 'Are you going to San Francisco?'

'Yes.' Adding, as if to ward off the charge of presumption against a nice girl (woman?), 'I have some brief business to do before everything closes for Christmas.' I am nearly forty, she thought. I am not a girl. She longed to ask him what kind of business but said nothing.

He was not young, yet carried himself easily. The face was smooth, fine boned, and set in a rather melancholy cast. She breathed a soothing whiff of pipe tobacco and soap. Why was it always easier with strangers?

'Will you be staying in San Francisco?' He inhaled deeply, a relaxed man.

'No, just stopping over. We're bound for Chicago.'

'A pity. San Francisco is very pleasant. My favourite city in this country.'

'Is Chicago so different then?' America was America. Or was it?

'Very different and very ugly. Very ugly indeed. You certainly haven't chosen the best time of year for your visit.'

'One can't always choose.' Her voice sounded strained. Why did he have to tell what she already felt in her bones? She remembered Max Weber's description of that city. He had likened it to a man whose skin had been peeled and whose entrails could be seen at work. She shivered, remembering reading the passage aloud to her husband a few days before they'd left home: 'He would see it like that,' had been his response. 'That's your typical depressive reaction. It's probably no better and no worse than any other large city.' Even so, she felt she would never learn enough cunning or toughness to survive what was coming. Passing through the sinister-looking metal detector frame to enter the waiting lounge she had again experienced the same chill fear. More suspicions (what *were* in all those bags?). More fears. That was what wars and uprooting did to people. Heavy at heart she had

turned away from the terrible lack of expression in the eyes of
the young soldiers. And the trouble wasn't over yet. The weather.
The time changes. Her head felt leaden, her body slow. At home
it was summer. The oleanders bloomed thick and white, the nights
warm and balmy. She recalled packing the last case with toys and
Jill's little dresses, her brooch with the white opal shining green
in the moonlight, a new Italian wallet for her husband — a late
present from old friends. As fresh tears sprang to her eyes she
resolved to remember to wear sunglasses more often.

A jet appeared unexpectedly from between two palm trees,
rising almost vertically in front of them. As her eyes followed the
sun strips on the wings her husband shut the book with a snap.

'It must be time soon. Where are the children?'

The children! She was suddenly enveloped in panic, the stranger
at her side forgotten. She'd been keeping Jill's blue dress in sight
(or so she thought). Her husband was already cutting his way
through the silent rows.

'You stay with the bags. I'll go after them.' His voice sounded
very faint in her ears. She had sprung to her feet feeling giddy,
dazed.

The man beside her looked up. 'Why don't you sit down? They
surely can't be far.'

The pink stewardesses had also risen and were moving towards
the Exit sign, clattering their heels like castanets. The vaulted
concrete roof seemed towering, the spaces between the vast arches
depthless.

'Yes, I suppose I should sit down.' Trying to steady herself the
words came automatically. Her husband had disappeared from
view. Every second became an intolerable span as if, inch by inch,
she were being stretched on an iron cross. He had been drawn
away from her as by some powerful undertow of that grey-green
sea.

A negro soldier sitting close by but away from the others
signalled with his hand. 'Behind you, ma'am.' Turning round she
saw Jill in her blue dress stumbling over a military bag. She was
crying. Jumping up, she ran behind the row of seats and grabbed
the child to her.

'Jill! Where's Mark? Didn't you see Daddy? What's the matter?

Why are you crying?' Like aimless gunshots the questions burst out.

'Mummy, you're hurting me.' Of course. She loosened her hold on the child. Her *feelings*. Those useless treacherous stirrings. But she kept her hands tight across the child's chest feeling the quick delicate heart-beat against her own hammering pulses. The stewardesses had disappeared.

'Mark wanted an icecream. He's looking for the shop.'

She felt the blood beat in her eardrums, a terrible pressure building up in her head. 'Which way did he go? Daddy's looking for him. Tell me, Jilly, for God's sake stop crying and tell me.' But the child, panicked by her mother's face, was white and speechless.

'Come over here and sit next to me.' The stooped stranger was now leaning forward to the child, patting the seat beside him. Caught in her mother's arms the child looked at him for one still moment. And then began to scream. And scream. The air was hot and close. The stranger continued to beckon.

'Please, Jill, please darling!' But the screams grew louder and the child writhed and struggled frantically, thrashing about with her head to keep it away from the stranger's gaze.

The first boarding call came. A distant crackle, barely audible above the stricken cries in the now buzzing murmurous building. She turned to the man who had risen along with wave after wave of green uniforms, close-cropped heads. As the stranger bent to pick up his bag he looked at her long and hard. Suddenly she discerned a certain thickening in his face, an incipient grossness that she had not seen before. He bowed to her and smiled.

'A pity that you must go to Chicago,' he said and walked away. The child was quieter now. She had buried her head against her mother's breast, moving convulsively. Everything was very silent and empty around them. 'It's all right, darling. It's all right. Daddy will come. Daddy will find Marky. There! There! It won't be long.' Her heart now thudding with terror in the silence, she cradled the soft head and began in a steady enough voice to tell her daughter about a very tall thin man with a black bag. 'And what do you think he had in the bag, sweetheart?'

NICK HYDE

BANG BANG

PERHAPS YOU'VE HEARD of the Chinese Theatre in L.A. where the stars tread in concrete for posterity. Well, Shirley's back patio a few canyons further east does its bit too in preserving the soul of Uncle Sam. Only two people really know the story behind the lump of iron that attracts questions by day and trips the unwary by night — myself and Buzz. And despite all kinds of inducements Buzz refuses to tell — and if I know him well, he never will — but as my liaison with Shirley has long since ended, I think the story can now be told. After all none of her friends will ever read this — they're too busy signing deals and drinking themselves into oblivion.

Shirley's parties were on the grand scale. If you live in Hollywood and have four beautiful daughters then people have certain expectations. She lived up to them. My infrequent visits, calling in from New Zealand or Australia on my way to the other side of the globe, always filled me with a sense of duty. As a lone man in a house full of women I offered my muscles in whatever capacity the ladies thought best. Usually it was mowing lawns or sawing trees, for Shirley owned a sizeable lump of real estate; but this one time it was laying concrete: extending the steps from the rear patio down to the pool. I performed the task on the day of the party, which is not as foolish as you might think. Guests at Hollywood parties never venture outdoors, and if they do it is always out front, under the lights, to parade like gaudy Druids below a full moon. So when I finished I thought my handiwork was safe, that the cement would harden gently in the cool of a Californian night. Sadly I hadn't allowed for the madness that followed. Soon as I had showered and changed Shirley caught hold of me in the hall.

'Mike-a! Where have you been?' — Shirley doesn't talk so much as sing — 'I'm so totally busy! Be an angel and go out on the

103

drive. We're expecting people. You know — be Eng-lish! Turn on the charm.'

Isiah rolled up in a stretched red Buick with white bucket seats and chromium trim. Jungle music boomed from the stereo.

'Hi, man. Couldn't make with an assist?'

I shook the dark hand. Inside the boot were two cases of Veuve de Veuvray. 'French champagne. For our little birthday girl.' I helped him unload.

Stevie arrived with his mother, which was most unusual. He clambered from the Rolls with the familiar stetson already clamped to his head. 'Staying with Patsy now?' I asked as he pounded my shoulder.

'Naw, we talked over some business last night.'

Stevie owned an airline among other things, running Lear jets from Long Beach to points east. Desert-dropping, he called it. Stevie was twenty-three and without the hat looked seventeen. Patsy as usual embraced everyone in sight. 'Mike-al! Hel-lo! Mmmmuh! So how long are you with us this time? Hon-ney! You always leave so soon! Come here you darling man, let me smell the sea. Shir-ley!'

The hostess had emerged, to be mauled by mother and son. Stevie stood back to admire the reaction.

'Yee-haw, Shirl! For a dame just turned forty, you're none too bad.'

Patsy agreed. 'Doesn't she look gorgeous! Hey, Isiah! Well hel-lo! Mmmmuh! Stevie, don't forget the gift, honey . . .'

We escaped the blazing sun and went inside the house. Party noises had begun. One of Shirley's kids had spilt ice across the kitchen floor and she was scooping up lumps in her hands. 'It's so cold, Mom,' she protested. 'I've gotta go feed Dancer!'

Samra was thirteen, and very fetching in her riding clothes. Unlike her sisters and mother she preferred four-legged friends to two, thereby inciting acts of bravado from half the males at Hollywood High.

From the laundry a baritone voice boomed: Brian Borthwick, otherwise known as Buzz, the only non-American save for myself able and willing to survive this Hollywood Hills soirée: 'Ice! We need ice!'

The immaculately suited Isiah skated over the kitchen floor, a case of Veuvray balanced on one shoulder.

'Champagne coming, Mr Buzz. Dig some holes in that ice.'

Two other daughters, one slim, dark and beautiful, the other slim, fair and almost beautiful, bent to Samra's assistance. From the driveway came the sounds of another arrival, a blast on a horn, followed by an equine cry of protest.

'Mother!' Samra glared, flustered by so many adult eyes, 'they're frightening Dancer!'

'Ooh, little Baby,' her mother kidded, 'that horse just loves automobiles.' Every one except Samra laughed. Shirley's Prelude had been odorously blessed by Dancer some days before.

Samra dropped her handful of ice and made for the door. She collided with an incoming body: Chester Groves, lawyer, part-time pianist and wit. With him was his lady of the moment — if five years can so be called, but both thrived upon tentativity — Macedoine Dupois, operatic singer and gourmette. Never one to miss an opportunity, Chester's hand enveloped Samra's bottom. She squealed, but the cry was lost amid his approving roar: 'Running from the party, Dena? Ho, ho, back we go. Show me where the liquor's stashed.'

'My name is Samra! Let me go!'

'Shir-ley! Bonne anniversaire!

'Ches-ter! Mac-cy! Hel-lo!'

Within the hour kitchen, lobby, lounge, driveway were one liquid flowing jostle of bodies, laughing, crying, arguing, greeting: the noise was intense. Los Angelenos at play. Attire ranged from semi-naked, various styles of après-tennis, après-swim, to the overdressed: diamonds and furs and fashionable silks. Temperature on the driveway: one hundred degrees dead. The occasion: the hostess's coming of age; plus the fourth daughter's graduation from college. That daughter had yet to arrive so until such time, Shirley held court. There were many eager suitors.

'My God, but you're beautiful,' growled Chester. 'Look at her, Buzz, look at that arse.'

'Ches-ter!' But the heroine's laugh was joyous.

'Mike ever turns you down Shirl, you just give old Chester a call.'

'And what about Macy? You're such an old devil.'

'So? I'll take the two of you. What you think, Buzz?'

Buzz was in law enforcement. No longer a weapon carrier, he lectured others. Today's demonstration was being held in the laundry.

'You hold it like this, see. Easy. Straight out in front of you.' His hands were wrapped around a half-empty San Miguel. 'Feet apart so's you're relaxed. Balanced. Aim for the body, never the head — too small a target. Then, blam!'

'Thanks,' I said. 'I'll remember.'

Buzz had been a cartoonist, back home in Liverpool, England. On a previous visit he told me why he'd left. 'Got too dull. Weren't no riots in my time, I guess.' Somehow he became my best friend in Los Angeles — apart from Shirley, of course. She made a point of inviting him round whenever I was in town. He now sat at a desk in the Scientific Investigation Unit of the L.A.P.D., the homicide department, drawing composites of suspects — murderers, kidnappers, rapists — the heavies. In that same conversation he'd called himself the Dali of Death, but I'd guessed the tequila was doing the talking. To look at him he was just a tubby little clerk in an ill-fitting suit.

Shirley never wore anything ill-fitting. A word for her would be voluptuous, but she had grace with it and the happy knack of mixing velvet with steel. A woman worth a whole story to herself.

And me? Michael Jones, a mere interloper, holder of an occasional ticket, usable whenever, to the real-life cartoon that is life in L.A., an open invitation, courtesy of the radiant Shirley, hostess extraordinary and long-distance lover. What am I saying? I nearly married the woman. But fantasy overtook fact. The truth of it was that flying Auckland to L.A. was like the adrenalin jolt of a *Miami Vice* feature after a cosy diet of *Country Calendar*, *Close to Home*, and a hundred lonely nights of solo living.

Every visit contained madness in some form. This was my third, and it promised to be no different. Already the drive from the airport had shaken me to the core. Just what are the responsibilities of the concerned citizen — even in a foreign land? For one frozen second a nightmare more chilling than any I'd seen enacted on celluloid had been caught in our headlights: a cop beside his car, legs spaced wide, fingers slipping off stars, joined at the groin by a gun to a kneeling desperado — just one flash in the night then gone, the finale to be acted out in the thousand fractured beams of headlights behind us. For ten seconds or more neither Shirley nor I spoke, just stared at tail light after tail light, hoping to make sense from the inexplicable. Then she turned to me, her voice as calm as a neighbour discussing the weather: 'Did you see that? He was wearing only one shoe.'

Twenty hours later I mentioned the incident to Buzz. He paused from digging a beer out of ice.

'What freeway was that? La Cienaga. Last night, huh? Saturday, busy night. And a shoe missing. Which foot?'

'Shirley said left.'

Buzz grunted. 'Easy, the left foot is non-operative when driving. So, the cop pulls a guy for speeding, the guy's running dope, he thinks it's a bust. He's got his stash in his shoe, he ditches the shoe when he's pulled over, finds the cop hasn't drawn his gun so he pulls out his own and is about to blast the poor sap's balls to bits when you drive past. Want a beer?'

I was unsure whether to laugh. Buzz noticed my reticence. 'C'mon, Mike, you probably saw a couple of cops fooling around.'

'Shirley saw it the same way I did.'

'Well believe me, if you'd interfered you'd both now be dead and there wouldn't be no party chez Shirley's this evening. Bystanders get shot in this town. They're called snoops. Take it from a pro, Mike, don't intrude on folks with guns.'

He handed me a chilled San Miguel. Buzz, sapient adviser to the innocent abroad. Each time I feel I know Shirley's friends they shock me anew: unpredictable as gypsies but a thousand times wealthier. And Buzz had once been an Englishman.

Buzz went in search of tequila. I went looking for sunshine.

On the front terrace below a Moorish archway Stevie had his arm around Dena. They were getting to know each other.

'How's it going, kid?'

'Okay, Stevie.'

'Working?'

'Oh, I do a bit. Gardening, pumping gas.'

'How old are you, Dena?'

'Seventeen.'

'Jesus, your age I was selling real estate. Get a decent job, kid. How about coming and work with me?'

'C'mon, Stevie, I'm still doing school.'

'So? Do school days, make bookings nights.'

'I'll have to ask Mom.'

'Sure.'

Stevie plucked a cigar from his shirt and a gold lighter from his jeans. Dena picked at her nails.

'Where's your mother, Stevie?' I asked.

'Patsy? Out back with Shirl some place. Checking out the present I guess.'

Dena squinted: 'Huh? Patsy bought Mom a present?'

'Sure. A wig. Crazy lady, Patsy.'

'Oh my God . . .!' And Dena raced back into the house to pass judgment upon her mother's new hair.

I followed, more slowly but equally curious.

In the master bedroom Shirley, Patsy and Macy were shrieking and jumping like schoolgirls. They shared one hundred and forty years if they shared a day but if you'd paid five dollars for every year you'd still be way short of buying that wig.

'God, Shirley,' Macy was crying, 'you look like a stripper!'

Patsy's eyes, too, ran with tears of laughter. 'Oh, shush, Macy — it needs some shaping, that's all.'

'You've been stung, Patsy: that's not real hair. It's llama fur!' Again Macy squealed.

Shirley stared at the unfamiliar reflection in her wall-length mirror. Five faces stared back.

'Oh, I don't know.' She pouted, and flicked at her fringe. 'Anyway, smart-arse, llamas don't have fur, they grow wool.'

Macy shrieked again, and Dena found her voice: 'Mo-om! You look terrible!'

'Oh, c'mon, Dena,' scolded a pink-faced Patsy: 'Give your Mom a break. What's so wrong with a change?'

'She looks like she's had a sex change!'

Macy was enjoying herself.

'Hey you guys,' Shirley spoke to the mirror. 'Stop ganging on me. Michael, what do you think?'

I chose to be honest.

'I think I like you better with it off.'

'Oh, men always say that,' said Patsy. 'Ignore them, Shirley, you look fine. Let's get out there and party. Macy, is that my margarita?'

Macy handed Patsy an empty glass: she looked in the mood for more.

'I wish Chester said it more often,' she said.

Our hostess caught hold of my arm, her fingers as cool as a silk shirt, and she guided me from the room. 'I'll keep it on for just five minutes — for a party piece. C'mon, let's go slay them.'

We passed by an open-mouthed Dena into the hall. The reaction was predictable: what we quiet people call going a bit over the top. I went in search of air.

On the rear patio steam was rising from the plants. The only moisture with a chance lay blue and neglected in the pool. Half a ton of ice and I could have swallowed it. A grove of trees screened most of the downtown L.A. smog, and as I continued across the patio I felt the heat singe my eyebrows, felt the beer turn warm in my glass. Then below my feet the floor began to vibrate: Samra was leading Dancer through her evening aerobics. At the far end of the lawn Dancer cantered in a tight circle, with Samra high in the saddle, her eyes half closed against the dust. I waved an arm, but Samra rode on, the boss in her own world, as if, like the hero of Lawrence's horsey tale, she possessed a secret that was unimaginable to the swarm of adults that partied on inside the house.

I watched a while; then a sudden movement among bushes distracted my glance. A face emerged from the foliage, then a brown body in baggy shorts and outsize gym shoes. We hadn't met, but instantly I knew who he was: Geoffrey, a boy from two houses further along the street. Shirley and Samra had spoken of him to me. Geoffrey's head looked rather too large for his body. He suffered from Down's syndrome.

'Hello, Geoffrey. I'm Michael.'

Geoffrey's smile was pleasant.

'Hello. I've seen you hosing the grass.'

'Yes, I do that when I'm here.'

'Do you have a car?'

'Well, not here in L.A.'

'Where?'

I told him. He looked over to where Patsy's Rolls Royce shimmered beside the house, stuck out a finger.

'I want one of those.'

I laughed: 'So do a lot of people, Geoffrey.' Curious, I asked if he could drive.

'Sammy's going to teach me,' he said, and added brightly, 'no one else will.'

Again I looked over to where moments before I had been lost in dreams: then suddenly Geoffrey made an odd purring noise; he rolled his left hand over his right and peered back over his shoulder at nothing. His foot kicked, and he reversed away from me in a careful arc. He paused, the foot kicked again, and he began trotting forwards in the direction of Samra and Dancer. I watched, fascinated. Every few seconds his head twitched, as though he was observing me in an invisible rear mirror. Samra saw his approach: she reigned Dancer to a powdery halt. But their conversation eluded me, and standing there alone, adult, and unoccupied, I quickly felt guilty: I'd become a snoop. My place was back inside the house.

The party was in full swing. From the recess near the aquarium Glenn Miller had come back to life and was frightening the fish; Buzz and Macy argued recipes for margaritas; Stevie had Shirley's third daughter pinned in a corner; Chester was singing an appalling blues to a startled Isiah . . . I raised my warm glass to the hostess: the party had every sign of being a success.

For the next few hours nothing mattered except what you held in your glass and who was helping you drink it. Bottles in bewildering varieties of size, colour and content became emptied or were misplaced, coloured lights splashed walls, floors and faces, trays of barbecued beef entered rooms and were devoured, salt-rimmed goblets sat abandoned while their owners made love, argued, sang, rocked and rolled. At one untimed point the happy graduation girl arrived escorted by an equally merry reinforcement. Introductions were made until people were no longer sure who was being introduced for whose benefit. It was time for a second intermission.

One of the striking features of Hollywood homes is the number of bathrooms. This house had three — four, including the Little Girls' Room at the rear of the stables. The master bathroom was too horrific to consider — its designer had been a disco-loving troglodyte — so I made my way to number two loo, the Big Boys' Room. Even here was a bath no smaller than most swimming pools. I resisted temptation, knowing I might never surface, and sat on that seat whose design welcomes us all. Beyond the door the babble of the party was now reduced to an even simmer and a wall of tiles made a cool pillow for a boiling brain.

Minutes passed during which I attempted to think of nothing. Water, probably of a high alcoholic content, gurgled along some hidden drain, darkness swallowed the last specks of colour from the Californian sky. Memories of South Sea beaches, of people who spoke with soft voices, nibbled inside my head. I must avoid hosing that lawn: every visit seemed to result in sunstroke. Then the floor began vibrating — was Samra now riding Dancer down the hall? A thudding rhythm. Music. Glenn Miller had been laid to rest: now Guns and Roses were entertaining the fish.

The scream was unnerving in its proximity — as though murder was happening outside the bathroom door. I leapt from my throne with an alacrity that would have shamed Edward the Eighth. The hall was deserted. Then, from a room opposite the bathroom, Samra's room, there came a stifled moan. If I knew one thing about Shirley's house it was how to enter a bedroom, either gently, with a loving glance, or forcefully, with a hard stare. I chose the latter, twisted a knob, shoved, and rushed in. Macy, half-naked, lay upon the bed, one hand over her mouth, the other searching among bedclothes . . . for knickers, rainbow-coloured, rather pretty. Her eyes held mine while she regained her modesty, then, still horror-struck, stared over at the other occupant of the room: Buzz, naked, crouched at a window. On the floor was a jumble of clothing. And a wig. The wig. Buzz also was having problems finding his underwear.

'Close that door for chrissake!'

I did as I was bid.

'Don't breathe a word about this, sweet Jesus!' Buzz spoke as he scrambled. 'I'll get that bastard, I'm going to get that bastard . . .'

'There's a prowler, Mike,' Macy moaned. 'I saw a prowler. In the window. He was watching us.'

Then a knocking on the door: and a voice, Patsy's voice.

'Hey in there! What's going on?'

Buzz grunted: Macy gasped: and for once I thought quickly.

'The wig, Buzz, put on the wig!'

He stared at me, frazzled, wide-eyed.

'Open up in there,' came Patsy's excited cry, and other voices repeated the demand.

Sudden realisation dawned: Buzz jammed the pile of hair upon his head, buckled trousers . . . Macy smoothed her dress. Then I opened the door.

One look was enough. Patsy shrieked.

'Oh my God! Hey you guys, come and look at this!'

'My God! Who is it . . .?'

'What is it!'

'Hey, it's Buzz! What are you doing, Buzz? Undercover work?'

'Hey, let me try on that thing . . .'

I pursued Buzz, now minus the hairpiece, into the hall. He turned, and held up a chubby palm: 'No, Mike, this is police work. I'm going to nail this bastard. Stay and look after Macy . . .' We reached the front of the house. 'No further, Mike. I've got my gun in the car. Go find Macy, go calm her down. Make sure she doesn't tell Chester, for chrissake.'

Something kicked at my rib. Coitus interruptus may be a most aggravating complaint, but was Buzz intent on shooting the guy? Suddenly he didn't look like a bank clerk any more: the ill-fitting suit and perspiring brow reminded me more of those grey but ruthless figures who shot their way through episode after episode of *The Untouchables*. Buzz meant business. A light flickered as he opened his car door: he bent beneath the wheel. I don't think he intended me to hear him, but I did: 'This bastard won't live to tell anybody nothin'.'

I was torn between restraining Buzz and searching for Macy. If she spoke to Chester then the man could end up in the darkness hunting an armed and angry cop. Chester set great store on asserting his rights. I stepped back into the house and closed the door. Every window now held a threat, every curtain concealed a snooper.

I found Chester in the lobby, demonstrating a wrestling hold on Dena. He beamed me a smile.

'Hi, Mike. These kids of Shirley's sure enjoy having fun.'

'Hello, Chester. Yes, it's a very physical family.' Dena did not look convinced. 'Chester, have you seen Macedoine recently?'

'C'mon, Mike, you trying to spoil things?'

A voice gave me the answer.

'She's in the bathroom, honey. I've just passed her a drink. The Big Boys' Room, y'know?'

So she hadn't moved far — a step across the hall. My passage was more difficult. Americans are gregarious people and this was a party. I finally won through to end stooped below a silently flashing 'ROOM'. There was a sound of sobbing.

'Macy, it's me, Mike.'

'Go away.'

'I've been speaking to Buzz. Let me in.'

The door opened a fraction.

'I want to die.'

'Macy, nobody knows except for me and Buzz.'

'What about the prowler? He saw us doing it!'

She had a point. The sobs returned. 'He could be looking for me right at this very moment . . . So he can have a turn! God, what have I done . . . I'll never forget that face, it was so ugly! And so big! The way he was looking at me . . . Like I was nothing! . . .'

Again I felt a kick in my rib. I looked at my watch: only eight-thirty. No lingering dusk in southern California. Could it have been him . . .? No, please, anybody but him . . .

I ran out the back way, out on to the patio, into hot silent darkness, and all the while the nightmare from the side of the freeway was playing havoc with my sight. Just as I called out, I heard the bang. The shot sounded deafening, but to the partygoers in the house it was just one more cork popping from one more Veuve de Veuvray. Again I shouted, and ran headlong over the lawn. The darker shadow of the stables loomed; and I remembered the lights: turn on the patio lights! Beside the door to the Little Girls' Room I found the switchboard: oh thank you Lord for little girls. I slapped at the buttons. Inside the stables behind the wall, Dancer stamped a reply.

A sheet of light flared across the sky; then again, at each corner of lawn. The pool leapt into view, startlingly iridescent, and above it the palms glowed pink and mauve. And a squat little figure stood between the spokes of his own shadow: Buzz, legs apart, arms outstretched, standing easy, frozen by the light in the centre of the lawn, his stance horribly like that of the cop from the previous night. In his hands he held a gun. And like the previous night there was something else, something eerie. His head was tilted, his jaw at an odd angle: already his neck was twisted from the hangman's noose. I was horrified — and then I understood. Buzz was gazing in astonishment at the lights.

I ran towards him. He turned, looked at me, half in shadow, his hair silver, his eyes bright.

'I know who it was, Buzz, I know who it was . . . It was a kid, Buzz, a retarded kid. He was looking for Samra . . . That was her room . . .'

Buzz's face seemed to change shape suddenly, from bewilderment to horror.

'You mean . . . I've just killed a kid?'

The answer came suddenly, and from an unexpected location: from a window of Patsy's Rolls Royce — a clear childish syllable.

'Bang!'

And out of the window a raised then lowered arm, and the sound again.

'Bang!'

Geoffrey was delivered to his home then Buzz and I returned to Shirley's rear patio. The steps gleamed white. I turned off the lights and told Buzz to be wary of treading in damp concrete. He spoke, hoarsely.

'Never again,' he said, 'never again,' then he leant forwards,

reached into his jacket and thrust out an arm. 'This damn thing
has fired its last!' He jammed the gun into the concrete of the step,
raised a foot and stamped down hard. 'That's what we oughta
do to the whole goddam arsenal!'

'One day,' I said.

'It won't come soon enough!'

We both stared a while at the little statue, then began across
the patio to the house. Suddenly Buzz again halted. He gripped
my shoulder and bent to remove a shoe.

'Damn thing's covered in cement. Can't drag muck all over
Shirley's carpet.'

We entered the house, Buzz carrying his shoe. I'd never noticed
he was left-handed. And left-footed. It was, I suppose, just another
of the night's little peculiarities.

Two days later I flew out of L.A.

OWEN MARSHALL

A VIEW OF OUR COUNTRY

SIMON PALLISER HAD spoken to the Blenheim Rotary Club on
his experiences as a noted traveller, and I agreed to drive him down
to Christchurch so he could see something of the country on the
way before flying out to Paris via Singapore. I was going on
business anyway, and the President thought that I could do our
scenery justice, so Palliser would have an impression of the place
to take with him.

As we crossed the high bridge close to Seddon, Simon Palliser
looked down to the blue, wild flowers and the pooled water. He
asked me if I'd ever been to the Ivory Coast. 'I flew in to Abidjan,'
he said. 'Some fifteen years or so I suppose after they got their
independence from the French. The heat was killing, and after a
few days I decided to move into the hinterland. I hired a car and
drove to Yamoussoukro where the President had his palace. I'm
telling you this because crossing that river reminded me of the
crocodiles of Yamoussoukro. I drove 240 kilometres to get there,
through Ouossou and Tomumodi, along a road more and more
enclosed by jungle and the red soil the jungle fed on. But at
Yamoussoukro itself the jungle had been cleared and a modern
city built alongside the President's family village. Great plantations
had been laid out too, of mangoes, pineapples and avocados.
Down one side of the President's palace an artificial lake had been
created and stocked with turtles, catfish and crocodiles. There had
been no crocodiles in that district before, I was told.

'The crocodiles were fed late in the afternoon, and the hotel hired
a driver from the Baoule tribe to take me to view them. The driver
met me on the broad boulevard in front of the foyer entrance.
He was a cheerful and talkative man with fair English. He began
to tell me about his country as we walked to the carpark. It was
a little cooler than the coast, and a mist gathered in the city of
Yamoussoukro; at once such a modern place, yet the site of chiefly

power for hundreds of years.

'There was a causeway across the lake to the palace gates lined with coconut palms and iron railings, and at the gate the Presidential Guard stood sentry. The crocodiles waited with their mouths agape, on a shelf of sand between the embankment and the lake, and the feeder came in a pick-up truck and took buckets of meat to feed them. He called lovingly in French as he threw pieces down to the crocodiles who seemed short-sighted and inefficient eaters. It began to rain heavily, and colours came up on the backs of the crocodiles, and more crocodiles and a few turtles came out of the lake. The mist crept closer and the rain dimpled the surface of the lake. The feeder then took a chicken from his truck, and swung it back and forth in the rain above the railings; all the time appealing in French to the crocodiles. Then he tossed the chicken into the air.

'The chicken gained courage from being free in the air and rain. It flapped stoutly and landed over the heads of the crocodiles and in the lake. As it landed a turtle surfaced, as if it had duplicated the flight beneath the water, and the chicken was seized. It was an auspicious thing to happen. The feeder was alarmed and angry; my Baoule driver was glum. The feeder climbed the fence and ran towards the water across the sand to frighten the turtle. Instead one of the largest crocodiles jumped forward like an ungainly rabbit and had the keeper's leg in its mouth. There were perhaps twenty or thirty people watching, and the feeling of all seemed not one of horror, or even active concern, but a deep hopelessness. The crocodile backed into the lake, giving several gulping changes of grip which drew the feeder more firmly to him. The feeder called out once in French, then was silent, and his long robe trailed behind him. One of the guards fired into the air, and the keeper's wide eyes were fixed on us, his audience, even as he disappeared.

'The rain dimpled the lake surface just the same; turtle and chicken, crocodile and man were gone, leaving us powerless in the wet. "Quickly come away with me now," my driver said. I was thinking that there had been no crocodiles at all at Yamoussoukro until the lake had been dug for the President's palace.'

It was a dry year in Marlborough. When we stopped a little

past Ward for a thermos of tea, the hills were very brown and the heat confused their outlines. Palliser said it reminded him of Spain. 'Emotionally, Spain was a turning point for me,' he said. 'A woman I was very much in love with left me to take up a United Nations job in the Mato Grosso, and I drifted south into Andalusia and was very drunk for several weeks. You know Andalusia I suppose? Of the several weeks I can remember nothing; a blank in my life, then I sobered up in the little town of Baeza in the hills above the Guadalquivir. I can feel the very evening; the air heavy with jasmine and orange blossom, the soil red as a heart. There were prickly pears at the roadside and within some of them the torreo bird had picked out small nests, and their heads watched at the entrances as I passed. My friend took me to the café to hear the gypsies sing the cante jondo, and all through it the more stolid locals sat at the back tables and continued with their dominoes. I didn't drink, and watched the gypsies under the influence of wine move from the plaintive cante jondo to a wild flamenco; all castanets and exclamation. In the midst of it a farmer brought in a lynx he had killed in his fields, and hung it from a beam by the door for his friends to admire, or to attract a buyer for the skin perhaps.

'As the gypsies danced and sang, as the domino players became steadily more absorbed in their own purpose, I sat with the scent of jasmine and orange blossom through the café door, and the Persian gleam of fur upon the lynx. It turned slowly on the cord, first one way then the other, as if its tufted ears still sought some magnetic north of freedom.'

The seaward Kaikouras crowd the main road to the ocean's edge south of the Clarence river and rise abruptly to over 3,000 metres. Simon Palliser had a love of mountains. 'Of course Switzerland has been something of a second home to me,' he said. 'Several times between expeditions I rested at Brunnen on the shores of Lake Luzern. Do you know it? A town of solid, unpretentious houses on a flat strip of land, while beyond it the steep, glaciated slopes descend into the lake like the sides of a fiord. I made a base at the guest-house of the Gotthardt's usually, and from my upstairs room I had a view of the small steamer berths, and the many trees of that part of the town. I remember on one of their election days taking the rack and pinion railway from Brunnen to Axenstein, a high resort with magnificent views across the lake. Because of the elections and the season there were few people travelling, and in my compartment only one other person; a Swedish woman, beautifully dressed, who spoke excellent German. She told me in a gentle, quite unselfconscious way that she had been travelling to overcome her grief at the recent death of her husband, and that her main difficulty was coping with the loss of sexual satisfaction brought about by the abrupt end of her marriage. She had found no opportunity for solace not repugnant to her she said, until seeing me who bore a singular resemblance to her husband.

'It was all so natural, so kind, so tinged with inevitability. We stood close in the corner of the rack and pinion carriage, with her lovely skirt folded up. Her tears were wet on my cheeks; perhaps I cried myself. She clasped her hands at the small of my back and pulled strongly. Past the blond hair fastened back from her smooth face, the lake seemed quite calm from such a height and pine forests rose up to the snow line on the mountains above the water. She murmured her husband's name through her tears, I recall. Have you travelled to Sweden? Sven is a common Christian name there.'

As we drove down the coast close to Kaikoura, Palliser thought he saw a seal on the rocky shore. He was interested because of the heavy swell also, and the scene reminded him of British Columbia. 'I had a temporary job in conservation there,' he said. 'I was camped in the magnificently unspoiled Pacific Rim National Park on Vancouver Island. My main task was checking on the sea lions which lived in groups on rocky islets off the coast. On the one day in three or four the swell allowed, I would circle the outcrops in the small boat provided, count the sea lions and record the colour of any tags recognised through the binoculars. Most days I couldn't go out, and I would walk through the stands of Sitka spruce which fringed the beaches, or I would push into the rain forest further inland. The garter snakes would sidle under salmonberry bushes as I approached, and in the cathedral quiet of the rain forest could be heard just the organ music echo of the great Pacific rollers breaking on the first American coast to obstruct them.

'It was cool rain forest, without many birds, and often difficult to walk through because of the swampy places and fallen trees. Ferns and mosses thrived on the decay, as did puff balls, stallion heads and frilled fungi which added the only vivid colours: visceral gleams of red, yellow and spotted black orange, powdered horns like those of a myriad snails sprouting electric blue from the cancerous side of a log.

'After storms I would walk the grey sand of the Pacific beach, see the heaped driftwood, whole trees sometimes, and piles of rotting seaweed which were alive with jumpers. Some of the driftwood still had soil and stones in its roots and gum on its branches, other pieces had been fully digested by the sea and were worn and pale like old soap. On one morning I was amazed to see the vast horns of a caribou caught in the cleft of a tree close to the water line. The tips of the tines were four metres apart, and the antlers would make an arch that two men could march through without stooping. I couldn't dislodge it from the driftwood, and overnight everything was carried away again by the tide and the storm. So are opportunities lost and nothing can be done. I've often thought that the only explanation of such size is that the horns and skull that held them must have been a prehistoric find, carried down to the sea at last from Alaska or the Yukon where some great bull died ten thousand years ago.'

Simon Palliser slept for a while then, his head jogging on his shoulder, and woke when we were coming through Parnassus. I was going to explain the origin of the name for him when we saw a small girl and her doll waiting patiently for the rural delivery man on the grassy roadside by her farm mail box. 'She reminds me of a child I met once in Mexico,' said Palliser. 'On my way to Tierra del Fuego I stopped in Mexico and took the opportunity to visit the Mayan ruins at Chichen Itza. I drove out from Mérida after a meal of tamale with black beans. Rather than the pyramids and temples it was the sacred well of sacrifice that interested me. A huge, circular limestone opening, and twenty metres down sheer rock walls to water which is twenty metres deep again. Young men and virgins were sacrificed in full finery there; the remnant of the jutting altar can still be seen. Government divers have recently managed to recover gold masks and skulls from the mud.

'I had my lunch of chocolate and melon by the stones and

shadow of the well's lip, and some Indian children squatted around me to beg a share. I could hear the murmur of the visitors and the more assured, single voices of the guides. I could see people clambering up the stepped side of the pyramid. I thought how this setting of absolute tyranny and religious death had become with time a picnic spot and oddity; the stones and pits denied the sacrifice which had given them their significance. When they had eaten my food the children left me, except for one small girl who calculated that I must have something hidden, or that I would tip her for the privilege of being rid of her. She sat by the rim of the well of sacrifice, and childlike twisted her fingers into the cracks of the wall while watching me intently. All in an instant her fingers drew out a ring of gold with blue amethyst centre, which had lain so long so close to all the people passing. While my mouth was still opening, she rolled the ring once in her fingers as a pebble, and still with her eyes fixed on mine, reached her thin hand over the rim of the well and dropped the jewel to the water and mud far below.

'She must have seen something in my face then that dismayed her, for she bounced up and skimmed away through the heat of Chichen Itza to join the other urchins. There was nothing I could do, you see; nothing that would bring back such a chance missed.'

I thought the Canterbury plains a good contrast to the landscape earlier in the day, and I told Palliser that the Waimakariri which was coming up, was one of our major rivers. 'For me,' he said, 'the river which has my soul is the Okavango, and I've seen both Niles, the Mekong, Mississippi, Rhine, Ganges, Amazon, Yangtze, Congo, Euphrates, the Don and the Orinoco. The Okavango flows away from the sea into the Kalahari; wonderful incongruity. In ancient times there was a huge lake over most of Botswana, but earthquakes altered the courses of the other rivers which fed it, and now only the Okavango continues spreading over 18,000 kilometres into a million channels and lagoons: the inland estuary of a once inland sea. The great Okavango flows into the sand, holds back the shimmering menace of the desert each year. It's one of the most beautiful and luxuriant places in the world, and protected from the worst of modern encroachment by the tsetse fly and sleeping sickness. I've been drawn back again and again, as perhaps you have yourself. On an early visit I was charged by a tusker while hunting zebra, and had to shoot. The authorities made me pay an excessive elephant licence fee despite my protests that I had acted only in self-defence. The ivory was confiscated, although I kept the tail and later had an ebony stock fitted to it, making a fly swat.

'On that visit to the Okavango old Johannes de Wette was still alive, and living on one of the estuary islands in the south. He was 87 years old and his brother in-law had captured Winston Churchill during the Boer War. De Wette was one of the true white hunters and we sat overlooking the papyrus beds, listening to the slap of catfish and myungobis, the ugly cries of the malibu stork, while he told me of the old days on the Okavango. They used to make hippo rafts to navigate the swamps by shooting four hippo in the head and sewing their mouths closed. After twelve hours the heat so blew their bellies up that they had the buoyancy of gigantic corks, and were used one at each corner of a log raft. De Wette and his comrades would drift through the channels raised up on hippo carcasses as if on a dais. Among the Botswana in those days they were treated like royalty, and de Wette said that a bed of Botswana maidens was provided for the hunters — 18 or 20 girls, their bodies gleaming with fig oil, would lie with arms and legs intertwined to make a couch for the night. De Wette's seamed, Afrikaner face was impassive as he told me, but his deep eyes were wistful as we watched a magnificent white-necked fish eagle plummet from the sky into the deep channels of the Okavango.'

As we came into the quiet, spread suburbs of Christchurch, Palliser contrasted them with the intensity of Calcutta. He had come down from Tibet to convalesce he said, after suffering from frost-bite, and to avoid the tourist traps had found a room in the Ashin district of Calcutta. 'It's always been my object to take part in the real life of any place I find myself in,' he said. 'You will remember no doubt the typical stench that part of Calcutta has; the cooking fires, exhaust fumes, oil and dung, the smell of the river and of the cremation grounds further out. Part of that smell too is poverty and loss of dignity. All within sight of the domed Victorian Railway Terminus, memorial to the Raj, and not far from the *maidan* — the lungs of Calcutta.

'My room was made of tar paper and the sides of packing cases from the Bala engineering works. As I lay on my sleeping bag at night I could see stamped on the boards above the curtained doorway the words, Store Away From Boilers.

'My small-time landlord liked to entertain me by taking me to the bazaars in the evening, spurning the untouchables from our path with the hauteur of a man of property. Street after street where life went on; everything is done in the streets because there is no option. Past the pumps in the street for household water, past the stall holders and beggars, the people crouched in doorways, the goat boy selling milk as required from his animal's udder, the banana sellers, hooded rickshaws with their drivers squatted between the poles and resting. One night we saw a goldfish and ball-bearing eater outside a flower shop and a potter's. There are no ends to the way a man can be demeaned in search of a living. Up to ten goldfish and ball-bearings I saw him swallow, then sing for a while, then regurgitate them into a plastic bag of water, so that they swam again apparently unharmed. In the narrow alley at the side of the potter's shop were piles of clay and wood, shards of pottery, trays of small images of Kali set out to dry. The sideshow swallower may have noticed me watching with more interest than most of the passing crowd, or perhaps it was just as a European who gave him an American dollar that I received attention. He stood before me with a smooth, handsome face, and swallowed five ball-bearings the size of golf balls and in good English told me that he was a B.A. "You are seeing what a person will be doing for sake of a family," he said. "What we are brought to is a terrible thing." Behind his personal misery was all the beauty of the flower shop; garlands of jasmine and marigolds from the red soil, roses even, and a few sacred lotus blooms set further back. The swallower became vehement at his plight; shouting to be heard above the transistors and bazaar noise. In his misery he forgot to maintain muscular control of the ball-bearings in his gut, and they must have moved down for suddenly he screamed with pain and fell back amongst the marigolds and jasmine. It drew more people and more interest than his former act, and all the watchers loudly gave advice as to the best way to cure him. The flower seller called loudest of all about the dying man. I asked my landlord what he was saying and was told the vendor demanded to know who would pay for the crushed jasmine and roses.'

I left Simon Palliser at his hotel by the Square. He was grateful he said to have had the opportunity to see something of the nature of the country here, and to spend time getting to know me. We could see the Cathedral quite clearly, and Palliser said as I left that it reminded him of a peculiar thing that happened while he was staying in Strasbourg some years before.

ELIZABETH JOLLEY

THE LIBATION

THE WOMAN WHO was in this room last week is dead. The Fräulein told me yesterday, after her little speech of welcome. She hesitated before telling me, afraid of spoiling my holiday, our holiday I should say, because stupidly, I am not travelling alone.

The Pension Heiligtum is run by an old woman and her elderly daughter. Neither of them speaks much English. Both do their utmost to make us comfortable.

'Euer Zufluchtstätte!' the old woman said knowing from before how much I need sanctuary, especially when I am travelling. All the rooms look out into the green arbours and the lilacs of a small enclosed garden. The quiet hall is lined with porcelain and hand-painted cherubs.

We have a double room without a bath and, in spite of being in the shadow of the Stephansdom, without magic. There has been no magic on this holiday. I knew there would be none before we left. All the time I have been asking myself why I ever made the suggestion that she should accompany me.

Neither of us is young. Between us there is the inevitable intimacy of bowels and false teeth.

This morning Miss Ainsley ordered quantities of hot water to be brought to her. As soon as it was cool enough, she gulped it like medicine from the little enamelled jugs, explaining that she was constipated. Later she said, 'Excuse me,' and has not yet returned.

I have known Ainsley for a long time. For many years she was my father's secretary and, after his death, when she found she could not attach herself to me or to my work, she left. Later, she came back, needing a home which I have grudgingly given her. I am not always kind to Ainsley. I am not even nice to her. She irritates me.

I have seen her tears, however, and that should be enough to

125

alter my attitude. The point about her tears is that I was humbled by them. I don't love Ainsley and, what is worse, I don't like her. No one loves her, no one except perhaps an insignificant mother, a long time ago, has ever loved her. Her tears did not make me care about her but, for some strange reason, during one of my more prolonged and unpleasant remarks she, by crying, suddenly made me see myself as I really am.

Though I forget now what the incident was, I remember all too clearly the huge tears trembling along her eye lashes. I couldn't help noticing too how the act of weeping distorted her slack cheeks and lips, crumpling her face into a soft, red, puffed shapelessness.

'It's all right for you,' she sobbed to me then like an upset school girl, 'it's all right for you to say the things you say and to act the way you do. You're a sort of wealthy goddess. You've got everything going for you.' For some minutes she howled aloud uttering the most appalling clichés about me and about my selfish, cruel, extravagant ways. Lately, I admit I have been guilty of the things she was saying. I stared at her with horror. I patted her quivering shoulder and, briefly, I felt real pity for her. Mixed with the pity was an unexpected curiosity as well as the distaste I knew I felt. That's why I did what I did to her and why I offered her the holiday.

'Don't cry, Ainsley!' I said to her. 'Look here,' I said, 'of course you must come to Europe with me. Cheer up! I'll arrange everything.' I kissed her and stroked her and comforted her and she responded so quickly to my unwilling hands that even now, when I think about it, I feel ashamed. Ashamed of knowing her response to my unwillingness I mean.

So, while the hot water is dealing with Ainsley's inside I am sitting here by the embroidered table cloth trying to imagine the last thoughts of the dead woman because I have discovered something about her which amazes me.

I do not want to be a tourist really. Travelling with Ainsley, being a tourist cannot be avoided. To anyone who can understand English, she explains that she finds a diet of campari and prunes very sustaining. Thus well nourished she stands, legs straddled, to be cultured, in the Beethoven Museum, in the Haydn Museum and in the Schubert Museum. Obediently she turns her head,

chattering aimlessly, as we drive by, to gaze at the entrance to
the ancient and famous hospital repeatedly entered by Schubert.

'*To wander is the miller's joy*,' she sings. 'We had this at school,'
she tells me and joins the crowd flocking to see the Schubert
Sterbezimmer.

I made up my mind, years ago, never to travel again.

. . . 'there must be no letters, not even thinking,' I said once
to a young woman with whom I was very much in love. 'I shall
not come after you,' I told her then. And I meant it. I did not
write and I did not travel across continents to follow her. We never
saw each other again, though nothing could stop me from thinking
about her. And now, all at once, in this apartment, dark with oiled
wood and overstuffed with heavy furniture, I am reminded of
her because something which no one knows about, something
belonging to the dead woman, was left in this room.

Since the discovery I made yesterday I have been unable to think
of anything else.

All the time on the bus tour yesterday afternoon I was thinking
of this woman while Ainsley chattered about the different ways
of 'taking one's own life' as she calls suicide. We were making
a tour through the Wiener Wald to Mayerling. Ainsley expressed
her eagerness to see the hunting lodge where Crown Prince
Rudolph and Maria Vetsera are said to have carried out a suicide
pact. We were not able to see the Lodge as it has been converted
into a chapel where an order of nuns are housed. All the way back
Ainsley talked of what it must be like to 'take the veil' till her
speech, thickened with campari, slurred off comfortably into sleep.
Her round, blue-grey head bounced softly on my shoulder and
unwillingly I smelled her soap.

The amazing thing is that we were so near. For some time, in fact
the whole time while she was here in the Pension, we were
journeying nearer and nearer. All the time while we were in the
Hotel Traube in Salzburg eating ham with sauerkraut and
dumplings or looking out vacantly over the wide view from the
Hohensalzburg Castle, she was here in this room.

I am thinking back over those long evenings. While time was
creeping slowly forward for her, we sat in suspended time gazing

at the life-like figures in the marionette theatre listening to the radiance of love reflected in Mozart's music. Had I known she was here in Vienna at that time I do not think I would have remained a moment longer in Salzburg. And certainly I would have had thoughts other than those of longing to be back in the quiet paddocks at home. It is strange to think that in order to endure Ainsley during *Die Zauberflöte* and *Don Giovanni* I occupied my mind with complicated plans to end the holiday and get back to my farm as quickly as possible.

And the woman in this room must have been writing a letter to someone whose name I shall never know. She must have been contemplating, perhaps in this chair by this table, the action which led to her death and subsequent removal, with as little publicity as possible, from the Pension Heiligtum.

The letter has no beginning and no end.

The Fräulein, when she told me, was very grave and assured me, with dignity, that the room had been thoroughly cleaned and well aired since the unhappy event.

That I am the subject of a novel, possibly a rejected one, is incredible.

I asked the Fräulein what the name of the dead woman was. At first she felt she could not tell me. She uttered a name which had no meaning for me. It occurs to me now that the dead woman could have been travelling under an assumed name. Or she could, after leaving me, have married.

It is disconcerting being the subject of someone's fiction. To be the subject might be quite usual but it is not usually known or realised by the person who is the subject. My name is not Helena and the young woman with whom I was so deeply in love was not called Lois. That is of no consequence. The writer would naturally use made-up names.

All fiction springs from moments of human experience and truth. The writer of the story must have seen and observed and must have been completely aware of certain things about me and about my life. I have not seen the novel in question only some pages of an incomplete letter which is a reply to an obviously insensitive attack on the manuscript. I have seen in this half-written letter a desperate attempt at self-defence.

In order to have written this book the writer must have perceived my most secret feelings, must have known everything about my farm, every detail of its geography, and everything about the derelict people with their avid intention in the wretched house adjoining mine. The writer must have known all the intimate details of my thoughts and feelings and my passion for this young woman which, for a time, altered my whole life. A life which was then so different from my boredom and disgust, yes disgust, which I feel now and which I envisaged then, at that time, years ago, and so brought our sensuous and idyllic happiness to an end before it could turn into a profane bondage.

Who can have written the novel? And who is the person who was writing the letter which I found?

The Viennese are very clean people. This room was thoroughly cleaned and aired, how then could I find the sheets of paper which have revealed to me so much of the dead woman — and so little. That she wrote a book and that the book was being rejected by someone unpleasant seems clear. Her name is not on any of the pages.

The Viennese are clean and they are thrifty too. I can follow the reasoning. The paper has been written on one side only and it is of good quality, new and white and clean. The drawers of the little chest and the writing desk have been carefully lined with the sheets laid flat and pressed into the corners. I discovered the handwriting on one of them by chance and then, one by one, drew out all the others.

I have them here, all the neatly written pages . . .

. . . Thank you for reading my book . . .

. . . Your notes and questions are anonymous so I do not know how to address you . . .

'What is the goddess?' This is your last question at the end of twenty-three pages of questions. 'What is the goddess? What is the goddess?' It's your last question typed out twice as if in exasperation.

You ask on the same page, 'Is "a deep spiritual and emotional experience" a euphemism for orgasm?' And still on the same page, 'What would Mr Byrnes and Helena be doing to the carcass if

129

it had been trapped, struggling and in a panic on the fencing wire for several days and full of maggots? Surely not butchering it to eat? I can see that it provides an approach to drama but, please correct me if I am wrong, at the expense of realism? ...'

I'll come to that part in a minute. I'll start at the end with your last question, the one about the goddess. She is an ornamental statue.

> ... In front of the Berghof is a wide gravel drive which encircles a white stone goddess seated in her waterlily fountain. A car turning slowly here sounds like a car on the track at Helena's ...

The sound of a car turning slowly and pausing and then turning again on the gravel path round the goddess reminds Lois of the same sound which she heard often at night when Helena was returning to the farm. Now of course she is not with Helena as they have parted for ever. Hearing the familiar sound in an unfamiliar place fills Lois with longing and sadness.

The goddess is both an image and a symbol. Earlier in the story Helena sings part of Schiller's *Ode to Joy*. She sings in the car when she is driving off with Lois taking her to the farm. It is the middle of the night and she has rescued Lois from an intolerable situation. She sings,

> 'Daughter of Elysium. We approach with hearts aflame
> O Goddess your sanctuary.
>   'It's Schiller, Ode to Joy,' she explained.

As they approach Helena's farm it is as if they are approaching her sanctuary. Helena says,

> 'When I go through the gate and am actually on my land I feel no harm can ever come to me ...'

She is a good deal older than Lois, perhaps she values safety more after previous experience. She wants to share this safety with Lois.

The goddess in the poem and the safety of the farm represent the strength of Helena's love as the tender relationship develops between the two women. The goddess in the lily pool suggests that love and safety are to be found, for a time, in the seclusion of the vegetarian guest house. This guest house in the mountains becomes, at the end of the story, a sanctuary for Lois.

The libation which you have failed to notice or mention, belongs with the goddess and the sanctuary. Lois is describing her new and passionate friend,

> *Every morning Helena pours a little water carefully, a libation, she calls it, into the tins and pots to sustain her little pomegranates and the myrtle and the rosemary . . . The water stays sparkling to the brim of every pot for a few seconds and then disappears into the grey sand . . .*

From your notes I see that you want the goddess removed from the book. I would like to keep her in as she is essential to the story.

Now, about the maggots and the carcass. There is a passage where Byrne and Helena deal with a sick ram. Lois is watching from the house and the scene is described by her,

> *. . . I never saw Helena do anything violent before. I saw Helena with the gun, she was behind Byrne's house, in a wired off yard . . . I saw Byrne agitated . . . and Helena at the edge of the barn with her gun. I saw the strength and grace with which she took aim . . .*

Helena shoots the ram, it is a mercy killing; and after the shooting, Helena and Byrne clear away the carcass. For the purposes of the novel it is not, as you suggest, just the provision of a dramatic moment, it is to show that certain circumstances require definite actions. Helena does not like shooting. She does not want to kill anything, she says so. And she does not want to end the idyllic happiness she and Lois have together. The shooting of the ram shows that she will do whatever is necessary at specific times. It shows too that in spite of Helena being rich and independent she knows how much she needs a man like Byrne on her farm. The incident is there too to show that a change is coming and Lois, fearing this and yet wanting it, is hysterical.

Your irrelevant question demonstrates your lack of

understanding of quite simple and ordinary human needs and human behaviour. To answer your question, no they wouldn't eat the ram themselves, perhaps the dogs might, but this has nothing whatever to do with the story.

The words 'a deep spiritual and emotional experience' lifted out of context do not appear as they are meant to. The words do not mean an orgasm. If I want to write orgasm I will write it. The experience referred to means something else as described in the text.

I do not understand your constant use of the word euphemism. Three questions all together, you ask,

1 Love — is it a euphemism for sexual intercourse?
2 Sexual intercourse equals the highest form of love?
3 Do either of these concepts for the protagonists hold water?
My answers are 'no' to question one.
'No' to question two.
I do not know what you mean in question three.

You are mistaken in your suggestion that Helena is blackmailing Lois. Like other human beings Helena has her needs. She is simply suggesting an arrangement which might be of use to them both. Lois needs to be somewhere while she has her baby. The views expressed on abortion and childbirth are not necessarily my own. No, I do not wish to enter into a correspondence with you about either.

Repeatedly you accuse me of being 'romantic' about pregnancy. The radiance I have written about is a fact of pregnancy. There are other observations about pregnancy in the novel. Obviously you missed them because you did not realise that Lois was pregnant.

Yes, Helena does have 'a past' as you call it but she would never use it to push the publicity of a sensational book as you suggest she might. Helena explains to Lois that now she is no longer able to practise as a doctor and she lives in seclusion because it is the only possible way she can live.

You must understand Lois! I can't put my name or my opinion forward. I write but only for myself. I don't even have a trading name here for anything I might produce. And I could never publish anything again.

No, I do not mention how the record player operates. Does a novel have to contain every detail of a household? Though I have described the big high comfortable bed and the verandahs I have not stated how many cupboards the house has, how many wash basins, lavatories, fireplaces, doors and windows. Should a novel have an appendix with these listed?

You say that the love scene between the two women is 'direct and purposeful' but the secrets of the two women puzzle you. If everything was made clear in the first pages there would be no novel.

Yes, the incestuous relationship with the brother is fact, so is the murder of the elderly doctor, you are quite right, neither of these are the secrets.

You say that the discovery of Beethoven is tiresome because you discovered him on a wind-up gramophone in 1930. Your discovery does not mean that Beethoven has been discovered for ever. Every day Beethoven is a fresh discovery for someone. For Helena a repeated discovery and pleasure,

> *How wonderful to have her here with me. Her presence alters the whole house. It is like the first cautious phrases of a Beethoven Symphony, the Fourth perhaps, or the Ninth. I hope this cautious movement lasts and goes forward as it must surely do, nothing ever stays the same, with the same grace and harmony and pleasure as the symphony does ...*

Your next note reads, 'Are the generalisations on the mature woman and the pregnant woman, "the healthy prima para", Helena's or yours? They are extremely romantic and idealised. The tender beauty of a pregnant woman seems ludicrous. Is there never a depressed pregnant woman? An ugly one? One with mottled thighs? One with three chins? ...'

Oh Get Stuffed! You clearly hate the idea of being pregnant! Of course the generalisations are not mine. I do not use the novel to express my own views on any subject. I have not tried to write a thesis or a dissertation on pregnancy or on lesbianism. You seem to wish for or need a different kind of book, one which I have not written. All sorts of pictures of pregnancy are given quite early in the story. One is Mrs Byrne's production of a wizened baby, almost out of spite, and certainly for convenience. And, there is too the memory, in prison, of the nauseating smell of pregnant women.

Later on as the loving relationship develops between the two women, pregnancy is seen as a predicament —

> But I didn't want her near me. 'It's too hot for that,' I said crossly. 'I'm too big! And I hate being pregnant, so big! It's awful Helena! How can you think it's anything special! I hate it, I hate the baby. I hate this hot wind! I hate everything!' I burst out crying . . .

How can you accuse me of 'perpetuating a myth about lesbianism' it is just one person's views about love making. Lois — and her thoughts about Helena,

> Even in her love making she is controlled, she waits for me; very occasionally, on purpose, I have made her lose control of herself . . . and when this happens and it is over she is terribly sorry. Once she wept and was afraid she had hurt me physically. I suppose it seemed so violent to her. Love making with a woman is different. What seems violent to her is not to me. She knows nothing of the full violence of it, she doesn't know the hardness of a man's body and the weight and fierceness of a man's passion . . .

Lois is merely describing her own feeling and her own experience and I do not consider her to be speaking on behalf of all sexual partners.

You suggest in your notes that the book ends badly for Helena and Lois. You ask why did I set up their lives with such grim sordid (your words) backgrounds and circumstances.

In the writing I have tried to make it clear that the relationship between the two women is a tender one with healing qualities. Helena realises that they must separate. She knows that she cannot keep Lois with her for ever. The life on the lonely farm, especially in the harsh summer, is not right for Lois. Helena is afraid of the inevitable bitterness and unhappiness in the years ahead. She decides that Lois should go away. Lois is remembering,

And she talked a bit about our lives. 'Once there was a German poet, you'll have to brush up your German!' Helena said. 'He said something like this: "if I can make a fruitful land between rock and stream" or, "if I can find an orchard between rock and stream", the idea appeals to me immensely. We can both be doing that wherever we are . . . '

Ainsley is looking forward so much to Grinzing. I am too much occupied with thoughts to know exactly what I look forward to.

Near my farm, where the road curves in a wide bend, there is an ugly dam. It looks as if the water in the dam is sloping towards the road. I have always been pleased to see this dam, even though it is not mine. It simply means I am near the boundaries of my place when I see it. Now I have no wish at all to go back to the farm. I am remembering all over again my return after I had taken her to the airport. I had never seen the farm before as I saw it then. The bald paddocks stretched into a dismal distance. The sheds and even the house itself seemed deserted, grey as if in perpetual twilight, empty beyond belief, without her.

The harsh voices of the crows cried loneliness into the still sad morning.

Ainsley has not stopped talking about the wine festival at Grinzing. The thought of the sentimental music and people wandering through the wine halls and the flower gardens, drinking and singing together, wearies me. Ainsley is excited because she has heard that wine is sold cheaply there in quarter-litre mugs.

Wine should be an offering, poured out in reverence.

I feel certain that the woman whose blood so recently darkened this oil-dark floor is the woman I loved years ago. The 'direct and purposeful love scene' was mine and hers. But there were many such scenes, not one.

I am the person who said those words quoted in the notes. I shot the ram too. There were other things as well, memories keep coming fast, one after another.

'You are so cool and smooth,' I told her once in a warm summer night. In our nakedness we did not need bed clothes. We seemed to only half sleep all night and the steady moonlight stripped the room of reality. She lay naked along my thigh with her little face pressed to my breast. Close outside the bedroom window the moon-ghosted loquats held their breath and our happiness in their stillness.

This Pension Heiligtum was a temporary stopping place in her long journey. I too am making this same pilgrimage though, when I set out, I did not know this.

'Ooo! Who's spilling her wine all over the place! In reply, I tell Ainsley that she is drunk.

'Well, Dear, perhaps a teensy trifle tipsy,' she agrees. 'But you are spilling your wine,' she insists. 'Here,' she says, 'have some more, Dear. There's plenty more where that came from. I mean, that's what a wine festival's all about isn't it.'

'We never exactly made a suicide pact,' I tell her.

'No, Dear! Of course not, why ever should we? Live and let live I always say.'

'I mean someone else, not you, someone else . . .'

'You need more wine, Dear,' she says, 'you know it doesn't suit you not to have enough. Sit down here, Dear, under these trees,' she says, 'while I toddle along and fetch some more.'

It's such a nuisance. I don't like having to depend on Ainsley. I don't like having to ask, in front of her, for hot water in a little row of enamelled jugs.

'Oops! You're spilling again, Dear!'

'No, it's not spilling, it's only sloping.'

'There! What did I tell you. You have spilled it everywhere.'

'No, not spilled. It's poured, it's a libation.'

'What! It's a what? It's a whatter what?'

I want to be private from Ainsley. We have a double room without a bath. There is no privacy here. She will be the one to make the discovery. She will see the stain of the offering, renewing itself, darkening these oil-dark boards so recently and so carefully cleaned. I wonder if, when the time comes, I will be able to hear her frightened voice calling as she makes her way along to the rosy cherubs in the hall. She speaks hardly any German. She will have difficulty. There will be consolation if I am able to hear her having difficulty.

She might even cry. Knowing the effect her tears have on me I would prefer that she did not.

ANTHONY McCARTEN

THE BACHELOR

ROGER STOUTMAN WAS wealthy and fat. Also he was alone. I don't mean he never saw anybody. He had a secretary in the next room who at that precise moment was peeling a hard-boiled egg and wondering from which end she would begin eating. And not that he was unloved. His landlady, with whom he had boarded for fifteen years, was dedicated to his comfort and washed his underwear with a special formulation usually twice a week, but it would be three times a week if Stoutman ever asked. He was alone because he didn't have a partner. That's how it goes. Just as simple as being wealthy or fat.

Roger Stoutman was, at age 42, a successful businessman who, though he had worked hard, had fed from every pleasurable dish, so to speak, that had come his wealthy way. Still, he was a bachelor. Women? He had not allowed them too close to him. Frankly, he had always been afraid they would marry him and then maybe take half of everything he had. He didn't trust them, as he didn't trust cheap shoes, homeopaths and people who openly spoke of God. The women he wanted he bought and let them go. In the past fifteen years he had not ended up a single night in any other bed but his own. He was an incorrigible bachelor. People would say, when they saw him coming down the street, 'Here comes Stoutman. You'd think he'd get tired of being alone.'

But recently Roger Stoutman had become uncomfortable. He did not know why but his work, as a mercantile agent moving stockings and women's finery all round the world, did not interest him as much as always. He was bored with his landlady's stupid gossip about this, that and the other. Even Maracaibo, an energetic city all year round, was beginning to bore him. He was 42 and though he'd never really done anything truly spontaneous, he was making more money than ever and should have been on top of the world. Occasionally a colleague would enter his office and ask Stoutman to come out for a drink. Once Stoutman took up the offer. The colleague merely wanted to discover something of how Stoutman made so much money. When Stoutman sensed this, after five straight questions about Swiss banks, he finished his drink and left, leaving the colleague with the comment, 'Money is like a woman,' he said. 'Death in the wrong hands.'

Anyway, it was at this time, one bright afternoon when Stoutman's secretary had bought three hard-boiled eggs to work, that Roger Stoutman leaned back in his sleek black vinyl swivel chair, gazed across his office to his bookcase, and caught sight of an outsized atlas sticking out of file with the many smaller books. He got up from his desk, crossed the office and took hold of it. It had never before been opened and was kept only for decoration. Stoutman took the book back to his desk and in one bold movement opened it midway through. The intensity of the coloured plate startled him. It was a wonderful map, though almost completely without feature. The plate concerned Mongolia, the desert republic that is the filling in the sandwich between the broad practice of communism in Soviet Russia and China. Stoutman gazed, mesmerised at the plate. You would think it was a picture of his mother, or of someone he had not seen for years, or perhaps of something which he had not known was the reason why he was rich, or fat, or alone.

Yet it was only a simple map, without a lot of interest and he'd never even thought of opening the book before. Roger Stoutman was the sort of man the world did not understand. What sort of man would rather die than risk going out with a woman for fear he would wake up in the morning married? And he *would* rather die too. As he once said to his landlady, 'I would rather the ambassador of death came to my door and asked my name than I wake up next to some whore who wanted half of everything.' There was a great barrenness to Mongolia and it took hold of Roger Stoutman's mind and wouldn't let go.

The next day he was gone from Maracaibo . . .

. . . by car, east, through Carora, Valencia and Maracay, to Caracas, and by air across the North Atlantic to Madrid where he was off-loaded due to industrial action and stayed there for two days in the same chair in the corner of the terminal, smoking cigars and sipping mineral water. The airport was full of students. If one of them tried to sit beside him he asked them to move. While there he also put in a phone call to his landlady, whose name was Anastasia, telling her he would not be in for dinner and to close the window in his bedroom. Then he was gone, flying to Hong Kong via Rome, Tehran and Delhi. In Hong Kong it took Stoutman fourteen days to get a Chinese visa for the train journey. The man at the embassy was a fool with a nervous tic. Stoutman went every day from his hotel to the customs office to demand his visa and when it finally came and the customs officer smiled as he held it out over the counter Stoutman did not even say thank you.

'Before I go,' said Roger Stoutman, 'have you ever been to Mandalgovi?'

'Mandalgovi? No sir. Where is Mandalgovi?'

'Mongolia. It is in the middle of Mongolia.'

'No sir. I have not heard of Mandalgovi. It must be a very bad place. One should be careful of places others have not heard of.'

'Do you know where I can buy a good hat with a very large brim?'

'Just round the corner is a place that sells hats.'

Wearing a bright yellow hat whose brim projected out from just above his thick eyebrows, Roger Stoutman boarded the train heading north, up the south China coast, through the cities of Shantou, Kiamen, Fuzhou and Wenzhou to Shanghai, swapping trains to reach Nanking, stopping many times. It was then relatively easy to reach Jinan across the Grand Canal and from there you could almost smell Peking on the breeze.

All this travel was having an effect on Roger Stoutman. He was losing weight. And resting against a fountain near one of Peking's sixteen gates leading into the Inner City, he watched a small one-legged girl begin hopping up a set of steps that seemed to go up so far that wisps of cloud obscured the top. It caused a peculiar shifting sensation in his heart and in his discomfort he hurried through the gate and into the crowds.

He stayed in Peking for eight days so that he could rest. On his second day he ate a vegetable concoction which made him vomit throughout that night. He spent most of his time there in his room. Prostitution was illegal in Peking but it did not bother him. He had not thought about women since he'd passed by his secretary's desk in Maracaibo three weeks before and watched her begin eating the second of her three hard-boiled eggs. He was scared of syphilis and of being robbed too. At night he lay in bed and wrote in a notebook a few thoughts. In his writings he tried to divine the reasons for his spontaneous and completely un-Stoutmanlike journey but he usually fell asleep with the light on before he could get to the heart of the matter. One night however he came close to a realisation. He wrote, 'Something calls me. Its name is destiny. Anyway, if I stayed in Maracaibo I'd probably wake up next to some whore.'

On his fifth day in Peking, driven for some reason to return to the fountain outside the gate to the Inner City, perhaps still to see the one-legged girl only half way up her climb to the clouds, he was spoken to by a very old man who smelt of death. The old man was walking up the road into the Tatar when he looked up to see Roger Stoutman leaning against the fountain.

'So, you have come,' said the old man looking in Roger Stoutman's eyes.

'I beg your pardon?' said Stoutman.

'I have been expecting you. Come.' The old man motioned him forward and Roger Stoutman went, perhaps only because the smell of death was so unmistakable.

Not looking back to check that Stoutman was following, the old man, with white hair and the terribly wrinkled face of China itself, led Stoutman through street after street, until, turning into a little alley, he entered a little house.

Inside the old man shouted out commands in Chinese. The household, of whom there were many, came out of many rooms and started to chatter quickly. The old man kept making orders and the woman ran away to soon reappear with a costume of clothes, a tremendous robe and an ornate headpiece.

'Where you go great fat man?' asked the old man who smelt like death.

'Mandalgovi,' Roger Stoutman replied, quite overcome by what was happening to him. One little boy under a table giggled.

'Ah, Mandalgovi.' The old man looked over his shoulder and translated the reply to which the household gave a collective 'Aaaaaaahhhhhhh.'

Within what seemed seconds, Roger Stoutman found himself clothed in robes and finements that you would imagine belonged to the Manchu emperors of the Ch'ing dynasty. Stoutman was helpless to resist the wardrobe but would not permit the removal of his wide-brimmed yellow hat. The old man finally waved the headpiece away. Three younger men then physically carried Stoutman out in the street, put him onto a high seat on top of a cart and wheeled him into the square, and, as it turned out, a huge parade. Roger Stoutman had no idea who these people thought he was but convinced himself that when the opportunity came he would make his escape and return to his hotel and lock the door. However, for the moment this was impossible. He seemed to be something of the focus of the parade. There were carts before him and after him but they were full only of flower arrangements. People were gathered in great numbers either side of the street and they shouted and waved painted flags. Indeed, with his large hat blown to the back of his head, the face of Roger Stoutman did seem to be somewhat backed by a yellow and glowing halo. Was it possible that for all these years, unknown to himself, the best mercantile stocking agent in Maracaibo was really a misunderstood prophet, a holy man?

The thought disgusted and terrified the overweight tourist. His fear of religious involvement ran deep and was as old as his knowledge of the certain ruination of bachelors by romance. Religion was a mental cancer. Back, way back in Maracaibo, his business associates had often quoted Stoutman, 'I would sooner throw up my arms and breathe my last than be seen kowtowing to those ridiculous book-thumping imbeciles.' The crowd sang songs of praise.

With the agility of a much smaller human being Stoutman threw himself out of his ceremonial chair. The crowd parted as Stoutman darted through. He was not athletic but this day he ran. He ran until an unattended bicycle presented itself, then he cycled like a madman. In his hotel room he bolted the door and collapsed in a distraught fever onto his bed. Alone, he waited like a criminal for night to fall.

Two days later he was on a train again, heading northwest this time, more physically wary than ever, and this was a slow and arduous leg, to Zhangjikou, southwest to Datong, then north-wards past Jining to the flatlands of the Nei Mongol Zizhiqu, across the 500 miles of that arid plain to the city of Erenhot on the Chinese Mongolian border.

Awaiting papers for two days, he pushed forward into the dry July Mongolian interior, taking a slower cattle train to Saynshand, Daramjargalam, Sumber and the capital Ulaanbaatar. Stepping off the train the wealthy mercantile agent rushed for the nearest available hotel, a bath and bed. At least he was in Mongolia. He felt better for that.

The following day, having recovered somewhat, he encountered an English-speaking Mongolian entrepreneur named Altay Hara, a skinny brown man with a large scything nose, who for 550 tugriks agreed to provide transport through the desert, 200 miles, to Mandalgovi.

'What is Mandalgovi like now?' Stoutman asked Altay Hara, as an emperor might ask when re-entering a city after years in exile.

'Oh, very nice! It is very nice place.'

It was two days before Stoutman saw Altay Hara again. The Mongolian businessman rushed into the hotel early in the morning during breakfast and said, 'Quickly Mr Stoutman, your transport is ready!'

For two and a half days Roger Stoutman travelled in the back of a goat herder's diesel truck, maintaining a steady 15 miles an hour on the one-lane cart track through the Gobi. Nothing but sand separated the Mongolian capital from Mandalgovi. Stoutman saw all of it, lying in a hollow between sacks of grain being taken to a nomadic tribe far out in the desert. At one point a fly flew into the mouth of the bachelor. He thought about it for a moment, then swallowed. Travel changes a man, he concluded.

The driver did not speak English and made no effort to communicate. To him Stoutman was no different from a sack of grain except that he complained more. At night the driver slept in the cab which had a picture of Elvis Presley stuck to the dash. Stoutman dragged one of the sacks of grain over him and slept in the middle of the cargo. In the morning the journey would begin again. Finally the truck stopped.

Climbing from the back, Stoutman looked down the track which forked just ahead. The driver started yelling things out of the cab window in what Stoutman suspected was Mongolian, and was pointing straight down the track, past the turn-off veering right. Then he started up his truck. Stoutman jumped up to the door in protest saying he had paid for transport all the way to Mandalgovi. 'Mandalgovi! Mandalgovi!' Stoutman shouted.

'Mandalgovi! Mandalgovi!' shouted back the driver pointing straight down the road, putting the truck in gear and rumbling off, taking the right-hand fork. In his loose-fitting white suit and big-brimmed yellow hat, Stoutman watched the truck depart. He looked back down the track where he had come, thinking he could wait for the next truck. There must be many trucks in and out of Mandalgovi.

'In the meantime I may as well walk on,' he thought, and did so. For his effort, five minutes later, not far in the distance, he saw the outline of a city. It was surely Mandalgovi! It shimmered in the heat, and in sympathy, so did his heart, a movement that brought the vaguest touch of water to his eyes.

The road dipped into a hollow and he lost sight of the city for a while. His uneasiness was intense as he walked on, deprived of a view. Rather than a fresh arrival, it seemed to Roger Stoutman that he was at last returning. The road rose again and, topping the rise, he inhaled to survey his strange Mongolian estate, this place that destiny had prevailed upon him so painfully to seek out.

'Oh my God!' murmured Roger Stoutman. 'Oh my dear God!'

Set out on the plain was a little town of only fifteen to twenty adobe-style huts. There was a main trail between the huts. In it nobody moved. Stoutman looked grimly beyond the town for the fulfilment of his vision but there was only sand. It looked as though nobody had been near the town in a hundred years. The businessman inside Roger Stoutman told him this was disaster. He felt, for the first time in his life, that he had lost everything.

Then he smelt death again. It filled his nostrils like a subtle perfume. He turned, half-pie expecting to see the old Chinese man coming toward him over the sand but there was only sand where sand should be. And an empty town where an empty town should be. A ghastly thought came to him. He had been brought here to die. Hadn't he even been given his funeral in Peking, that mad procession? The words of the old man returned. To have travelled half way around the world and find only sand and huts made of dung. Roger Stoutman, mopping his brow with a soiled handkerchief, wondered now only how his end would come. By thirst, by hunger. He remembered that four years before an ulcer in his gut had perforated. He strode toward the town, his thick figure sinking deep in the sand, his collapsing mind turning oddly to the matter of life insurance.

A dog, with its ribs pronounced in ugly proportions, ran falteringly between two huts in the distance. It was the only sign of life in Mandalgovi. Roger Stoutman moved down the track through the middle of the town. Open-mouthed he looked left and right as he walked; the evidence of quick evacuation, a hut half painted with whitewash; another hut half built. He stepped on a lizard and he had to swallow a cry of fright. There was a well at the other end of the town. He dropped a pebble into it and heard it bounce. Perhaps it would be thirst then. He began to laugh. Some emperor, he thought. Master of lizards and sand! King of flies!

Laughing made him dizzy, and turning to sit his bottom down on the edge of the well he almost fell into it in absolute surprise. Standing in the middle of the main street was the figure of an old man, and an ass.

The old man was completely motionless. At first Roger Stoutman thought it was the old Chinese man from Peking.

'Hello!' Roger Stoutman called.

The old man, turbaned and grotesquely thin in a tattered black burnous, didn't respond. Stoutman took a few steps toward him, the features of a gaunt dark face becoming clearer.

'Hello!' Roger Stoutman repeated, a panic rising in him. There was a silence. The two men looked at each other — the stranger impassive.

'Hell-loo,' the old man said.

'Thank God!' Roger Stoutman shouted and ran to the old man. 'You won't believe this but I thought I was stuck out here alone!' The ass shied at the onrushing fat man. 'I thought Mandalgovi was gonna be the last place on earth!' Stoutman stopped at arm's length before the old man. 'My name is Roger Stoutman.' The old man tilted his head quizzically. 'Hello,' Stoutman said.

'Hel-loo,' said the old man after a pause. If a heavy crease in a face was worth ten years then he was at least two hundred and fifty.

'Well, how can we get out of here, I s'pose that's the thing?'

'Hel-loo,' the old man replied.

Surprised, Roger Stoutman enquired, 'Where is everyone?'

The old man smiled, revealing a collection of smashed and rotten items. 'Hel-loo,' he said.

'Oh no,' Roger Stoutman said. The old man touched him on the shoulder as if in sympathy, but Stoutman could not be soothed.

'Trucks! When are the trucks? My God, what sort of town is this? You've got to help me get out of here!'

The old man kept smiling, and when Stoutman stopped shouting he merely raised an arm and indicated they go into one of the huts across the street. Roger Stoutman was a large man but he followed the garmented skeleton to the hut like a small boy. He passed by the ass and patted it on the nose. The animal didn't look too bad. As he bent to enter the dark hut, a spark of imagination flared into an image — himself, riding on a donkey, out of Mongolia. It faded.

The hut had no windows. It took some seconds for Stoutman's eyes to adjust to the lack of light, but when they did they settled on the squatting figure of a small woman about 40, her head covered. The old man muttered something to her and she got up and left, passing by Stoutman at the door. To his surprise her garments were of a fine silk that once he would have been pleased to move around the world. She was perfumed too. She must be the old man's daughter. He noticed her eyes never looked up.

The old man sat on the ground and bid Stoutman do the same. They sat silent, hopeless to communicate, for several minutes, looking intently into each other's face. After wondering how to bring up the matter of the old man's ass, Roger Stoutman's mind wandered into wondering what he was doing with himself this time last year. Beyond that he thought of his landlady's legs. She had rheumatic symptoms, got no doubt from years of climbing the stairs to his room to tidy his things. He was thousands of miles away from her rheumatism now, he thought, and yet in great trouble. Also, this old man never blinked.

The daughter re-entered the hut with a wooden cup of water which she handed to Stoutman. He drank it and handed it back. She had waited, looking at the ground.

Stoutman now wished to talk business and feeling a bit of old energy returning, produced from inside his white suit a wallet, removing a sum of cash. The old man held out his hand to receive the gift but Stoutman raised his arm, pointing out the door, to the ass. The old man leant forward to see out the door, then smiled. He understood. Stoutman held out the cash but the old man did not take it, giving only one of his dreadful grins. Stoutman had, in his wallet, enough money to fill Mandalgovi with merchants two times over yet he refused to offer more than a fair price. It was part of the foundation of his life. The old man bent forward, kicked Stoutman's hand with his foot and the money fell in a great flutter to the floor.

Stoutman blinked in confusion. He did not understand the old man's tactics. Though he tried to suppress it, the thought worked forward in his mind that this old man, who looked near death's door, did not respect money at all, that presumably the world had not yet come to Mandalgovi, and that once again he was back to square one, helpless, where a thousand square miles of fatal waste pressed in on him cruelly, wanting submission.

'What, what do you want then? Tell me. I know you understand.'

In a world designed to get you it could have been only one thing, and by some precognisance of this fact, Stoutman's eyes turned toward the squatting daughter even before the old man could point. She did not look up.

So, Roger Stoutman thought, I have been brought all the way to Mandalgovi for this, these tens of thousands of miles to be forced to relieve an old man of his middle-aged daughter who wears a permanent expression of shame on her face! But instead of being defiant, he surprised himself. Perhaps he could do it? Perhaps he could take her with him on the ass, through the desert. She wouldn't want to go with him beyond the border. But then she might. She might be one of those who are loyal till death. Perhaps he could live with her, even open himself up to her, love her? He wasn't a corpse. He could love. Why not? He wasn't qualified to know, never having tried it. And her ugliness? What was ugliness compared to life or death.

Roger Stoutman could feel that loosening of control, that cranial dizziness, that is the preface, he suspected, to going mad. There were tears coming from his eyes, though he did not feel that he was in fact shedding them.

Then came another voice inside him.

'I am a bachelor,' he said aloud. The strangers did not understand *bachelor*. 'Do you hear me? I am a BACHELOR!' and they echoed BACHELOR — BACHELOR — as if it was being shouted down into a deep hole, say a grave.

'I WOULD RATHER DIE!'

But he believed in these words less than ever.

Affected by some force, probably the same one that brought him so far, Roger Stoutman rose shakily and felt his feet take a step toward the downcast daughter. His face was reflective with moisture. The old man and the daughter rose to their feet.

'DON'T BE A FOOL STOUTMAN!' came the words for the last time, as the daughter looked up at last, eyes so clear and dark they may never have looked up before. She reached out her small hand toward him. Closing his eyes and dreaming of an improved world he raised his arm, and groping in the darkness for a second, found her hand, took hold of it, and squeezed.

It did not take long, perhaps only a moment, but in touching her he felt, as somehow he had always known he would feel at that moment, an oppressive pang of pain and joy in the region of his heart, and he knew, suddenly, that it was a mistake. Sometimes you shouldn't hope for better. He was a bachelor through and through, and alone, designed for nothing more. He hit his chest once with his fist, feeling a strangulation of his lungs, and with a cry slouched limply to the floor, his yellow hat coming off and rolling toward the door like the bright soul escaping.

With gleaming eyes the old man looked at his daughter. She smiled, revealing no front teeth, and not the slightest hint of surprise. Then, without a word the old man bent over the large, now still, white-suited figure and slowly drew out his knife from Roger Stoutman's back, as the daughter began to go through the pockets for a fool's money.

Back across a not-so-wide world a landlady cleaned out her spare room, once occupied by a quiet, wealthy fat man. She hummed a popular tune she'd heard on the radio. Into a large cardboard box she finally put a mantel clock, an empty fish bowl and two pairs of Italian black leather shoes. She was to show the room again that day to an unattached clerk with a mild manner. She was only interested in bachelors. They were not any bother at all.

PETER WELLS

THE GOOD TOURIST AND THE
LAUGHING CADAVER

EVEN THE GUIDEBOOKS — index of the anodyne — described
the city as 'faintly sinister'.

Visitors are advised, the guidebook said, *to avoid attracting attention
to themselves either by their behaviour or their way of dress, to refrain from
night-time strolls and, in particular, to be on the alert at all times.*

He could, with effort, restrain himself from 'night-time strolls'.
But how, Eric Westmore wondered, could he, a gay man, avoid
attracting attention to himself? His 'way of dress' in his own
country would be considered, perhaps, a little too emphatic,
colours a bit too carefully orchestrated with key aspects — thick
leather belt, shaven shortness of his hair — sending signals to those
interested in reading them. But, in this city, *this* particular circle
of hell, it wasn't simply a 'way of dress', he knew, which caused
people to look sharply at him — or worse, turn away from him
as if his very existence offended them.

Already within twenty yards of leaving the hotel, a man had
turned and spat, with contemptuous accuracy, right by Eric's feet.
The day before a woman, a mother, had come very close to his
face as if she bore a personal message, then her expression pincered
into disgust, almost as if she were, involuntarily, going to vomit
at the sight of him.

Eric now knew this was not to be an exception. He caught
himself returned, with astonishing clarity, to the paranoid world
of his childhood: when to be sexually different was to be
extraordinarily obvious, almost an amusement for a majority so
complacent in its selected paranoias.

But he was not a child, he told himself angrily — he was nearing
what would be the midway section of *other* people's lives: and his
knowledge of himself and the world was gained at considerable
cost: for men of his age and type there had been no established
learning: that was, he told himself ironically, beyond those

provided by psychiatric hospitals, prisons and the occasional morgue.

This was, he knew, to be paranoid himself: but this city of gargoyles, tortured saints — proud possessor indeed, of seventeen (how joyously particular) thorns, thirteen pieces of the Cross, a sponge, flails and even, it was passionately believed, a liquefying phial of the blood of Christ — was not exactly unacquainted with the tinctures of the curdled mood.

Yet with what quixotic fervour had Eric and his two friends — Tim, an Australian of unshakable self-possession and Guiseppe, his Italian ex-lover, a languid man from the North — chosen to stay within the heart of the old, decaying, *sinister* city.

Each held to the *snobbisme* that they were not so much tourists, perhaps, as cultivated men intent upon experiencing 'the spirit of place': yet the Sunday of their arrival was enough to shake Eric. The taxi-driver had almost killed them taking them the wrong way up a one-way street not far from the station. Their night-time stroll — Guiseppe said in his charmingly enpebbled English, 'Please not to stray far from another' — had revealed a miniature view of hell: an alley cut deep into ancient slums, shop windows behind steel shutters. The sky, high above the street-lights, had the look of flesh several days after a beating.

Eric's immediate response, on returning to their spartan hotel, was to lie down on his bed and close his eyes. It was, in a way, his idea of nightmare. He had been paranoid — that word again — about even going away. He had fought a mounting feeling of panic as he was driven out to Auckland's airport that he wanted to do one single thing: to turn around and stay at home. But this would have meant hiding from his friends and acquaintances, all of whom viewed his departure as the beginning of the one true joy, which lies in departing from New Zealand's shores: a rest from its repetitions, a holiday from its isolation: it would be as if he were trying to elude the 'time of his life'.

Perhaps he was. Eric, at the age of 39, had now to face the fact that in a foreign city, this positively sinister place, he might have to call a doctor, face the horror of an unknown hospital. A complaint he had almost managed to shake off only days before his departure had returned, like an avenging angel, to haunt him.

It was an intolerable itch which had begun approximately two months before: a small squadron of upraised pores which became, soon enough, a squabbling storm of pain, an armada of acute irritation: before long he was reduced to something akin to an animal: lying in bed at three in the morning, ripping the heads off sores with septic fingernails, trying to claim some relief. Then, as a refinement of his torture, there was the scratchy irritability of flesh forming a scab: worse still, anything which attacked his equilibrium sent him off, uncontrollably, onto a mission — hopeless as it always turned out, self-defeating, lacerating in its very futility — to soothe the ache, the itch.

Uncontrollable was of the essence. Eric was faced, immediately and close up, with the reality that he had a nervous condition he could not control. Doctors in New Zealand had offered balms, lotions, ointments, all as useless as they were expensive. (Indeed in the expense lay the inverse potential of salvation.) And now he was here, participating in his own worse nightmare: to be in a foreign land and ill.

He had worked it out at home before he left what was so peculiarly threatening about this thought: to be ill in a foreign country was simply to experience in advance the reality of all illness, which is to be homeless.

It was to be in a permanent foreign land — one where the language used is barely comprehensible, or at least where words seem to match, only clumsily, what they stand to represent. Worse still, you had to adjust to customs you barely comprehend in a place which you never can be, you never actually want to be, at home. It was to be in permanent exile from the world you knew. You were a refugee before you even knew it. A refugee in your own world too, perhaps.

Yet was he really ill? If he could only calm his nerves — evade the uneasiness which held him in its grip — he might escape back to that once-known, fondly remembered homeland: *health*.

Yet he was in search of no medicine that afternoon as he made his way down the Via Duomo. Eric had quietly got out of his bed towards the end of the siesta hour on their second day in the city. He had left Tim and Guiseppe dozing in their room, blind softly tapping against the window.

He was driven out of their room, restlessly searching for nothing so salving as a miracle. Rather he sought to solve all his earthly problems by an eminently materialist quest: a pair of Italian shoes.

He knew he must return to his own country with a few selected totems which signal the returning tourist: not to do so would be viewed as almost scandalous: as if all those kept at home, entrapped in the two small islands — no strangers to paranoia themselves — were being denied the news of exactly what people were wearing, eating, saying in that miraculous world which lay beyond New Zealand's three international airports.

Eric now took his *passigata* past the ancient duomo, looking in shop windows. He carefully manoeuvred himself around passers-by, avoiding ostensible eye-contact, rejecting, seemingly invisibly, the many intense stares which passed over his body, sought an entrance through his eyes, as if to snare out and hook, like an obdurate oyster, the moist matter of his soul.

Instead he concentrated on the saving safety of leathern objects. The shoes were displayed in ranks, their prices discreetly placed by their toes. Yet even as he stood there, the soothing practicality of his quest lost its focus.

He could not precisely name the feeling which overcame him at these times: yet all the time it was as if he were waiting: everything seemed a preparation yet, simultaneously, nothing was enough. If anything this trip, as everyone in New Zealand called it, this voyage into the outer world, served only to exasperate his problem. Behind every destination lay another appointment, so everything seemed slightly out of focus, as if his eyes were always and nervously straining to something beyond: his smiles felt false, his attention flickering, his logic obtuse in its connections: the fact was he was already listening, with an almost manic intensity, to the silence within his own body.

Almost on impulse, to escape this introspection, he entered the shoe shop he had halted by.

Immediately an elderly gentleman, petitioner to a quattrocento court, came forward with crossed palms.

Eric, who possessed no Italian, mimed the shoes he had seen: they were supple plaited shoes of a kind you could safely not find in his own country. The shop owner — his proprietorial hauteur was such that he could only own the shop — now mimed his own appreciation of true good taste. He ushered Eric to a low-backed chair set against 1960s mirrors. Eric sank back, murmuring, like a curtsey, a self-conscious *grazie*.

To travel, Eric now knew, was to be stripped of all your assets: you were simply what you were, in flesh, or, perhaps, to that more indefinable thing, the spirit. Was it an accident, then, he had come to a country so loaded with the detritus of spirit when he felt almost spiritually fractured: in need of integration? Yet how could he hope to find solace in a religion so offensive in its hatred for his type: not so long ago — that is, in the margin of this place, four centuries — he might have been burnt, broken on the wheel, crucified.

Comforting, then, to be alive, even in *this* haunted present.

As if in answer to his prayers, the shop owner came back with a pair of shoes. No, the shoes did not quite fit. Now Eric became subsumed into the shop-owner's drama: that he should make a sale: and in fact the flattery of the shop-owner's attention — after the outright affrontery of the streets — was curiously relaxing.

The shop-owner turned and, with the dismissive gesture of a great theatre director to a bit player, sent a boy along the road to another shop. Eric waited now, paused. And perhaps because waiting had become almost his natural state — a kind of anxious anticipation, or foreboding, underlying every event — he oddly, even luxuriantly, relaxed into this lacuna.

He looked at the other customers. In the women's section, a dowdy middle-aged mama was crouched beside her daughter aged no more than nine. The child was dressed as an infanta in white. All around them lay an army of shoeboxes, all in disarray, routed in the quest for the perfect bridesmaid slipper. A grandmother, a more withered version of the mother, gazed on while a shop assistant crouched down in genuflection at the infanta's tiny feet.

The child, Eric could see, was luxuriating in her brief regnum of power. Her legs swung to and fro, brow petulant with the perfect vision of the golden slipper, no doubt, that would take her away from all of *this*. Yet Eric wondered at her chances of evading the fate of her mother and grandmother, women visibly soured by life, beatings probably, premature deaths, men indifferent to them: no wonder these people clung to superstition, as a compensating, even avenging faith.

Eric caught his own image in the mirror opposite: or rather, his image betrayed him. Yes, looking at his smooth unfurrowed face, there was privilege in its softness. He was not visibly ravaged by any unhappiness: his unease was internal: he was simply looking on, almost a spy.

As if in answer to his self-doubt — did he really exist beside these people? — a man outside the door casually cantilevered his hips towards Eric. Behind the cheap cloth of his trousers, the man, possibly a gypsy, displayed a hand, frottaging a not-inconsiderable erection. The man's eyes hungrily fed off Eric's homosexual face. This was as much a part of the paranoia of the place, Eric now knew: the flagrant tumescence of the men.

Only the day before as he and Tim and Guiseppe went up in the funicular, a beautiful youth had engaged his attention. As they ascended — suitably upwards, as if only in a heavenly sphere this youth could exist — the young man had turned himself towards Eric, and under the eyes of everyone in the compartment — these people who saw everything — the youth had begun to leisurely, silkenly, squeeze his erection. All the while his grape-green eyes never left Eric's face.

Thoughts had sped through Eric's head: to spend an afternoon, even an hour — or let's get basic, several hectic minutes — with a boy so beautiful (he had an atypical colouring of honeyed skin, dusky gilt hair, the eyes of peeled grapes) would be, well, heaven: yet was he, Eric, even capable of the magic which was sex, when he was so full of indecision? Finally, abruptly, the youth had broken off the gaze, the tenure of which had, as much as the wires pulling the funicular upwards, kept Eric's mood in ascension.

The funicular had lurched to a stop. The youth turned and walked away. Was it some small compensation that he who had appeared so perfect stationary — or ascending — walked away unevenly: he had a club foot. Even so, he did not turn back.

'*Si, si,*' Eric said to a pair of shoes which matched, approximately, the shape of his foot. Ah, the happy curve of an act completed. Now, almost bowing, in a flutter of money exchanging hands, the transaction complete, Eric walked out of the shop with his totem. He awaited, wryly, that de-escalation of mood which followed the efflorescence — or was it defloration? — which was purchase. In his room he would discover, perhaps, the leather was not quite so: perhaps the heels were packed with cardboard. There was any number of deceits for those people passing forever through: among the permanent inhabitants in the panorama of life, a tourist.

As he turned back towards the hotel, Eric's eye, elated by the victory which goes with any sort of possession, happened to snag on the typography of an English-speaking newspaper. He hurried into the shop — really only a booth, maintained by a severely sceptical woman who eyed his money now, intently, as if he were a bona fide counterfeiter. Eric felt at this now-familiar affront a rush of irritation: involuntarily, yet as if it physically expressed his emotion, he sneezed. The woman shrank back angrily, crossed herself, and handed him the paper, a chill dismissal.

Outside the shop, the paper in his hand, Eric felt an unreasonable anticipation of pleasure overtake him. He would celebrate his good luck — his return to the world of language, and the logic which lay inside language — by an espresso, an aperitif.

He turned and went instinctively to the small coffee place where he had seen, the day before, an astonishing male beauty. This, too, would restore him.

As he made his way towards it — the streets growing busier as the siesta hour fell further behind — he thought to himself, amusingly, of Tim, Guiseppe and himself going, the day before, into one of those religious shops which specialise in items to ward off evil spirits. They had settled on some votives — small silver objects reproducing part of the anatomy which requires God's healing intervention. Eric had chosen a leg as gratifyingly shapely as an All Black's; Guiseppe had fallen for the Grecian profile of an eye and a nose: Tim who always went the whole hog sexually, went for an entire body, in toto.

A perfectly hypocritical madame had encased their purchases

in whispering tissue-paper. Outside Eric and Tim had screamed with laughter as they walked away, imagining how the women would think they were men with very extreme illnesses to placate, whereas their hidden humour was that the objects were purely decorative: interesting totems to prove they had been to that particular place. The votives would end up sitting on a bookshelf, dusty and forgotten.

The coffee place had several men standing by the zinc counter: a woman sat behind her cash register, bored as a magistrate facing a daily line-up of recidivists. The male beauty had his arms in suds, washing cups and glasses, an act which piquantly feminised him. Eric's eyes magnetically found the young man who, withdrawing his ruddy forearms, marble-white above the elbow, pulled off an espresso for Eric.

'*Grazie, grazie.*'

Eric took the coffee and leant a discreet viewing distance away on a counter. He looked once more, appreciatively, at the young man. His face was Egyptian in cast, like those entombed replicas gaudily painted — eyes outlined not with kohl but lashes, with lips made for love, for kissing and sucking and teeth for biting. Eric quickly looked away.

He opened the paper with gusto: even the biscuity aroma of the pages he enjoyed. He caught up, speed-reading, the latest world news, the usual combination of catastrophe and calumny, then his eye, almost automatically, as if selecting the one true item of personal importance, found the celebrated capital letters.

In a profound silence during which Eric lost his presence in that city, in that coffee place, before that male beauty, he read the simple statement which had appeared a decade ago, that exact day in a New York paper.

An unknown cancer had appeared. Forty-one homosexual men had already died. It was possibly contagious.

He reached for his aperitif — an ouzo. He drank it numbly. Suddenly it tasted too sweet, too intense. What exactly, after all, was he celebrating? He looked up speedily. The male beauty was holding up to the light a glass, the cleanliness of which appeared suspect. Outside a clatter of horns battered the air.

Eric returned to the few lines and as he re-read, as if to find in them some further intelligence, an awareness settled in him — the reality of what these few lines conveyed.

It was that date, he knew, that the fateful diaspora had begun.

He sighed heavily and thought of what it had meant in his own life: friends he had not appreciated were so particular until they were wrenched, like garden plants too early, from his life: then the disease crept closer, robbing his heart of his best friend, Perrin, infiltrating his existence until it became an unavoidable, a central reality: a prism, as it were, to gaze upon a world.

Manners, over time, dictated that not too much was made of it. With so many people ill, it was grossly self-indulgent — risking even exhibitionism — to make much of the disease. The deflective language of the theatre was deployed: characteristic turns such as 'scene-hogging', 'spotlight hugging', 'prima donna swansongs' marked painful, humiliating demises.

In such simple ways the enormity had been reduced: the stark phrase 'having health problems' signified the advent: from here the stigmata varied in their elliptical progress: a 'seizure', 'in hospital', 'on morphine' and finally — usually, thankfully — dead. Thankful because out of pain — thankful, too, because the difficult business of being a witness was over.

But what about when you were the witness to your own — not death exactly — but the presence? There were as few rules here as there had been in the wilderness days of sex: to follow your instinct, to try and have courage in your convictions, your choice. What did that mean exactly when you awoke in the morning with unanswerable questions: what have I done with my life? To be more precise: what am I doing with my future?

Future, an interesting concept, that.

Eric laid the paper down.

Oh, irony, his saving grace, his god, almost — could it desert him now when he needed it most? Yet how could its deflective nature, its silvern armour save him from such sharp and piercing shafts of self-doubt? It could not, it would not. Yet really, when he thought of it, closing the paper thoughtfully, was there not a certain mordant irony in the fact that he found himself, at this moment, now, on such a personally historic anniversary, in the very city which had suffered a plague so terrible that at its end so many were dead there had not been enough living left to bury them?

He suddenly thought of the night before. Guiseppe, Tim and he were returning from dinner. The rubbish, in a nearby alley, was being collected. Eric could hear the threshing truck yet there was another sound his ears could decipher. He listened acutely. It was the scream of a cat in pain or abject terror. The truck's roar drew closer. The cat's terror rose in syncopation. A cat-lover himself, Eric knew instinctively what was happening.

Sitting in the café, newsprint moist against his fingerpads, the exact tune of the cat's torture returned to Eric.

Sometimes it seemed to him the echo of this scream pervaded the entire universe. It underlaid everything, it was a basic note. At times, of festivity, of *amour*, this note was overlaid, forgotten. But then, at other moments — the silent moments, in the immobility which is doubt — or, again, in moments of great violence, this sound returned. It filled all space as if it were the one true essence of existence: chaos.

Eric hurriedly left the café, nodding at the young man who nodded back, as automatically as a dancestep in the waltz of living.

He walked home to his hotel among Caravaggio's saints and executioners.

Tim had the way, he mused as he walked along: there were few agues that marijuana, booze and a raunchy sense of humour could not cure: and what could not be cured was faced with a blatant bray of black humour not indivisible from courage. Tim had lost more friends than other people had family. And Guiseppe, Tim's ex-lover, was a charmingly vague man, as imprisoned perhaps in his own language as Eric was by his own lack of Italian: yet there was peace between them, no linguistic war.

Yes, Tim had the right idea. Every daily dilemma narrowed down to a choice of restaurant, then of dishes, a particularity of wine: and those moments after a meal, having eaten slightly too much, definitely drunk too well: to a sense of well-being as re-juvenative as good sex, yet somehow infinitely easier to obtain and of course, in this world now, this *fin de siècle* present — a century running out of monstrosities with which to haunt itself
   much safer.

Eric passed on the street an ancient metal skull on which a few pinched blossoms had already wilted. This living with death, this fond familiarity, even fatalism, was a reality for these people. They, their cynicism intact, had survived.

It was not good enough, he told himself, firmly: he simply must adjust his mood.

As if in answer to his prayer he remembered something he had seen the day before. He had come across a crowd of people clapping. Over their heads he saw a cascade of fireworks: like toitoi feathers dipped in emerald, ruby and gold they painted the air, fading even as others appeared. He had always loved fireworks, their evanescence. The fragility of their beauty comforted him.

He had stopped to watch in the cold wind, then moved on.

But the yowl of that cat apprehending its own death returned, now, to haunt him. Why was it he in particular who heard it, while neither Guiseppe nor Tim appeared to? Was it that it tuned into his own frequency, as it were, of paranoia: which was that he might, in a more hauntingly real sense of the cliché, see the city and die? Or was it that his mood at present constrained him only to hear the descant notes: to view, mordantly, blackly, everything he was seeing on his voyage? And did this not mean, precisely, that he saw everything blackly. He must find — not the courage for optimism, that was foolhardy — he must locate at least an appetite for life: it was the essence, after all, of being a good tourist.

'*Ciao bello!*'

Tim pulled him into his embrace, and Eric let his thin frame lean into the large, comfortingly fat form of his friend. Tim's stomach ground companionably into Eric's penis, as if by the rotation of his belly, its content, Eric might share in his happiness.

Guiseppe smiled and waved an elegant semaphore with a cigarette. He was lying down, reading *Vanity Fair*.

This, *this* was real now, this room with two friends, with whom he could share his thoughts.

He was suddenly tired. He eased his shoes off, and recounted, in as amusing a way as possible, the man outside the shoe shop, his proud display of an erection. Lastly, and self-deprecatingly, he produced his newly bought shoes.

Tim immediately said he himself had seen the shoes for half the price in another city.

To compensate for Eric's natural national disability ('the Pacific's True Boat People', 'Irish of the Pacific'), Tim poured him a glass of an exquisitely fresh rosé wine.

It tasted, on Eric's tongue, momentarily, of strawberries and mountain water, of ice and watermelon.

Eric let it enter his body, easing, cooling, numbing, soothing. His particular ache, for one moment, lessened.

Now Tim, who enjoyed being naked, stood there stripped for a shower. Eric, who had missed being Tim's lover more by accident than design, averted his eyes, caught Guiseppe's drowsy gaze and they exchanged a momentary jag, a snippet of shared amusement. How good it was to share a fondness about a mutual friend's peccadilloes!

Tim removed his magnificence and, for one moment, his psychological presence occupied the room, as if his rotund physical shape were indented on air.

Water splayed on concrete.

Eric had instinctively not alluded to the epochal anniversary in the paper. An event so major in all their lives was better left to after dinner, perhaps, when satisfied appetite could better combat what would inevitably attempt to spread a pall.

A pleasant silence fell in the room. Guiseppe turned a page. Tim, from the bathroom, took up his anthem, all the more personal for being tunelessly defiant: *'I'm going to live forever! I'm going to learn how to fly!'*

'Those fireworks I saw yesterday,' Eric said slowly to Guiseppe, having deliberately saved the best, most private part of his thought for someone less proprietorial of pleasure than Tim.

His question was carefully un-elliptical.

'I wonder what the fireworks were for?'

'Oh, the fireworks,' said Guiseppe, thoughtfully, listening abstractly to Tim's watery ode to joy, 'that day was . . . I t'ink' — he could never quite manage that hurdle of the esoteric, that particular consonant which divided the world into the English-speaking and the forever-foreign, the aspirant 'h' — Guiseppe paused, searching his English inventory for the correct word, 'the

Day of the 'appy Cadaver, I t'ink.'

Eric said nothing for a moment.

Then a shout, a flag of irony, escaped his lips.

And Eric Westmore, a good tourist for the first time that day, began to laugh.

DEBRA DALEY

A BENT CUCUMBER

ON A COOL autumn night after heavy rain, the San Romeo English Conversation Café in downtown Kobe opened its doors, as usual, at five o'clock. Hilary's shift, from seven until ten three nights a week, reliably drew a fair-sized crowd who paid a cover charge for her services. She was advertised as an exponent of British English, as opposed to the far less stylish American English which every Tom, Dick and Haruko confronted at high school. The sign promoting Hilary, pasted on the wall of San Romeo's vestibule, featured a sketch of a man in cap and plus-fours swinging a golf club and in the background a meticulous drawing of Westminster Palace.

Hilary was Australian, but fortunately her original accent, already compromised by a number of years in London, went undetected in the café. The only material proof of her migrations lay in her passport which was thick with additional pages. Determined to avoid the taint of tourism, she kept no journal, carried no camera. (True, she had bought a kimono last Sunday, but this did not have to mean she had succumbed to collecting.) She offered up herself and in return was accepted and liked in many languages and diverse landscapes. This was the premise of her compulsive voyaging: to confirm her personality, to find herself cultivated on even the most alien soil. She imagined her progress around the world to be marked by a series of flags stuck in the hearts and minds of foreigners. These tiny conquests filled her with pride, urging her to seek fresh fields. This sentiment, however, remained undeclared. When asked why she was in Japan, Hilary waved a casual hand and said that nothing more significant than an appreciation of sand gardens and lacquered bento boxes had borne her there, carelessly, like a seed on the wind.

The San Remeo's patrons sat on high stools at the bar or at tables and booths where, immersed in anglo-rustic decor, they ate curry-rice and cake. As a conversation hostess, Hilary had only to smile and encourage the sale of refreshments while extracting sentences in English. During the first half hour of her shift, she worked behind the bar attending to innocuous details. She took scalding handtowels from the microwave, replaced coffee filters and chalked the Phrase of the Day on a blackboard, all the time aware of furtive, shy glances from the San Romeo disciples who at this point conversed securely in Japanese. Hilary's Japanese was passable but Tommy-san the proprietor (given name, Toshio), a relentless anglophile, watched her vigilantly to ensure that only English passed her lips.

After this reassuringly domestic exposition of her presence, she began her educational chit-chat, although still confined behind the bar. Hilary obligingly introduced words like 'frightfully', 'splendid' and 'absolute wally', while not yet singling out any one person for attention, and was humorous on Cockney rhyming slang. Two or three confident regulars, grizzled businessmen who had been posted overseas in their nostalgic past, enlisted from her fragments of Beatles lyrics and Shakespearean quotation. But these men were exceptions. Most of her audience had never left Japan, even during their brief sorties abroad. The stay-at-homes charged their glasses, scenting the agony that was Individual Conversation, a theatrical in which Hilary was cast as a sort of linguistic dominatrix. She did not wish to humiliate them but they insisted.

Smiling, she stepped from behind the bar.

At once the café prickled with anticipation. The women, disguised as soubrettes, preferred booths at the hinterland of the room. When Hilary breached their territory they buried their glossy heads in their Hello Kitty handbags, epileptic with laughter. Taking pity on them, as they had hoped, she turned away to the tables, searching for an opening. At once salarymen averted their blushing faces from the power of her blue-eyed stare. They held fast to their headgear as if bracing themselves against a typhoon. These defences required a firm approach; in fact the salarymen, her guys, adored the firm approach and proved it by bringing her presents, manicure sets and fans, pickled ginger and reproduction Buddhist scrolls while also contributing collectively to her store of unprocessed memories and international anecdotes. That was the way of it, give and take.

Inflicting herself on a slender middle-aged man in bifocals and tartan tam, Hilary uttered the terrifying phrase, 'Hello, how are you?' Explosively relieved to find themselves spared, the man's companions howled gleefully while his attempt at a reply sailed beyond futility. Hilary knelt at his side.

'What is your name?'

Possibly revived by her perfume, he exerted himself. 'Machida.'

'Okay. And your first name, Machida-san? Or christian name, as it's sometimes known.'

Machida was overcome by a generalised spasm.

'Ooo-ooo-hoo — First name! First name! First name!' The furies that were his friends thumped the tables.

Machida's mouth fell open as an aspirate fought its way into the world. 'Ha-Hajime.' Hajime shut his eyes tight.

'And so Hajime, what kind of work do you do?'

Probably he was a PhD in Middle English or the veteran of a fortnight in Honolulu or similar, who had boasted to his colleagues of mastering that ubiquitous English. Nothing to it. Infinitely penetrable. But now, thrashing around in the trap of pronunciation, Hajime expressed nothing but halting gibberish. His companions hooted anew, joined by a confederation of hecklers at surrounding tables. Idiot! Idiot! Mush-brain! Despite Hilary's murmuring small-talk, the conversation expired. Yet remarkably, as soon as she released him from her gaze, Hajime beamed with satisfaction and committed himself to the raillery of her next victim. This ritual of command and cringe played, with variations, until Tommy recalled Hilary to the bar at ten.

While he was peeling her wages from the cash-box, Hilary said cheerfully, 'Well, I don't know, Tommy. I still strike fear into them. They don't really think I'm such a dragon though, do they?'

'That right,' said Tommy. He gazed up at her as if she were a long way off, making her feel taller than necessary. 'You a pussycat.'

Kobe is an industrial city, a port, in the Kansai region of Japan. In the suburb of Rokko, a street called Nagaminedai winds up a steep mountainside before unravelling in a stone forest of Shinto obelisks which is the Rokko cemetery. Statuettes of pert little dogs, dressed in crimson aprons, guard the dead. Osaka Bay lies hugely below, a final vista for those denied perspective during their lifetime. Hilary lived just outside the cemetery gates and took advantage of this convenient site to enjoy a daily walk along the rocky pathways surrounding the graveyard. Brilliant maples grew thickly here; occasional snakes crawled from the undergrowth. It pleased her to live close to this unexpected wilderness which was largely ignored by Rokko's inhabitants, except for ritualised visits on designated dates, such as National Physical Fitness Day or Moonviewing Day.

The flat-roofed wooden house which Hilary shared with three other foreigners, although poorly maintained, was remarkable for its generous proportions. Where its suburban neighbours were compact, economical, trim, this dwelling drew itself up from the neglected garden to an expansive two storeys. Its broad face featured large sash-windows and a massive front door. A number of these big, peculiar properties existed in Kobe, built decades ago for foreign merchants who once settled in the city in the name of import-export. Now the house was rented by shadows of those previous entrepreneurs whose exchange of goods and services was more diffuse.

Thankful to escape Zac's percussive carpentry, Hilary strode out of the house, and was halfway down the mountain when a very short thin young woman sprang at her from behind a persimmon tree. Her lovely face was round and flat, her skin pearly, her bouncy jet hair permed and swept into a topknot to reveal the essential nape of the neck. She wore a 'We Are Gay Boys' sweat-shirt and distressed jeans. Hilary paused, used to the passing curiosity of strangers.

'Konnichi wa.'

'Sorry, sorry,' the apparition whispered.

'Ah. You speak English.'

Shaking her head violently, the woman expressed a tense 'Good afternoon,' before clamping her hand to her mouth.

'Good afternoon. Hi. I know you don't I?'

'Mori Shizue,' cried Shizue. 'San Romeo!'

Now Hilary recognised a mute regular from the Conversation Café.

'Ikaga desu ka? How are you, Shizue? Samui desu ne? It's quite a cold afternoon don't you think?' Hilary almost winced herself as her booming voice buffeted the tender creature hovering on the verge. Shizue's face became rigid with concentration.

'Soon the beautiful leaves will begin to climb down from the spinney, I believe.' Then screwing up her eyes in anguish, 'I am in good spirits, Miss Smith.'

Touched by this difficult announcement, Hilary sought to put Shizue at ease. 'I'm glad to hear it. And I couldn't agree more about the leaves.'

'Thank you, thank you, Miss Smith.'

'Please, call me Hilary.'

But this invitation to commit phonological suicide caused Shizue to enter a temporary trance. Clasping her face in her hands she stared into the grey sky. In sympathy Hilary too raised her eyes. Eventually, addressing an ulterior plane, Shizue said 'May I —, may I — oh —, may I *company* you?'

'By all means. I'm just on my way to the supermarket to get some Instant Ramen. It's my staple diet.'

'Ha-ha-ha!'

While the two women were sharing this moment of hilarity, Hilary's flatmate Bennie materialised, hurtling down Nagaminedai on his customised Suzuki. Skinny throbbing bike; skinny throbbing rider. Hilary watched Shizue consume Bennie's throwback rebel appearance: his leopard-skin jacket and tight jeans encasing pipe-cleaner legs which concluded in gold shoes of an extreme pointiness. Bennie's hair, sculptured by gel and spray, jutted out above his narrow forehead like a cliff. Although Hilary judged Bennie to be an insistently shallow human being whose sojourn in Japan was nothing more than a cunning kind of procrastination, she got on with him here as she never would have if they had been thrown together in the west. In Japan, the stereotype that was Bennie — Essex Man: 'What can I do you for, darling?' — was translated into a model of singularity, an antidote to conformism. At least, in some eyes.

'Got a date with the visa men?' Hilary called.

'Those tosspots,' he shouted, wrenching the bike into a lingering lower gear so he could appraise the Japanese. Shizue wisely made a spectacle of herself by means of twitching hands and paroxysmal giggles which instantly suppressed his interest. Bennie had immigration problems. A master of pretexts and promises, he had managed to loiter in Kobe for nearly five years, but now it seemed that only marriage would save him from being deported to, he had hinted, criminal retribution at home and worse, obscurity. Bennie liked to stand out in a crowd. His best hope was to find a phlegmatic bride from a son-less family who would pay him to adopt the family name. Then he could achieve permanent residence and financial security while maintaining lack of responsibility. Just before disappearing around a curve, Bennie rose up on his pedals and wiggled his arse. Slightly convulsed, Shizue covered her face.

By the time they began patrolling the aisles of the supermarket, Shizue had become composed and quiet. She walked one step behind Hilary, intensely contemplating the items Hilary placed in her basket, Instant Ramen, mayonnaise, Glico Pocky chocolate, Pocare Sweat soft drink, salted fish.

'Fish, why?'

'Well, to eat.'

'Difficult for you. Japanese fish.'

'I've got used to it.'

'Ha-ha-ha.'

It bothered Hilary that even this simple procedure, gaijin girl goes shopping, seemed mysterious to her companion. She felt a great desire to make herself clear, to prove her expertise in foreign relations.

They were standing in the produce section, when Shizue said suddenly, 'Boy on motorbicycle. Is he bent cucumber?'

Hilary smiled. 'Well bent, I'd say. And he's no boy, my dear. Bennie's thirty-five and counting.'

'So.' Shizue's grave expression rebuked Hilary's grin.

It was hard to get this sense of humour thing in synch. 'I don't know what you mean, Shizue. What's a bent cucumber?'

'You see. Here is crowd of cucumbers.'

The telegraph cucumbers, like all the produce, were acutely arranged. They lay perfect and glowing, uniformly green and straight, in a basket-weave pattern on the shelves.

'Put bent cucumber on shelf, nobody buy. It still taste good but —' Shizue assumed an attitude of censure, her index finger pointing at the ceiling. 'It is — it is — it is — REJECT!'

Engaged by this display of opinion, Hilary perceived that Shizue might be speaking about her own, Shizue's, situation. But before she could draw the woman out, Shizue made one of those characteristic gestures of diversion which complicate Japanese life, just as the language is complicated with honorific forms and conditions, for the foreigner.

In a *coup de politesse*, she wrenched the basket from Hilary's hands, saying, 'I pay completely.'

There followed a desperately courteous to-and-fro over the question of payment, to the amusement of the many, many onlookers at the checkout, but Hilary prevailed by insisting that it would be unkind of Shizue to put her under obligation. More truthfully, she felt it necessary to neutralise the formidable power of Japanese etiquette in order to make a personal connection with the overlooked bent cucumber.

Shizue waited, disadvantaged, outside the supermarket, her hands demurely clasped, her shoulders slumped.

Joining her, Hilary said in the breezy manner she relied on to leap many a cultural trough and pothole, 'So why haven't you ever talked to me at San Romeo? Your English is okay. You could have a conversation.'

Shizue shook her head, grinning. Her eyes were moist.

'Shizue? Speak to me.'

She sighed. 'I study hard. I listen to BBC World Service. I am age twenty-six. I have no boyfriend.'

Hilary felt immensely gratified by this confidence. So. Left on the shelf. She wanted to say that there were advantages in not being prepared as a dish, flavoured with sugar and vinegar. But this was too metaphorical. She thought it simpler to change Shizue's life by example.

'I'm the same age as you and I don't have a boyfriend. Who cares? Listen Shizue, you don't need a boyfriend. Don't you have a job?'

Shizue smoothed her sweatshirt. 'When I would speak splendid

English, I work in Japanese company in London. I have lots of frightful fun like you.' Removing her earrings, she offered them to Hilary. 'Please take.'

A quartet of schoolboys wearing Prussian uniforms strolled by 'Hello,' they cried, flashing peace signs at Hilary. 'Michael Jackson!' Hilary waved automatically while her heart swelled with purpose.

'Thank you for the earrings. And in return you must have tea with me. At my house.' By which she meant, please inspect a charmingly eccentric situation populated by free spirits such as myself, an inspiration to those constricted by decorum and duty.

When Hilary and Shizue entered the kitchen they found Zac reclining in the sawdust, draining a can of beer while he looked on his handiwork and found it good. Hilary introduced Shizue, who unsurprisingly could find nothing to say. Zac's appearance did tend to render strangers speechless in this neck of the woods. A tsunami of iron grey hair surged halfway down his back. An equally overwhelming beard blended with the hair on his chest. Gold hoops glinted in his ears. His shirt was unbuttoned, his trousers splattered with paint. His attributes, hammer, power-drill and spirit-level, lay at his side. Saluting with his beer, Zac rose to his feet. He stroked the framing on the unfinished counter.

'Got the fittings in for the lights.' He shied the can into a corner, where it struck a hundred other empties. 'I'll have it finished by the time Tyler gets back.' He sloped from the room.

'Tyler's our other flatmate. He's in Kyushu right now travelling round playing pool. That's how he makes his money. You know "pool"?' Shizue made a swimming motion. Hilary countered with a mime of cue and ball. She set the kettle to boil. Shizue was staring at the structure in what was once a dining room.

'Zac is building a bar. He's been building it for years apparently.'

'This is bar?' The incipient bar, built of brick, an incomplete country pub lexicon of brass carriage lamps, printed mirrors and complex shelving, harked back to Zac's days pulling pints in Derby. Sheets of thick yellow frosted glass were stacked against the window seat.

'Zac's putting lights in so that when that yellow glass is fixed in as a counter, it will be all lit up from underneath.'

Shizue raised her hands helplessly. The discretion of tatami and ricepaper screen seemed a million miles away.

'But the point is that he will never finish it. Just when it seems on the verge of completion, some defect causes him to pull most of it down and start again. Well isn't that like a Zen thing? The master misses the target.'

Shizue's face said, 'Huh?'

'He's a New Zealander. I think he had a Japanese wife once. Please, sit down.'

Shizue perched at the long oak kitchen table, taking care not to disturb teetering columns of CDs and magazines, while absorbing the chaotic environment in which she found herself. The kitchen was large enough to accommodate four separate refrigerators, one for each tenant, (their doors elaborated with magnets restraining postcards and bills and advertisements for nightclubs) and two dressers crowded with pointless bric-a-brac plundered from the inorganic rubbish deposited once every six months on the streets of Rokko for collection. Banquets of plastic sushi occupied the wide sills of the curtainless windows overlooking the street. Bennie's paintings of androids in samurai armour, executed in housepaint on hardboard, jostled for wall space along with Zac's tribal souvenirs from New Guinea, where he had been a surveyor in the seventies. Tinsel decorations and deflated balloons, left over from a summer party, hung from the remote ceiling. If Shizue had dared to investigate the living room she would have found an intensification of this involved decor. The bedrooms, on the other hand, were spartan as if their occupants, having made an exhibition of themselves down stairs, could retire to sex or sleep without the encumbrance of personality.

Zac, now attired in a massive army coat, hair tucked under a bulging green beret, stomped through the kitchen. 'Going down to drink at City Dog with Bennie. If Yoshiko calls you don't know where I am.' Windchimes clanked as he pulled the door to.

Wiping crumbs of breakfast toast from the table, Hilary set down mugs of tea. 'Do you know City Dog?'

Shizue hefted a mug to her mouth and took a tiny sip. 'That

is yakuza place.'

'I think that's its attraction. Bennie likes to walk on the wild side. He told me how the name yakuza came about, from a game called kabu. It's to do with the scores. Ya equals eight, ku equals nine, za is three which adds up to twenty. He says in a game of kabu, which is strictly played by low-lifes, ten or twenty is the worst score you can get. So yakuza really means a kind of defeat. It means nothing. Is that right?'

Shizue was emphatic. 'Don't understand.'

'Never mind.' Silence fell. The yakuza topic was a mistake. Best to get straight to the problem at hand. 'Anyway, what kind of job do you want to get in London?'

Shizue, apparently not yet cognisant of the significance this conversation held for her future, was distracted by the appearance of a cemetery-bound family outside enjoying a hiatus in their ascent. The father held up a small girl to his shoulder and pointed at the tea-drinkers in the merchant-house. The jaunty bunny ears on the child's fluffy pink hat trembled in the gusts blowing off the moutain.

'Shizue?'

'Um. Secretary maybe.'

'And what do you do now?'

'Work in mother's kissaten.'

'A waitress?'

'Café au lait, Earl Grey, pizza toasto.'

'Okay, I get the picture. And why do you want to go to London?'

Shizue squirmed in her seat, wrestling with amnesia. 'London?'

'I have an idea,' said Hilary, trying to sound harmless, although she felt excited at the possibility of asserting her identity in this most convivial and indifferent of countries. 'Why don't you come to me once a week for English lessons?'

'Oh? You are a university girl?'

'No, not exactly. I'm sort of like you. I worked for a coffee importer before I came here. Among other things. It wasn't much of a job, but look at me now, I'm travelling, I'm independent. Do you know "independent"?'

Shizue looked over her shoulder.

'You could see how we live. You know, language and customs. I don't really have a chance to teach anyone at the San Romeo. That's just entertainment. Do you understand what I'm saying?'

'Language and custom. In this house.'

'Yes. You don't have to pay me. In return you can help me with my Japanese.'

'Japanese very very difficult for you.'

'What do you think?'

Shizue laid down her mug and overcome with emotion, stroked the table with her fingertips.

Having directed Shizue to the bathroom and explained the peculiarities of the flushing mechanism, Hilary hurried to her room and removed from a hanger the black kimono she had recently bought secondhand. She believed it to be an autumn kimono, judging from its design and thought to ask Shizue for her opinion. She held the silk against her chest, only able to see her head and shoulders in the small mirror propped on a tea-chest. The sandy hair, the freckled face, the wide shoulders. Impossible of course actually to wear the kimono without looking like a complete fool; she had breasts and hips that ruined its definition. But she was thinking of starting a collection.

The holland blind rattled in the burgeoning wind. While tugging at the window, which had warped in its framework over the summer, Hilary saw Shizue running from the house. She almost cannoned into the bunny-ears family returning from the graveyard. Shizue pulled up short, bowed, then resumed her flight down Nagaminedai.

On the kitchen table lay a leaf of pastel Little Twin Stars notepaper on which Shizue had written, in roman alphabet rather than mysterious kanji so that Hilary might better understand: *Goyo ga oari no tokoro o taihen ojama itashimashita.*

'I'm afraid I have taken up a lot of your time when you have so much work.'

That evening in the San Romeo, when Hilary approached her ducking-and-bobbing facsimiles of students, of whom Shizue was not one tonight, Hilary silenced them and surprised herself.

Addressing generally the tables, she said, in an unassailable tone and with extravagant gesture which did finally truly alarm them:

This box is large.

Is that a window too?

No, it isn't. It is a door.

The customers craned their heads this way and that, gazing in confusion at doors and windows, assuming at first that these declarations had some meaning.

As cool as a cucumber, Hilary continued her one-woman dialogue.

Is that pencil over there red?

Yes, it is.

What is this?

It is a watch.

This watch is not low-priced; it is expensive.

It's fine weather isn't it?

Not at all. The leaves are climbing down from the spinney. So to speak.

Then her sentences were submerged by 'Ferry Across the Mersey' as Tommy cranked up the sound system. He terminated her.

'What is this stupid pencils?' he roared as Hilary slid into her coat.

'I was speaking existentially, Tommy.'

'Go. Go! You are no conversation girl.'

With nothing left to say, Hilary took the bus. She took the plane.

MURRAY BAIL

FROM HERE TO TIMBUKTU

FOR MANY YEARS it never occurred to me that Timbuktu actually existed. I had only heard its name used jokingly by certain members of my family in Adelaide, who shouted 'From here to Timbuktu!' whenever they wanted to denote hopelessly long distances or banishment. So the moment I stumbled across it on the map — faint dot in the southern Sahara — I wanted to go there.

To Europeans, 'Timbuktu' has always represented remoteness, mystery. Its reputation has been helped along by the infectious camel-gait in its syllables. Gounden, not far from Timbuktu, would hardly work in the same way; and 'From here to Ayers Rock' never really gets off the ground. But always giving support to its name was Timbuktu's forbidding location — literally in the middle of nowhere, and for many centuries surrounded by warring kingdoms.

Difficult to get to, Timbuktu was even more difficult to get back from. In 1826, a certain Major Gordon Laing became the first European to get there, enduring the most dreadful hardships, only to be decapitated not long afterwards. Two years later a Frenchman, René Caillié, disguised as a Muslim trader, made it to the mythical city and lived to tell the tale. He stayed for two weeks.

To this day, Timbuktu continues to resist the casual visitor, although its power is weakening.

Mali itself is in the interior of west Africa. And it is large: four times larger than New Zealand, with two or three Tasmanias tossed in. The seven African states surrounding it are in various stages of decline. Their names are splendidly evocative: Ivory Coast, Niger, Upper Volta. All remain more or less time-warped in Islam, agricultural poverty and the effects of European occupation. Mauritania, the enormous north-west neighbour to Mali, abolished slavery only in 1980, and until very recently had no building of more than one storey in the entire country. And along these worn paths of Africa there is the vague feeling of dislocation. Unlike Europe or across Russia or India even there are no cultural references; no touchstones along the way, such as a cathedral breaking the horizon, or a woodcock flying up in front, straight out of the sketches of Turgenev.

I travelled first to Senegal, then inland to Mali's melancholy capital, Bamako, and, after an unseemly dash into the southern Sahara, finally entered Timbuktu. It was early in November; I did not imagine it would be hot. Small boys ran forward and called out, *'Toubabou! Toubabou!'* ('White man! White man!') The heat and sand soon had me dressing like a Tuareg: winding a *chayta*, usually indigo, around the face, just the eyes showing. It is why the Tuareg are called the 'blue men of the desert'. Women do not cover their faces, but carry a shawl called an *afar*; occasionally when they meet a man who is a stranger, they cover their mouths.

Timbuktu emerges from the sand: a scab on the camel-coloured desert.

The houses are mostly mud and clay, sliced off horizontally, north–African style. Sand is everywhere ankle-deep, dappled with footprints. It is like an immense vacant beach where a collection of interlocking cubes has been established, for no apparent reason. The streets and alleyways are dry rivers of sand, and at the end of them begin the dunes of the Sahara in their hypnotic monotony. Walking can become an effort. Sand is always underfoot, even in the two mud mosques and the houses, where there is usually no floor, just sand, ankle-deep. An exception is the mayor's house. It has a concrete floor. But when he has a meal he lays a blanket outside, and sits cross-legged or reclines, happier on sand.

Sand kept getting in my ears, eyes, nostrils and hair. There was sand in the food. The rice tastes of sand. Biting into the flat bread baked in the mud ovens half blocking the alleyways, sand can be heard and felt grating on the teeth. Every day I was in Timbuktu there was a steady desert wind, although it never reached the pitch of a sandstorm when, I was told, it turns into night, bringing all movement to a grinding halt.

Beyond the town the dunes, pale, polished and scalloped by

the wind, offer a series of circular patterns rising and falling to infinity. The silence out there is immediate and impressive. Stranger still is the endless cleanliness; nothing loose; everything smooth; and the silence becomes just another part of the cleanliness, as smooth and as widespread as the sand. Homesick Bedouin are drawn into the desert at dusk, and can be seen sitting alone on top of a sandhill, or throwing themselves down on the sand like children, then rolling on their backs to gaze up at the sky. Large glossy-black beetles are the only other signs of life on the dunes.

Meanwhile, sand builds up against all vertical surfaces in the town, as the Sahara continues its formidable spread south.

Aside from the military green of a few mimosa and tamarind trees, and a tiny bird dusted a pinkish-red, the Senegal Fire Finch, which darted about as if someone was throwing red-hot coals, Timbuktu has virtually no colour. And because the only solid objects, the houses, are the same dry mud-brown of the surrounding sand, and the same texture, as if the sand has merely continued vertically, Timbuktu has the unusual feeling of not being solid at all. In this way it matched the vagueness of Timbuktu in my imagination. It was solid, a settlement, yet it didn't seem to exist at all.

Unlike other towns of west Africa, Timbuktu is instantly Arab and medieval. It is lean. And it has geometry in the air.

Figures are separated by large spaces, duplicating the immense distance between the occasional low bushes in the desert. An additional separation is displayed between the sexes, at least in public. And this double separation has the town appearing half-empty.

A man is rarely seen walking with a woman. The men apparently prefer to sit around in groups sipping mint tea in small glasses. Some carry daggers; I saw one with a rusty sword. Often two men walking would be holding hands. Now and then I felt one brush past on a donkey, rhythmically kicking with the heel and making a curious tongue-clicking sound.

The women sit cross-legged in the market or against a wall, offering on a piece of cloth a few lumps of rock-salt or dried fish, herbs and spices, or dyes in tiny envelopes. Others float past balancing a load on their heads — a tin of water, a bundle of firewood — very handsome and quick to smile. It is the women who make all the noise! A group of women a hundred yards away sound as if they are arguing, though I believe it is their normal way of conversing.

In Timbuktu, as in all of Mali, the practice of female circumcision has hardly diminished. It is supervised by the women in seclusion when a girl turns twelve. They hold the girl down during an operation which is performed by an older woman who is said to know the healing qualities of mud and herbs.

An expressionless young Tuareg explained how marriages were arranged. Sight unseen a woman was worth twenty camels, and up to fifty camels if she can be inspected and is found to be beautiful. An unseen bride wasn't so bad. 'There is value,' he told me, 'just as you pay for a packet of cigarettes without knowing what is inside.'

I glanced at his wife, now eighteen, pounding maize in the courtyard of his house. Mohammed was pleased with the deal. She had cost his father twenty-five camels, twelve sheep and some gold.

Timbuktu came into existence around 1100AD when some nomads left an old woman to wait at a well. In Tamacheck — the Tuareg's language — '*Tim*' is well or water; '*buktu*' is woman. Timbuktu grew as the main trading stop for the caravans from the infamous rock-salt mines at Taoudénni, 900 km to the north. By the sixteenth century it was one of the great intellectual centres of Islam, already rumoured as the mystical city, although still unvisited by a European.

Salt still accounts for something like 50 per cent of the local economy; from Timbuktu it is distributed to Mopti on the Niger and throughout much of west Africa. It is dearer than sea-salt, but people prefer its distinctive taste. Caravans still arrive most days; each camel carrying in a sling on either side a 50-kilo slab which looks like muddy marble. Not long ago 10,000 camels laden with salt would be in a train. Now it is more likely to number 100 or so.

Similarly, at the turn of the century Timbuktu's population was 100,000. Nowadays it is between 30,000 and 40,000 depending on the numbers of nomads in from the deserts and on which aid agency needs to be impressed.

A drought which has already lasted 15 years has strained the composition of Timbuktu.

The Songhai, the black agriculturalists of the Niger, have been resident the longest; next the aristocrats of the region, the Tuareg, comprising warriors, literates and pastoralists (in that interesting social order) who regard the town as merely a mercantile centre — but have been forced in from the dunes by the surrounding famine; then there are the Arabs, including Moors, and the Bedouin — their numbers too have swollen after losing their animals in the drought.

'I wouldn't go to Timbuktu,' a recent traveller had clutched my arm in London. 'It's like the Klondike, full of starving Bedouin. They'll skin you alive.'

But these lean and harshly handsome men were proud and courteous. Shaking hands was like shaking hands with a king: the hand offered limply, pointing down. Then they would touch their hearts in the traditional way.

The dispossessed nomads can be seen camped around the fringes of town. And here they are among a minority group also flung out by some centrifugal force, the Bella people, descended from slaves, reduced to living in dome shelters like Buckminster Fuller geospheres made from matting, bits of cloth and tin.

Four or five wealthy families in Timbuktu still have slaves; or rather, descendants of slaves when slavery was legal. It was still possible, I was told, to buy or exchange a slave — although there was now little wealth in Timbuktu.

At dawn I walked out into the desert. It was chilly. The dunes were smooth as skin, pale yellow, with sand blowing off the ridges like smoke; and as I waited they gradually shifted to silver, like an immense snowfield, then to grey-brown streaked with shadows. A small caravan was setting out, the Tuareg holding a rope walking ahead with a set expression. High on the second camel sat his wife wrapped entirely in black. A stain of disappointment spread as I took in the scene: almost certainly I would never be seeing this part of the world again.

I wandered inside the town until it became too hot. Women were firing the street-ovens for baking bread. Two goats (male) began fighting, a colliding of horns, drawing an appraising crowd of half-smiling men. I saw a blind man shuffling in step behind a boy. Where his hand held onto the boy's shoulder it had worn a ragged hole in the shirt. The boy was holding a white chicken. There was a sign on a wall: 'Place of 333 saints.' And a man kneeling with hands on his knees, peering underneath a broken-down Land-Rover, looked as if he was praying to Mecca.

Blue rubber thongs have made noticeable inroads in Timbuktu. Men otherwise wear black sandals with broad straps, or the leather chappals curved up at the front like sledges, or else white slippers without heels. A young man with one leg who somehow scratched out a living making musical instruments told me he broke his leg several years ago and got gangrene. Using hi-tech walking sticks donated by a UN agency he had perfected a way of hobbling at a great rate alongside me.

I climbed the roof of the Djinguereber mosque. The *muezzin* in electric-blue had a thick-lipped voluptuous vanity. He confided that he worked much harder than the *imam* because he broadcast the prayers five times a day, and yet he was paid less. The mosque of mud, straw and clay was among the oldest in west Africa and stood up like colossal anthills, with joists and gutters jutting horizontally. Inside I raised my arm against the bats flitting about and realised that coolness and half-darkness are perhaps essential for worship.

Of the twenty or so Europeans living in Timbuktu there was a Baptist missionary. For twelve years he had toiled away spreading the Word. But his efforts were almost wiped out by a small incident, probably unknown to him. It happened shortly before I arrived.

A visitor from America had called bringing him messages and things like tinned peaches and zinc cream. To reach Timbuktu he had crossed oceans and rivers, not to mention the harsh interior of Africa. And yet the missionary received him at his gate, and didn't invite him in. Hospitality is almost a law among desert people; and the Baptist's discourtesy spread around the town in minutes.

When I went to see this missionary I found a large house in a bare compound surrounded by a high wall. The gate — the only picket gate in Timbuktu — was padlocked.

I had pictured a gaunt crew-cut figure, in his sixties. But a much younger, solid man, in his early forties, came out wearing shorts and RICHARD printed across the chest of his T-shirt.

Resting an arm on the gate, as if we were chatting in Michigan, he explained the original missionary had retired, and that he had arrived only two months before. He was somewhat haggard, recovering from malaria. When I expressed sympathy Richard shrugged, 'I am spreading the Word of God, I am working for the Lord.'

As we spoke his wife in a cotton dress and holding a child stood looking at us through a screen door.

When I asked how many converts they could claim so far in Timbuktu with its population of 40,000 he said, 'Twenty.' After twelve years that seemed an amazingly high cost/conversion ratio which must be causing concern back at headquarters.

Later I passed the tiny Catholic church, rather more like a holiday shack, its cross on the roof positively defiant. There was singing inside. The slow mournful hymn from the small congregation; a tiny building of stubborn appearance.

Opposite — and demonstrating not so much tolerance as indifference — was an Islamic study centre and library. Stored in glass cases, its Koranic texts and commentaries, many of them illuminated, its lives of the Muslim saints, were mostly from the old Timbuktu university.

In the courtyard as sand swirled around my eyes I told a scholar wearing sunglasses I was from Australia.

It was my last day in Timbuktu. And I noticed all the skin was peeling off my fingers and hands.

Speaking through his *chayta* he of course saw things differently.

'For us,' he said, 'Australia is the Timbuktu — *le bout du monde* — the end of the world.'

ELIZABETH SMITHER

IN THE BLUE MOUNTAINS

SUSAN WEDLAKE WOKE to a silver train crossing the valley floor, out of sight under the eucalyptus trees. She recognised the sound as she blinked and in the same instant the knowledge of silver. The Blue Mountains stretched away beyond the verandah until, in the distance, they formed a rim as indeterminate and wavering, if seen through binoculars, as the sea. At the same time, like the line on the sea, the blueness was definite and bold. The double-decker trains shot among the rocks and eucalyptus leaves like spent silver arrows, a firework skidding over grass. The same train the frail and hopeful elderly writer, accompanied by her nephew, had fallen into the aisle of and no one had stirred to help.

Susan's own surroundings were far from agreeable as well: an exercycle propped against an ochre-coloured sofa and herself in a bottom bunk with a frilled valance. A fireplace with a bunch of teazles in the grate, a black guitar case, a model train set against the wall under the venetians. Still the basement had its own shower, hastily and apologetically cleaned by her hostess, and it was a place of retreat, if necessary, to prepare her speech which she hoped to memorise as a compliment. Through the venetians she could see the clothesline and then the lawn sloped away with a few stalwart fruit trees, like children climbing up a hill.

Upstairs the furniture was heavy and solid: a splendid jarrah dining table practically filled the room where she and Margery had sat, looking out over the mountains, listening to 'Eine kleine Nachtmusik' until the farthest horizon seemed to be outlining the melody.

Before coming to the Blue Mountains Susan had been billeted in a Sydney suburb whose name she had forgotten with a woman called Anne. Together they had crossed the Harbour Bridge on the top deck of one of the silver trains and Anne had pointed out

Luna Park, dark and closed, but with the distant suburbs making a ghostly carnival behind and, on the other side, the Opera House striped by the bridge's girders. Eventually the train stopped at a well-preserved lace-edged station with geraniums in window boxes and an ornate exit ramp. Here there were no footpaths or fences; instead the houses had long sloping lawns and more gum trees. Susan was pleased to see Anne's front door had a stained glass window with parrots and near the verandah a large magnolia tree in full bloom. Once again she was given a child's room, but a large child with a double bed, a duvet with Indians and horses and a mattress stiffened by a sheet of hardboard against which she grazed the back of her leg — it overhung slightly — in the morning.

It would take two hours to reach the Blue Mountains and to show Susan the lie of the land Anne's husband, Dermot, produced a map which showed the Blue Mountains in padded bubbles rising from a yellow plain. They leaned over it while they drank their breakfast coffee.

'It might be braille,' Susan said wonderingly, running her fingers up the first ridge. 'The plain feels like a plate.'

The thought of something heaped up preceded by something scooped out was rather appealing, if obvious.

But in reality the Blue Mountains, after an hour on the plain, seemed no closer. Nor was there the least hint of blue. A blueness caused by 'the scattering of light as it comes in contact with dust and droplets of oil emitted by the leaves of the eucalyptus (gum) trees' and rising like a nimbus. Numinous mountains, like someone standing in a doorway, someone with a woolly perm lit from behind by a house light or a street lamp. The thought of all those fuzzy ridges caused Susan to smile from the back seat of the car where she had insisted on taking her turn. They would change over when, if they ever did, the Blue Mountains came in sight.

Anne and Dermot were explaining that the Blue Mountains, desirable as they were, thanks to the silver trains, had the highest divorce rates, the most spectacular property crashes and repossessions imaginable. In the true Blue Mountains, discounting the little towns that clung to the flanks as children to a mother's skirts or a fag to a prefect's gown, Susan could expect to see no property that wasn't the acme of desire. Homes to which lawyers and surgeons and advertising managers would drive in the evening, away from smog and towers into the blue air, sniffing the eucalyptus drops as they rose towards wife and children in a blue eyrie.

By now they had crossed a wide river, brown in its bed, and were climbing, past common little settlements with caravans parked under gums and washing hanging on strings, a hot dog stand. But in case Susan should miss something it was suggested they change seats now.

It was the next afternoon, before the launching at the library, in the presence of the mayor, one lady councillor and the director of the local art gallery, that Susan, Margery, Dermot and Anne had a chance to inspect any of the grander residences. They had driven higher and higher and down some new roads where the brick houses seemed the size of small castles. Some had turrets, some mansard roofs, some were exceedingly elongated and pressed close to the earth as though listening for subterranean sounds; one a Gothic arch of stained glass, another a wall of glass bricks.

Susan listened intently, half-expecting sounds of a violent quarrel, a slammed door, even a gunshot from a padded study, but there was nothing. Only the susurration of hoses sprinkling the emerald green lawns and flower beds. Lawns and flowers that eschewed the decor available to everyone for free: the rocks and eucalyptus leaves that took control of everything, requiring only the simplest path of buried stumps or stepping stones.

The publisher of the book of antipodean poetesses, *Kangaroo & Tuatara*, lived in a smaller version on a lower plateau, approached by a path that was too new even for eucalyptus mulch. Margery had driven Susan there shortly after her arrival at Blaxland to secure a copy. A child had answered the door and said his father was out. Then, after a pause, during which her name was repeated inside, a book was poked through the gap and the door firmly closed.

Kangaroo & Tuatara showed the two emblematic creatures lying side by side as though speared onto the laminated surface. Instead of their natural colours they were stippled by a leaf pattern, reminiscent of bamboo. And their names, in case of foreign sales, were enclosed in signposts so Susan half-expected to see *Kangaroo: 12,000 miles*.

There was a great pile of them at the launching, some spread flat, and, at the rear, towers like the glimpse of Sydney from the Blue Mountains. More were in boxes under the table for the new desktop publisher had wanted a bold beginning.

Quite a few people were lifting one up to look at, as though seeing if the animals were correctly labelled. A few were turning the pages where the authors' photographs, black and white and rather savagely trimmed, began each contribution.

Susan's own photo was a horror because in zooming in on what she imagined was a 'poetic' expression — dark intense staring eyes, serious ruminative mouth — the softening and far more pleasing frame of hair had been cut off. If a number had been affixed as it was to the kangaroo she might have made a convincing criminal. To her chagrin others with far more relaxed devil-may-care expressions now looked the epitome of a lady poet.

A few of these were standing about, almost recognisable once one added a wig. And Ruth, the elderly but exceedingly vivacious poetess who had had the unfortunate experience on the train was obviously fully recovered.

'I expect they were mainly teenagers, high on drugs,' she said gaily. 'A new experience for me, having myself and my baggage stuck in an automatic door. Luckily Oliver here is strong and was able to give us both a shove.'

But Oliver, though he smiled at his aunt, looked a great deal less convinced.

'One of the pleasures of travel,' Susan remarked to him. 'The uncertainty even in what is supposed to be a moment of triumph.'

'A moment or a week,' he responded, smiling. 'Luckily my aunt is very resilient and has already thought of turning it into a poem. *Fall from a silver train*. Something like that. It's an enviable facility. Whereas I thought she was going to be crushed.'

'Perhaps to travel well one needs a companion, like yourself. Someone to prise doors open and attend to all the details.'

'Well, she's paying for it all, you know, and certainly not out of her royalties.'

Before they could get onto a discussion of royalties however there was a great deal of throat-clearing somewhere near the back of the room and the publisher stood on a chair and said the formal part of the launch was about to begin. So Susan rapidly practised her technique of clenching her stomach muscles very tight and pressing her two palms together with her utmost force while hoping this didn't alter her facial expression or show in her posture.

That night, seated at the over-large table, one end of which was set with napkins, a carafe, two wine glasses, Margery suggested the elderly writer and her nephew might be glad of a day trip in the mountains. They were planning, since there were no further engagements until a publisher's dinner in two days' time, to spend the whole day touring, stopping where they pleased, circling the blue circumference ridge by ridge.

Ruth and Oliver had no car and had talked of taking one of the silver trains further but there had been a touch of hesitation about this, as though the incident with the doors and lack of assistance was not quite buried. Susan, after her five-minute speech had gone not too badly and her spirits were restored, felt a little doubtful, as though she ought to be conveyed about in solitude on her own reputation; then she concurred. Oliver was very pleasant and Ruth, who had presented herself in her reading as slightly eccentric, could be relied on for admiring the scenery.

Scenery, Susan thought, as she refilled her wine glass while Margery went to phone, did take rather a lot of admiring. Wordsworth must have had quite a lot of stamina to be out in it all day and unflagged enough to write about it in the evening.

Over her shoulder the Blue Mountains were becoming black. The blue drops had done their work of levitation for the day and were sinking into the same darkness as any other eminence, private apart from the stirrings of nesting birds.

'They'd be delighted,' Margery said, coming back into the room. 'They particularly want to thank you for including them.'

At this Susan couldn't help feeling a little ashamed and determined to make up for it by offering the front seat. A faint, very faint last light played on the mountains now. A faint emanation from the dying coals of fire for remarks uttered during the day by hordes of tourists.

'Katoomba is a place where you could spend a considerable amount of time and it caters for all tastes. For those who just wish to sightsee, the area is superb,' Ruth read from the guidebook on her knee. 'The population swells in the summer as the temperature here is far more pleasant than on the coastal or plains areas.'

'In spite of that, Aunt, I wonder about small towns, even in the Blue Mountains. Are they civilised? I especially wonder about the ones with picturesque teashops and restaurants converted from general stores with board floors and batik hangings where you bring a bottle of wine in a sacking bag.'

'Ridiculous boy! You'll be able to find out at the publisher's dinner because we're coming back here. *The Coq d'Or*, I think he said.'

'The very thing. A golden cockerel. A blue mountain. Blue sky. My suspicions are aroused.'

They drove on, climbing all the time, on roads that after a day of blue drops appeared almost white. Though they were on the Blue Mountains they did not see them until they stopped from time to time at a lookout. Then the drops rose like so many notes from an organ or blue mermaids from the sea, as Oliver, turning unexpectedly poetic, put it.

'A new blue rinse, that's what it makes me think of,' said Ruth as they stood looking across a vast valley with escarpments and plateaus at Echo Point.

The valley was wide enough for parts of it to be in shadow: having baked in the sun for most of the day now sections were mercifully cool and almost ordinary looking. Susan imagined an explorer reaching one of these bluffs and resting his weary back against a ridge.

Because the whole valley was composed of treetops it was impossible to imagine how any explorer might proceed. Flight seemed likeliest: skimming over the tops and coming to rest against a promontory rendered soft and restful and bare like worndown upholstery in the sinking rays of the sun.

'The sun always seems extra strong at this time of day,' Margery remarked. 'Even in a small garden like mine I can't help noticing how it attaches to the trunks of trees or the underside of leaves.'

'An extra venom. Or the last energy before dying,' Susan offered. What was the word she was thinking of? *Canalise*, though she could not remember the exact meaning.

They lunched at the Hydro Majestic, a huge spa hotel with picture windows, leather seats and rather dusty unkempt-looking waiters. The selection of cakes and cold meats were displayed on refrigerated shelves.

Below them another angle of the valley sloped away to be subsumed in the first trees, then, as the trees thickened, the same perm-like appearance recommenced. An evenness so soft and gentle Susan wanted to run her hand over it. A metaphoric hand of course. Then she imagined tired figures climbing up from the valley floor, perhaps leading a packhorse, an exhausted woman and a child at her skirts, looking up in amazement at this vast and surely forbidding hotel. Unlikely they would be invited in to use the cake forks.

To walk off their lunch they strolled along the maroon-carpeted corridors, peering in through the ballroom door where chairs were stacked against the walls, the cinema, the massage rooms and a curious indoor pool with tepid pale blue water.

Afterwards they continued their circling of the mountains, stopping only cursorily at the most popular lookouts where huge airconditioned buses were disgorging neat Japanese tourists to trip nimbly down steps and under an artificial pagoda bordered by rose beds. *The Three Sisters* and the tiny cable car, swinging in its descent, were like a vast novel, the Three Sisters drawn aside in conference, the swinging car, from which it was possible to imagine squeals of fear, a bookmark.

On the evening of the publisher's dinner, while the authors and guests were assembling in the foyer of the little BYO restaurant at Katoomba, the sales manager produced a review from that day's *Sydney Morning Herald*. An artist had drawn a stylised tuatara dancing with a kangaroo and judging merely by space it was a handsome first notice. But the publisher was very upset by certain sentences: 'There is perhaps something of the textbook in the conception . . .' and 'The enthusiasm of several contributors fails to cover a preface with little substance.' There were other glancing blows: tuataras and kangaroos were unlikely bedfellows; where did the press (its name was *Dandelion*) intend to scatter its next seed? But Susan thought on the whole it was very satisfactory: almost a quarter page, including the artistic frieze, of a prestigious paper, the notice of a powerful editor.

It was unfortunate that she was seated opposite the publisher and had to hear his grievances in full. More unfortunate that she tried to contradict him. Soon they were locked in battle like two horned creatures. Wouldn't he reconsider the letter his editor had drafted at least until the morning? Wasn't it the Persians who slept on such missives before affixing a stamp? When he swept the Persians aside wouldn't he think of his own future publications and their hopeful authors whose advance notices might be consigned to the dustbin? Margery joined in here, holding her dessertspoon aloft. 'The authors to come,' she repeated. 'It sounds like a dormitory or a row of cradles.'

It was only by an effort of will that Susan remembered it was the publisher who had paid half her fare. She felt sure, though he accepted her apology gallantly enough, they were now enemies. The dinner had been a mistake, she thought. What she had said seemed good sense and would seem good sense when she considered it on the morrow like the Persians. But ultimately it was not her concern. Coming after a day in the Blue Mountains it was unnerving to discover such ferocious antipathy towards a benefactor.

'You fought like two elands. I've not enjoyed anything so much for ages. It made my night,' the woman further along the table wrote a month later when Susan was home again. She tried to recall the woman: fair and vivacious, with mocking eyes. Something about a broken marriage or a toy boy and a cottage bought with alimony. An obsession with gardening or did it even go as far as compost? It was a shock to discover that what had seemed conspiracy was in fact categorising, mocking.

The last engagement arranged by the now huffy publicity manager was a reading in a smoky Sydney tavern with black walls to an audience capable of hostility who imbibed and smoked and talked. Sometimes they addressed the stage where a black lectern and the microphone cord were invisible and a hazard. They had been billed as four women poets from the *Kangaroo & Tuatara* anthology and a gust of mirth swept the audience when they were introduced by the editor, wearing a brushed angora jersey with a kangaroo design.

Ruth had asked to read last and when her turn came she subdued her audience with a grandmotherly pose. Oliver was enticed to join her onstage and she recounted her near-fall from the silver train. And shrewdly assessing the audience's tolerance she wove a commentary around each poem. It all ended in great good humour and a certain amount of nonchalant hanging about waiting for fees in envelopes.

For Susan, the final two nights, to be spent in Sydney, had been arranged and she had already seen her bed. She was feeling as secure and confident as a counsellor as she exchanged some last remarks about adolescents with Margery. All the talk they had had in the Blue Mountains, climbing and descending the endless white roads, the slow walks among the gums and metallic rocks was obliterated by the sight of an elegant narrow bed under a canopy in a dormer room.

Yet two days before, at another small function in a local bookshop, while she was drinking wine and talking to two charming elderly ladies, Susan had become uneasily aware that arrangements had broken down and nothing was planned for Sydney. She could hardly ask for an advance of royalties from the publisher who now avoided her and she doubted she had enough money for even a cheap hotel.

There had been another quarrel between Margery and her son Paul while Susan was resting on her bunk and she had heard the screen door slam and feet rushing along the deck. Then came the sound of sobbing and a little later running water. When she climbed the steps half an hour before they needed to leave, the house was in darkness.

Yet Margery had enjoyed the outing, Susan thought, remembering how her hunched body at one of the little rickety tables where they had sat drinking had slowly unwound. When one of the regular readers and something of a star had joined them Margery became almost animated.

More adult company, Susan thought, as though this was something one could write on a prescription pad. Paul was nice too: sensitive under all the door slamming: he simply wanted his own life. Anne and Margery were two heroic women to whom membership of their writing circle was far more than therapy. A tiny amount of unbelievable pain was being released each month: Anne who had been wrongly accused of negligence by bitter relatives at the nursing home where she worked and Margery slowly releasing the terrible death of her husband.

The poems they had held out to Susan on the day they were all together in Margery's house, with Dermot having to watch his diet and eat sardines, seemed to be on scorched paper. The spaces between the words burned and Susan had not recognised, until it was pointed out, they were about incest and sibling rivalry.

And here finally was Susan Wedlake in her third and superior bed, a bed in which Faustina's mother — for she was staying with a famous writer — had spent her last years. The soft-as-feathers mattress had formed a definite declivity onto which Susan's larger body would be superimposed like a covering shadow. Something from an old hymn — shadow of a mighty wing — teased her as she unpacked and set a few possessions on a little mosaic table.

Faustina had cooked a whole chicken stuffed with a whole lemon and then divided it and they had eaten half each. They drank glass after glass of retsina. Then a sorbet and some figs. Later there was Turkish coffee and some fine dark mints in gold foil.

Susan and Faustina sat companionably in a book-lined room holding art books open on their knees and talked about the sinister effect Norman Lindsay's house had had on Susan while she was in the Blue Mountains. Especially the studio which had been preserved in all its dust and turps and linseed so she half-expected a model in a faded yellow kimono to step from behind the screen and move languidly towards the throne on the dais.

'And the Blue Mountains?' Faustina asked. 'How did you find them?'

'I think ...' Susan replied slowly, because Faustina was a serious person who deserved serious answers 'they reminded me of the Romantics. I wonder what Wordsworth would have made of them? Would he have been content, for instance, to walk for days on the rim, delighted by the mirage, whipping out his notebook to write something to Orphan Rock or Chelmsford Bridge?'

'Wordsworth certainly might have liked the Three Sisters,' Faustina agreed.

Susan had already told Faustina of the quarrelsome dinner with the publisher at Katoomba. She had not mentioned the teenage son or Anne's impending court case. She had circled the Blue Mountains with two scorched survivors and a woman almost flung from a train and they had looked down on them and into them with an awe that was unreciprocated.

In the end it came down to something like a blue glass bottle or a blue Chinese plate. The strange thing was, it was only in the place commuters fled from to reach them, that the Blue Mountains had any effect at all.

LILY BRETT

CHOPIN'S PIANO

LOLA BENSKY WAS about to arrive in Warsaw. She tried to decide whether she was nervous or anxious. Nervous was all right. Being anxious made her dizzy. She wondered if she should take a Valium. She didn't want to take a Valium if what she was feeling was a normal kind of tension. If it was anxiety, she needed the Valium.

The plane landed. An indecipherable blast of blurred Polish came from the loudspeaker system. Lola began to feel breathless. She hated not being able to understand or to make herself understood. In the bleak immigration and customs hall, long queues of people stood waiting. Lola was dismayed. She always tried to avoid standing in queues. It was one of the things that made her very anxious. Her analyst had explained to her that she felt this anxiety because she could not bear to have to wait for the breast. That she was angry about the fact that she was dependent on her mother. That she was outraged that her mother had something that she didn't. That she was jealous and envious of her mother, but couldn't face the pain of these bad feelings, and so denied her need for her mother. This insight hadn't helped Lola with her queue problem.

The yellow-haired, sallow-faced young man behind the immigration desk tapped his blue biro violently as he asked Lola questions.

'Your nationality?' he snapped.

Lola tried not to panic. He was holding her passport. Why would he ask her her nationality?

'Australian,' she said meekly.

'Purpose of visit?' he barked.

'To see Poland,' Lola whispered. She could see that he thought that this was a reasonable answer. With a brusque gesture, he motioned her to move on.

Outside it was dark and bitterly cold. Lola was flushed and hot. She could feel drops of sweat trickling down between her breasts. She was wearing a woollen spencer and long woollen underpants, a three-piece woollen suit, angora socks, boots, an astrakhan hat, elbow-length gloves and a voluminous, thick coat. A cashmere scarf was wound around her neck. She caught a taxi to the Victoria Hotel. Driving in, she was astonished to see that Warsaw looked like an ordinary city. The streets were lined with graceful neoclassical four- and five-storey apartment buildings. A soft, yellow light that suggested happy family life seeped out from the sides of the curtained windows. There was no sign of menace in the air.

The Victoria Hotel was a 1960s late-modern building. Lola recognised the style. Caulfield was full of fine examples of this sort of building.

Lola was unnerved when she walked inside the hotel. The interior was a large replica of the loungerooms of Caulfield and Bellevue Hill. The same granite and marble surfaces, the same rich, rounded woodwork, the same heavy raw silk drapes, the same large leather lounge suites, and the same 1950s expressionist ashtrays and vases. Chandeliers hung from the ceiling.

The short, stocky woman who was to be her guide was waiting in the foyer. Lola explained to Mrs Potoki-Okolska that she had come to Poland to see her parents' past, the small piece of their past that was left.

She wanted to go to Lodz, she told Mrs Potoki-Okolska, to see where her parents had lived before the war. Where they had studied, where they had played, where they had walked. She would also like to see what was left of the Lodz ghetto. She explained that her parents had spent four and a half years in the Lodz ghetto before they were shipped to Auschwitz.

'My mother was the sole survivor of her family. Her brothers Shimek, Abramek, Jacob and Felek, and her sisters Fela, Bluma and Marilla, and her mother and father were gassed and then burnt. My father lost his parents, three brothers and a sister.'

'It was a terrible, terrible tragedy, yes,' said Mrs Potoki-Okolska. 'But Polish people lost people too. It was not just the Jews who were killed by the Nazis. We suffered. Oh, how we suffered! My mother's cousin lost her mother, an innocent woman who never hurt anybody.' Here, Mrs Potoki-Okolska had to pause. Tears were streaming down her face.

Mrs Potoki-Okolska showed Lola to her hotel room. A sign on the back of the door asked that no guests remain in the room after 10 pm. Lola assumed that that meant guests other than those who were paying.

The fridge in the room was full of bottles of blackcurrant juice, blackcurrant juice with vodka, and Coca-Cola. Mrs Potoki-Okolska drank four bottles of Coca-Cola. She thanked Lola profusely for the Coca-Cola, said goodnight and left.

Lola looked out of the window. Warsaw was asleep. The city was covered in a fine layer of snow. Everything looked peaceful.

'It will be the end of you. They will put you in jail,' Mrs Bensky had warned Lola. 'They won't let you leave Poland. The Poles were worse than the Germans. They used to laugh at us in our concentration-camp rags. Small children would kick us when we were walking to work in the towns near the camp. Oh, those nice Poles, those good people, they couldn't wait to point Jews out to the Germans. They couldn't wait to take over our apartments when we had to move to the ghetto. They took our clothes, our china, our furniture. They took over the Jewish businesses. They just helped themselves. The caretaker of my parents' building, who my mother had looked after like she was one of the family, went running to the Gestapo to report on us.

'And after the war, there was a miracle. Not one single Polish person did know anything about what happened to us. You could smell the flesh burning for kilometres from Auschwitz. Those chimneys were blowing smoke twenty-four hours a day. The sky was red day and night, but the Poles didn't notice.

'And when my cousin Adek went back after the war, what did he see? He saw that they were surprised that he was still alive. Mrs Boleswaf, the caretaker, said to him: "Oh, I thought all of you were dead." Her son was wearing my father's suit, Adek said. My brother's grand piano was in the middle of their living room. And Mrs Boleswaf offered him a cup of tea from the beautiful white-and-silver china that was part of my mother's dowry. What do you want to go to Poland for? Something terrible will happen to you.'

In the morning light, the city looked less vibrant. Lola was shocked at how depressed and oppressed the people looked. They walked with their heads down. Even the children were quiet and expressionless. Men and women wore grey clothes and grey faces. Their hair was lank and dull. No shampoo, Lola remembered.

Long queues of people waited outside the sparsely stocked shops. There was no movement in the queues. No one spoke. Lola found this collective depression frightening. She had always thought of depression as an individual and isolating experience.

At the bus stop, people stood in silence. The bus arrived. The crowd clambered aboard, elbowing each other and Lola out of the way. Lola was left behind. From the bus, Mrs Potoki-Okolska screamed at Lola that she would get off at the next stop and walk back.

By midday Lola had seen the Radziwill palace, the Potoki palace, the Tyszkiewicz palace, the Uruski palace, the Czapski palace, the Staszic palace, a dozen churches and several cathedrals. Mrs Potoki-Okolska left money in each church, and wept as she dedicated the gift to her mother. In the Church of St Cross there was an urn that contained Chopin's heart. The Old Town Market Square, like most of the city of Warsaw, had been destroyed by the Nazis. Mrs Potoki-Okolska pointed to one quaint seventeenth-century building after another and announced: 'Built in 1953,' or 'Built in 1956,' or 'This building is still being finished.'

Lola was exhausted. Her feet hurt. She was suffering from the anxiety that she experienced when she was ignored. Mrs Potoki-Okolska had refused to listen to her when she had expressed her lack of interest in churches, palaces or monuments to famous generals.

Lola had arranged to have lunch with Mr Konrad Serbin, the father of a friend of a friend. She felt that it could do her no harm to have a connection with Mr Serbin, who was one of Poland's leading barristers, and his wife, a highly acclaimed surgeon.

Lola wanted to buy some flowers for Mrs Serbin. Mrs Potoki-Okolska took Lola to a small, dimly lit, shabby shop. The back wall of the shop was lined with shelves. Each shelf held three vases, and each vase contained two flowers. A carnation and a freesia. A round, red-faced man was meticulously wrapping a pink carnation in a small square of butcher's paper.

Lola asked Mrs Potoki-Okolska to ask for a dozen carnations. Mrs Potoki-Okolska looked horrified.

'It is very rude to buy so many flowers,' she said. 'Your friend's father will think that you want to show him how much money you have. It is not good manners, no, not good manners.'

Mrs Potoki-Okolska was very concerned with good manners. This morning at breakfast she had wrenched a toothpick from Lola's hands. 'This is not good manners in Poland,' she had shouted.

The carnations were thin and stringy. Lola thought that twelve of them would at least produce some volume.

'What to do? What to do? What to do?' sighed Mrs Potoki-Okolska.

Mrs Potoki-Okolska ordered a dozen carnations. A rumble of hostility went through the waiting queue. The florist glared at Lola and wrapped the carnations carelessly. Twelve carnations cost as much as most people earned in a week. Flower-growers were the new rich in Poland.

Mrs Potoki-Okolska was right. Mrs Serbin looked furious when Lola gave her the flowers.

Mr and Mrs Serbin were wealthy Poles. Their two-room apartment was filled with nineteenth-century romantic and historical paintings, oriental rugs, leather-bound books, silver and crystal.

The Serbins were very pleased with the parcel of pencils, biros, soaps, toothpaste, pantihose, silver foil and kitchen cloths that Lola had brought from their daughter. Mr Serbin's brother and sister-in-law joined them for lunch. Mrs Serbin served an entrée of smoked trout with horseradish sauce. In the middle of a mouthful of trout, it occurred to Lola that all five Poles at the table were in their mid-sixties. The same age as Mr and Mrs Bensky. Where were they when the Jews were being rounded up for the ghetto? Where were they when the Warsaw ghetto was burning? Were they part of the heated, cheering crowd on the Aryan side? Were they watching Jews explode into the night?

Lola felt nauseous. She excused herself, and ran to the toilet.

The toilet was in a tiny room, ten feet away from the dining table. The door wouldn't close properly. Lola tried to hold the door shut with her foot while she sat on the toilet. She felt bilious and giddy. Sweat ran down her face. She could hear every word of the lunch-table conversation. She coughed loudly to disguise her own violent eruptions. Half an hour later, she emerged. Mrs Potoki-Okolska rushed to greet her. 'You look terrible. Was it your liver or your kidneys?' she asked.

Mrs Serbin brought in a large jar of Nescafé on an enormous Georgian silver platter. She put six spoonfuls of the coffee powder into each person's cup. Lola asked if she could have tea. The other guests drank their coffee with relish.

The next morning Lola met Mrs Potoki-Okolska at the railway station at eight-thirty. At eleven o'clock there was an announcement that the nine o'clock train to Lodz had been cancelled. Mrs Potoki-Okolska rushed Lola to the taxi stand.

Lola looked at the miserable faces in the taxi queue. She felt buoyed by their hardship.

'You've got what you deserve,' she whispered to the man standing on her left.

Lola sat in the back of the taxi. Mrs Potoki-Okolska sat in the front seat. She ordered the taxi driver to turn the heater on high, and settled down with a bag of boiled sweets.

Lola had packed her own provisions. She had packets of Life Savers, Minties and Steam Rollers. Steam Rollers, Lola felt, were particularly good for combating nausea.

After an hour in the car Lola felt sick. Her skin burned and itched. She unbuttoned her coat and jacket. Her chest was covered with angry red blotches. She thought that she was probably the only person in Poland suffering from a heat rash.

She opened the car window a little.

'What is that?' bellowed Mrs Potoki-Okolska. 'Shut it, shut it, shut it. You will catch a disease of the lungs. It is very dangerous. Very, very dangerous.' Lola closed the window.

They arrived at Zelazowa-Wola, Chopin's birthplace. Lola was glad to be able to get out of the car. An hour and a half later, Lola had seen Chopin's piano, Chopin's mother's piano, Chopin's bedroom, Chopin's mother's bedroom, Chopin's garden and Chopin's bathroom.

Lola thought that maybe she would never get to Lodz. She thought, once again, that maybe Lodz didn't exist. Maybe Mr and Mrs Bensky's past would always be inaccessible to her. Mrs Potoki-Okolska left Zelazowa-Wola reluctantly, humming *La Polonaise*.

They passed kilometre after kilometre of flat, snow-covered countryside. This soft, white stillness was punctuated occasionally by small forests of spindly, black fir trees.

They were now ten kilometres from Lodz. Lola was already weeping.

NORMAN BILBROUGH

EEL DANCE

OSCAR FLEW INTO Hong Kong late. He took a taxi into the back of Kowloon, but the driver could not find 8 Choi Hung Road. Oscar levered himself out, covered in luggage. People were strolling and eating in the street. It was midnight. Where Number 8 should have been there was the bulk of an institution, with a cross on its roof. There was a light high up in one of the buildings.

The fence was eight foot high and spiked. With some effort Oscar hung his luggage on the spikes, then climbed up after it. The traffic tore past, but nobody seemed to care about a huge white man scaling a fence. For terrible seconds he was poised above the spikes, then he was over. He pulled his luggage down and crossed a concrete playground. This was obviously a church school.

He climbed an echoing tower of stairs and beat at unresponsive doors. Sweat was popping out of his face when he came to one with a lighted bell. There was a metal door behind a grille, and when the bell rang it was smothered by interior walls. The place was like a fortress.

There was a pause, then the doors opened and light divulged itself sparsely. A small man peered at Oscar.

'Father Paul?' The man nodded. 'I'm Oscar Petty from New Zealand . . . I climbed the fence.'

Father Paul pulled aside the grille. 'I was going to meet you but I did not know your flight.'

He was dressed in a white shirt, nondescript trousers and jandals. He had the presence of a morose and emasculated flea, and he shook Oscar's hand with a child's hand.

The priests in Oscar's life had not been big men, but they had owned a certain sanctified bulk. And never jandals. Oscar could see he would have to revise his stereotypes.

Paul took a bag, and Oscar followed him through doors into

a large room which was dominated by a statue of the Virgin and a tank of brilliant fat goldfish. The furniture was solid. A heavy wooden dresser and sideboard. Crystal behind glass. The enamelled translucence of bowls. And heavy comfortable chairs.

A young woman in glasses came out of a kitchen. 'I am pleased to meet you,' she said, trying out her English.

'This is May,' Paul said.

May's hand was firm. It contained squeeze. Oscar felt heartened.

'Come to your room,' Paul said.

May took a bag and they went up two more flights of stairs. Corridors dived away on all sides, but the place seemed without presences. A rabbit warren of empty rooms.

'You've got a big place here,' Oscar commented.

'So so,' Paul said.

He showed Oscar into a room with tall windows obscured by clacking venetians. High ceiling and parquet floor. Oscar would have to lie between over-washed church sheets and sit at battered church furniture. But he was entranced. 'This is a lovely room.' It was his room in the East, with an ostrich fan about to circulate. 'It's a writer's room.'

'You are a writer?' May questioned. 'What will you write?'

'I'm going to try and get into the refugee camps,' Oscar said. 'I write about human rights.'

There was silence. Paul and May stared at Oscar as if he had come to Hong Kong on a mission that was not only absurd but inappropriate.

'Very difficult to get into the camps,' Paul muttered. 'Very difficult.'

'Oh, I think it'll be all right,' Oscar said blithely.

May remembered herself. 'You have a good flight?'

'So so,' Oscar said without thinking.

'You have photographs of New Zealand?'

'A few,' Oscar said.

'You show them to me tomorrow?'

'If you want?'

'I want,' May said

Paul showed him a dank bathroom which grew mushrooms, and a lavatory that groaned its way down three storeys when flushed.

'All yours now that Father Chiles is in America.'

Father Chiles was Oscar's contact in Hong Kong. He had arranged for Oscar to stay in the priest's house before he had gone off to a conference in the States. His room was across the corridor. It was spacious and comfortable, with television and an audio system. Oscar saw tapes of Carol King and the Rolling Stones. There was an exercise bike in one corner.

'You may use these things,' Paul gestured at the T.V. and the bike. 'You exercise?'

'I jog,' Oscar said. 'I've bought my running shoes.' He planned to do a shuffle through the Kowloon streets each morning. Perhaps even find a park somewhere.

'You run?' Paul looked horrified. 'You die!' He squeezed his narrow throat and made faces of asphyxiation. May giggled. 'Fumes kill you!'

'Yes,' Oscar considered. 'They probably would.'

'I teach you exercise bike,' May said, as if he was a European moron.

Before he slept that night Oscar imagined how he must look to her ... over-large, possibly erring towards inflation. Pasty, watery-eyed, and covered with pale hair. Perhaps she equated oversize with ineptness.

Jet lag snapped him awake early. Big dusty elms grew outside his window — relics of a colonial past — then there was a tidal creek. Beyond this an enormous block of flats filled the sky. Outside these a minute crippled woman was executing Tai Chi. Oscar breathed deeply. His lungs filled with diesel and old corrupted Chinese cooking, and sewerage from the creek. He did not mind. The East, the East! He was ready to dive into it, and reveal its cynicism and cruelty to the newspapers of New Zealand. Possibly even the world.

He splashed his face in the fungoid bathroom, gave his armpits a douse and scraped at his bristles. Feet came up the stairs.

'Hullo Oscar Rights,' May called. She was wearing a T-shirt and stretch pants. She had small brisk shoulders.

Later she knocked on his door. She was puffing and a tiny sweat lay upon her brow. 'I show you how to exercise,' she said.

'No thank you,' Oscar replied. 'I can use the bike quite well.'

Then he added, 'Do you live here?'

May giggled. 'Of course not. I come and go. I live with my mother and father.'

'What's your job?'

'I work in public housing,' she said dismissively. 'It is not interesting.' Without glasses she had small dark vulnerable eyes.

'Why do you wear glasses?' Oscar said. 'You can see all right.'

'Everybody wears glasses in Hong Kong,' she replied. 'What are you writing today?'

'I am ringing up a camp in the New Territories today.'

'You will get lost. I will take you.'

'No, I'll be fine,' Oscar said firmly.

'Where are your photographs?'

'I'll show them to you another day,' Oscar said.

Breakfast with Paul was toast, and porridge made from rice. It tasted like sweet sludge, with no milk to thin it. Paul read the paper. Oscar looked at it uncomprehendingly until Paul gave him the English section. There was a telephone in the room, but Oscar waited until Paul had disappeared before using it.

He dialled a long number and after some delays a Scottish voice came on the line. 'Janice McPherson?' Oscar enquired.

'Speaking.'

Oscar introduced himself as a friend of a mutual friend. He was a writer, and he wanted to see how the Vietnamese were adapting to the camps.

'You mean you're a nosy journalist?'

'I do human rights research.'

'Don't say those words! Did you say you were an entertainer?'

Oscar's mind did a frantic shift. Once he had put on a puppet show for his daughter, and he could play 'Jingle Bells' on a recorder. 'I can tell good stories.'

'Right, you're the storyteller from New Zealand. Can you come on Saturday morning?'

Saturday was five days away. Oscar was keen to get into a camp that afternoon. 'Saturday's fine,' he said.

For the next few days he desultorily explored Hong Kong. Not being a tourist or a big spender, he found little to interest him. He stayed in Kowloon and watched a lot of television.

But the house was always busy. Apart from an intimidating cook who only spoke Cantonese, many young people came in and out. They held long noisy discussions, and Paul flirted cryptically with the girls. They treated Oscar with smiles and politeness. Were they students? Paul's acolytes? Oscar never found out.

On Friday morning May cornered him after a meek sweat on the exercise bike. 'You haven't shown me your photographs,' she accused.

They sat on Oscar's bed. May sat close, brushing his arm with her body, and occasionally nudging him. Oscar did not respond, but he did not shift away either. He showed her photographs of empty hills. He showed her a photograph of his house and the street he lived in.

'Whose car is that?'

'Mine.'

'You must be rich.'

'Most people have cars in New Zealand.'

'Where are the people? Are they hiding in their cars?'

'There aren't many people there. There's plenty of space. Clean air. Beaches to swim on.'

May considered, and calculated. 'I will come to New Zealand on my next holiday. I will stay with you.' She held Oscar firmly by the arm. 'Will your wife mind?'

It occurred to Oscar that May's intimate overtures would only ever be of the machine-gun variety. 'I haven't got a wife,' he said.

May looked perplexed. 'You must have a wife,' she said. 'You have photographs of your children.'

'She is no longer my wife,' Oscar explained. 'But my children are still my children.'

'You and your wife have stopped marriage?'

'Yes,' Oscar said.

But May could not comprehend. 'My mother and father are very old. They are married forever,' she said with a certain superiority. 'My mother is strong. She looks after my father.'

Oscar remembered a tiny stooped woman in the subway when he was looking for 8 Choi Hung Road at midnight. She was carrying an enormous bag stuffed with obscure vegetables, but she still offered to carry one of his . . . Maybe she had been May's mother?

'Women don't do that in New Zealand,' he said.

May brushed at him impatiently. 'What do they do then?'

'They work. They do all the things you probably do. They've just left out that particular item.'

A week later Oscar visited two refugee camps — and returned feeling not a writer, but a man overburdened with privilege. He lay in his room. He felt like a sham. He slept, being a person who could partially lose his problems in sleep, and by late afternoon he felt better. He showered, and was sitting in his underpants when there was a knock on the door.

'Come in,' he said carelessly, knowing it was May. He would keep living with his privilege. After all, what was the alternative?

'You are hot!' May gave an uncertain smile, and stared. 'You have a big build too.'

Oscar grinned. 'That's a nice way of putting it.'

'Pardon?'

'I have a big build,' he agreed. He pulled on trousers and shirt — an act he knew to be far more intimate than showing his passive nakedness. May watched from behind goldfish spectacles.

She pointed. 'Shirt hanging out.' And in case he had forgotten, she added: 'Clean socks. I will take you out to dinner.'

'Really?'

'A good restaurant near.'

'I need a drink,' Oscar said.

'Water?'

'No — whisky, alcohol.'

May consulted her watch. 'It is Happy Hour at Airport Hotel. You go with Father Paul. Be back by seven.'

'Ahh,' Oscar said. Happy Hour with Paul would be mostly unhappy hour. 'I'll give it a miss.'

'Coffee then? I'll take you to a strong coffee shop.'

'Okay,' Oscar said, lacing his shoes.

'Brush your hair,' May ordered. Oscar sported wet, flattened spikes. 'You look like Wild Man from New Zealand.'

She walked ahead of him through the ceaseless streets of Kowloon as if she did not own him. Enormous naked bellies of jets slid a few feet above the roof tops, in their drop to Kai Tak. Oscar thought how one well-placed bullet could bring the whole screaming mechanism down . . . He hurried after May.

She took him into a restaurant with FAST FOOD emblazoned upon its windows. The room was packed with young people wearing the same clothes as May — white shirt and stone-washed jeans. Eyes looked curiously at Oscar, then slid off politely. He squeezed into a midget booth with May, and burnt his lip on a cardboard cup of coffee.

Later they went to a murky restaurant off Choi Hung Road. May rapped on the glass of a fish tank.

'Which do you want?'

'You mean I have to eat one of those?' The fish looked very depressed.

'Very tasty. Very fresh.'

'Can't I eat something else?' Oscar asked.

'Of course,' May said. 'Many dishes.'

'Which one are you going to have?'

May pointed at an eel lying at the bottom of the tank. It appeared to be having a nervous breakdown. 'That,' she said.

'Will you eat it all?' Oscar asked.

'I will keep for my mother and father what I do not eat.'

The waiter seemed reluctant to catch the eel. There was a terse exchange in Cantonese, then he shrugged and fetched a net. Oscar went over to watch.

Despite its depression the eel proved difficult to catch. The waiter dipped and cursed, and the eel squeezed itself along the angle of the tank. Oscar admired its cunning.

Exasperated, the waiter plunged his arms in. The fish swirled in terror, and the eel shot malevolently into the room.

Its mouth was open as if it was about to shriek, and attack Oscar's socks. But Oscar shrieked instead, and danced off between tables. The waiter dived and caught the eel which, after its hungry lunge at Oscar, seemed somewhat confused. It went docilely into the kitchen.

There was applause. Oscar bowed — to more applause. Patrons

shook his hand. Streams of language poured over him. May laughed.

'You are funny. A good dancer . . . The eel dance!'

Oscar liked it when she laughed. All the briskness left her face.

'Poor thing,' he said.

'I shall order for you?' May asked.

'Yes please. Anything except eel or pig.' The roads of Kowloon were jammed with taxis, Mercedes, BMWs, and trucks of pigs screaming like humans.

Soup, vegetables, prawns and rice arrived. Oscar tucked in heartily. May's dish was unrecognisable as eel.

'I've been into the camps,' Oscar announced.

'You did not get lost?'

'Terrible places,' Oscar continued with relish. 'Today I visited an old factory. Filthy! Thousands of refugees locked in it. Children with sores on their faces. The men were cutting each other with knives . . .' Oscar paused. 'I was offered lunch.'

'Did you eat?'

Oscar shook his head. 'How could I? I'm overfed already. Terrible food. Mush. A dog wouldn't eat it.'

'A dog would not be given it,' May said practically.

'Nobody is allowed out — only the children. They go to school in buses.'

'I know that camp,' May said suddenly. 'It is not permanent. Soon they will go to a better camp.'

'They've been there for six months!' Oscar exclaimed. 'They're treated like criminals.'

'They cannot agree,' May said. 'The North Vietnamese do not want to live with the South Vietnamese. They must remain there until other accommodation is found.'

'Accommodation!' Oscar scoffed. 'Prison.'

He was about to race on, but May said quietly: 'We do not want them here, the Vietnamese. But it is not good. It is a problem.' She looked directly at Oscar. 'We have many family in China. My parents were born in China, but our family are not allowed to come to Hong Kong. If they come they are sent back. The police hunt them . . . But the Vietnamese are allowed to stay.'

Oscar fell silent. Then he said, 'I wish you would take off your glasses.'

'Why?'

'You've got pretty eyes.'

May was amazed. 'I have pretty eyes?'

'Take off your glasses,' Oscar repeated.

She did so. They laughed. 'You like a sweet?' May said.

Oscar's stomach was awash with green tea. He did not feel like floating anything more on it. 'No thank you. I will walk you home.'

'I walk *you* home,' May corrected.

Outside 8 Choi Hung Road she offered him her hand. Oscar laughed.

'What is funny?'

'I get tired of shaking hands,' Oscar explained, and kissed her cheek. May did not rear back, or cuff him as he might have expected. She looked at him with some interest.

Oscar kissed her on the mouth, expecting an adolescent's kiss — a mere rubbing of lips — but May kissed him with some passion. Oscar stepped back, surprised. He stooped again, but May shifted her face and giggled.

'Goodnight Oscar Rights,' she said.

During his last few days Oscar watched television and thought too much about May. He avoided the sticky streets, but the day before his departure he bought flowers for the cook, English biscuits made in China for Paul, and a lozenge of jade for May.

She did not appear.

'A concert tonight in the church hall,' Paul informed him. 'You are invited.'

'Thank you,' Oscar said. 'What sort of concert?'

'Music. Drama. Items by individuals . . . Much fun,' Paul added morosely.

Oscar went along diffidently. Paul introduced him to a string of people. Children and adolescents and grannies filled up the seats. For two hours Oscar listened to Chinese rock, hymns, and watched Shakespearean episodes. He scanned neat rows of heads but could not see May.

Paul clambered onto the stage and announced a dance. The rock band returned and people pushed back the seats.

It was time to go, Oscar thought.

He rose stiffly, and May hastened up to him.

'Oscar, you dance with me.'

Oscar felt injured. 'I'm going tomorrow. I've got a present for you.'

'I cannot see you tomorrow, Oscar. I can dance with you now.'

'Okay,' Oscar said. He supposed they would joggle foolishly on the floor; but to his surprise the band launched into a waltz. May held on to his arm, maternal, yet unsure.

'You can dance to this?'

'Sure.' Oscar was suddenly emboldened by his stature. He swept May onto the floor, and the other couples spread away nervously. May giggled and they whirled. She was so light, she was insubstantial in Oscar's hands. The crazy music went on endlessly, and finally Oscar dropped into a seat. May disappeared, and Paul introduced him to yet more people.

Then May grabbed his hand. 'Come and meet my father and my mother!' She pulled Oscar across the hall to where a tiny alert woman sat next to a battered old man. The woman gave Oscar a smile, and the man looked at him as if he smelt bad. Oscar was not particularly offended; in fact the old man looked familiar. Probably he was one of the men pissing in a park that Oscar had crossed a week previously. He had been foolish enough to wear his New Zealand shorts, and there had been sarcastic comments about his legs.

'My mother would like to dance with you,' May said.

The old woman laughed, showing a mouth of discordant teeth. 'No, no!' she wheezed. She shook her head vigorously. 'No, no!' And her husband added a look of contempt.

Oscar waved good-naturedly and backed away.

He busied himself with a quickstep, then May danced with a girlfriend while the band blasted rock 'n' roll.

It was waltz time again. The floor became crowded. Old couples clasped each other in a relieved and friendly fashion. Oscar and May danced on the spot.

'I like your dress,' Oscar said. It showed her small pale legs.

'You say so many things,' May laughed. She snuggled closer, and Oscar kissed her forehead.

'I'm going tomorrow,' he insisted, pressing his hand against her cheap noisy silk.

'You have told me that, Oscar.' There seemed to be a note of irritation in May's voice, as if she was going to be brisk and officious to the last; but when Oscar glanced down she gave him a smile of pure warmth.

He swallowed. 'What about my present for you?'

'I'm sorry, Oscar, I won't see you again.' May looked inspired. 'Take it home with you. Take it back to the woman who is your wife.'

TIM WINTON

BUSINESS

for Ed in exile

WEAVER WAKES EARLY, dresses with care against the cold, and goes down into the dark morning street. The cobbles are icy. Already he yearns for the septic warmth of the Metro.

On the suburban line, he feels a growing excitement, and in the arrivals hall of Charles de Gaulle he resists hopping from foot to foot like his three-year-old son. From the clot of shovers at the electric doors, he sees his old friend, Darkie, grinning, complete with Akubra and oilskin.

'Gawd, look at you!'

Hugging his friend, he smells the wide brown land in him, or imagines he does, and becomes miserable.

Back at the flat, Weaver's wife and son cling to the oilskin and knock the Akubra clean to the floor in a mad, laughing stampede.

Darkie opens a box of presents from home: a fruitcake baked by Liz's mother, Bushells tea, a gumleaf, family photos, some books.

'Paris,' says Darkie, looking out the window, now pale with fatigue. 'Paris.'

'My oath,' says the three-year-old.

Through the close grey streets of the Marais, Weaver takes his friend, rolling suitcase and all, to a small hotel. Women and children smile at Darkie who doffs his hat with a steer-like grin.

'I thought you said the French were pigs.'

Weaver clamps his lips around his teeth and takes him into the shabby lobby, bracing himself for the agonising routine of being deliberately misunderstood, but the thin, bald little clerk sees Darkie and bursts forth in English.

'Ello, and welcome!'

'Five hundred bucks' worth of lessons,' Weaver says to Liz in the afternoon while they wait for Darkie to wake. 'And it gets you nowhere. You try not to be offensive, you blend in, best you can, stand in front of the mirror trying to make your lips soft as morning croissants, and still they ignore you. And in *he* flies, not a word of the lingo, sticking out like a dunny in a desert, camera round his neck and giving them all "Bongjewer!" and they carry him upstairs on a bed of flowers.'

Liz smiles in a way he hasn't seen her smile for a year.

In the Concorde station, Darkie gives a busking flautist ten dollars worth of francs, thinking it was forty cents' worth.

'Ello, cooboy,' says a lithe Parisienne schoolgirl on the stairs.

The four of them go from museum to monument up and down the rue de Rivoli, lunch at Le Train Bleu, hit the Bastille market and wander in the Tuileries talking with wild ocker accents. Weaver's son Bob rides on Darkie's back. Behind her scarf, Liz laughs, and Weaver feels free, free and young and capable of anything, even being on the wrong side of the world.

He tries calling a café waiter 'mate' and his bubble bursts.

'I'm quitting my job,' Darkie says as they cross the Pont Louis Phillipe full of champagne and raw meat, with the evening lights tizzying up the murk of the Seine.

'Quitting the meat trade?'

'Jim's been fiddling the till. The company's about to disappear up its own vent and I reckon they're already looking for a scapegoat. Last on, first off. They'll crucify me for the sake of their good name, Jim and his old man.'

'But he's a friend,' says Liz. 'You're godfather to their kids.'

'You've been away too long. This is Perth we're talking about, city of enterprise converts. They're true believers now, you see. It's business.'

'So you're quitting before they can smear you?'

'They'll smear me anyway, but I want to pull the plug before them. Two weeks, I'll fly home with my letter.'

'Ah,' says Weaver, troubled. 'You'll fall on your feet.'

A gust of wind rips along the bridge, and Darkie is swallowed up by his Drizabone with only the weakest of grins.

Paris just keeps raining, so the four of them pack a bag and head for Brittany. On the train they sing old *Playschool* songs and wilfully frighten the French.

At St Malo, beneath great sea walls, they sweep down on the wide, tide-bare beach and take up fistfuls of sand.

'Been a long time,' Weaver says. 'Eh, Bob?'

'My oath,' says the three-year-old, zig-zagging up the beach with his mittens over his ears.

'You might have stayed too long,' says Darkie.

'Tell me about it.'

The rest of the morning, Weaver walks ahead of them, just within earshot of their laughter.

Alone in their shared room at the pension, Weaver finds a postcard begun by Darkie. *Dear Chris, I have never been so cold in my life* . . . He turns it over. Barges on the Seine between autumn-gilt leaves.

Liz and Darkie are downstairs playing pool while he watches Bob sleep. The sound of their clumsy breaks rings in the floor.

Bob sleeps on while the three of them fill toothglasses with Ricard and tap water and drink into the small hours with their backs to the heating grilles.

'We all go back a long way,' says Liz. 'Back down the dirt roads of the past, and no *business* will, no business, no business.'

'You're pissed as a stick,' Darkie says.

'We all are,' says Liz.

'We should be going out more,' says Weaver. 'Seeing more places. We keep darting into cafés for steak frites.'

'Parting tribute to the meat industry,' says Darkie.

'It's because our ears hurt,' says Liz.

'It's costing us a fortune,' says Weaver.

'Weaver's gonna sack us as friends and partners,' Darkie mumbles. 'Another rationalisation measure.'

'Sack me,' says Liz. 'But the cold hurts my ears.'

Weaver looks at them. They're more drunk than him; he's certain. 'Darkie didn't come twelve thousand miles to eat lousy Chernobyl steak in provincial towns.'

'He didn't come that far to have sore ears.'

Weaver pulls himself upright. 'Darkie, do your ears hurt?'

Darkie blurts a laughing spray of pastis all over him. Weaver grabs coat, scarf and mittens and finds the door.

Back in Paris, the sky is the colour of the cobbles but it doesn't rain. Bob takes Darkie to the Tuileries to collect horse chestnuts while Liz works at her queer poems and Weaver stares from the window out across the river. Without Bob he is lost in this town. He doesn't miss his job, and he doesn't begrudge Liz this late chance at a literary life, but he knows he has no business being here.

'Poor Darkie,' says Liz, coming to the window.

'He'll be all right.'

But Darkie comes home with his Visa card cut in two.

'Looks like they're on the move,' he says.

'You better move in with us,' says Liz.

There is only one bedroom, but Darkie doesn't argue.

Weaver lies awake sweating with desire, listening to the farmyard breathings of the little flat. He feels Liz's thigh in the dark. He hears Darkie mutter in his sleep down on the floor, and he takes his hand away. In the morning there'll be the concierge. And every morning.

Heading for the toilet, Weaver comes afoul of the horse chestnuts on the floor by Bob, and goes down roaring.

A man in a stockman's outfit and a man with plaster on his broken nose stand together at a bar called Le Petit Fer à Cheval, and a blonde, anorexic Parisienne comes on to the stockman. The man with the broken nose offers no help with language, but stuffs himself with ham and Calvados. In the middle of the night he scrambles across bodies and a nutless floor and heaves, poisoned, into the washbasin. He had no idea how integral the nose muscles were for this operation. His groaning wakes up the others and

214

they take the plumbing apart and put him to bed.

Bob sleeps beside Weaver who reads month-old reports of the VFL finals. They're out there seeing a movie, Liz and Darkie. He waits, punishing himself with thoughts.

There's snow falling when he goes outside. Weaver can't help himself — he chases after snowflakes, swats them with his mittens, mouthbreathing and causing people to stare.

> *I love her far horizons,*
> *I love her jewelled sea,*
> *Her beauty and her terror —*
> *The wide brown land for me . . .*

He sings, nasal and wild. He's never seen snow before.

He goes home to discover that the flat is empty, and he checks the bed for signs, actually peels back the bedclothes and checks.

Back in the street again, vendors pretend to misunderstand him, a flic eyes him suspiciously, and outside a kosher butcher's he stumbles through a fresh pile of chickens' feet and beaks, swept neatly into the gutter. Bloodied and plaster-nosed, he walks the streets and thinks of spiriting his son away. Darkie'd be flapping around in his Drizabone, tilting his hat somewhere in the snowfall, and Liz'd be laughing up into his open face. Oh, yeah, they go back a long way on the dirt road of the past, the Meat Man and her. He's a failed export exec with a pair of blue eyes and she's not literary enough to resist that.

Weaver gets drunk on Belgian beer in a café on the Ile St Louis and goes home sliding wet-socked through the mush.

Darkie is packed and red-eyed at the flat when he staggers in. So it's true, Weaver thinks, and he's showing some honour late in the piece.

'Scarpering, are we?' he snarls.

'They beat him to it,' says Liz. 'They've already been ringing around.'

Weaver sits down heavily. 'Bloody hell.'

'We'll see him right with money, won't we?'

'Geez, we were gonna go to the Alps. Arles. Places.'

'They've buggered me, mate,' says Darkie.

'They know you in Perth,' says Weaver. 'People know what you're like. They won't believe this. Perth people know a fair bloke when they see him.'

Darkie wipes his nose on his oilskin sleeve. 'You've been away too long, mate.'

'So where you headed?'

'Melbourne,' says Liz. 'We got him a flight through Hong Kong.'

'Hey, clown nose,' says Bob. 'You got blood.'

'Jewish chooks,' Weaver says.

The taxi grinds through the traffic with the Arab driver hissing at all passers. Weaver counts out some money for Darkie as they go.

'Who's Chris?' he asks.

'Hm?'

'I've been reading your mail. Dear Chris.'

'Oh, this girl I was going to marry.'

'And?'

'And now I'm not.'

'You knew all this would happen, didn't you?'

Darkie nods. 'Disaster amongst friends, remember the old motto?'

'Yeah.'

At the departure gate Weaver shunts the French out of his way to make room for Darkie.

'Tell me what happens.'

Darkie shrugs. 'You look after them two. And here.'

Weaver feels the Akubra squashed down on his head and the Drizabone thrown across his arm. Darkie goes without a wave, his ancient TAA bag flapping against his hip. Weaver turns snarling at the mob around him, and they smile back.

BIOGRAPHICAL NOTES

Entries are listed in the order of the authors' contributions in this book. The author's nationality is indicated in brackets; (A) for Australian and (NZ) for New Zealand. A selection only of published works is given. For more information the reader is directed to *The Penguin New Literary History of Australia* ed. Hergenhan, Penguin 1988; *The Penguin History of New Zealand Literature* ed. Evans, Penguin 1990; and *The Oxford History of New Zealand Literature in English* ed. Sturm, Oxford 1991.

(NZ) **Shonagh Koea** (1943) novelist and short story writer: *The Woman Who Never Went Home* (1987), *The Grandiflora Tree* (1989), *Staying Home and Being Rotten* (1992).

(NZ) **Lloyd Jones** (1955) novelist and short story writer: *Gilmore's Dairy* (1985), *Splinter* (1988). *Swimming to Australia* (1991) was runner-up in the 1992 New Zealand Book Award for Fiction and was shortlisted for the 1992 Goodman Fielder Wattie Award.

(A) **Kate Grenville** (1950) novelist and short story writer: *Bearded Ladies* (1984), *Lilian's Story* (1985), *Dreamhouse* (1987), *Joan Makes History* (1990).

(NZ) **Fiona Farrell** (1947) poet, novelist, short story writer. *Cutting Out* (1987), *The Rock Garden* (1989) — both as Fiona Farrell Poole; *The Skinnie Louie Book* (1992). Winner of *Sunday Times*/Mobil and American Express short story competitions; Writer in Residence, University of Canterbury, 1992.

(A) **Barry Hill** (1943) novelist and short story writer: *A Rim of Blue* (1978), *Near the Refinery* (1980), *Headlocks* (1983). National Book Council prizewinner with *The Schools* (1976).

(A) **Frank Moorhouse** (1938) journalist, short story writer, scriptwriter. Eight collections of short stories include *Room Service* (1985) and *Forty-Seventeen* (1988).

(A) **Beverley Farmer** (1941) short story writer and novelist: *Milk* (1983), *Home Time* (1985). Winner of NSW Premier's Award.

(A) **Michael Wilding** (1943) novelist, critic and short story writer: ten volumes include *The Paraguayan Experiment* and *The Man of Slow Feeling* (both 1985). Reader in English at Sydney University.

(A) **Fay Zwicky** (1933) poet, critic, short story writer: *The Lyre in the Pawnshop: Essays on Literature and Survival 1974-1984* (1985).

(NZ) **Nick Hyde** (1951) novelist and short story writer: *Earthly Delights* (1989).

(NZ) **Owen Marshall** (1941) short story writer whose six collections include *Supper Waltz Wilson* (1979) and *Tomorrow We Save the Orphans* (1992), which was shortlisted for the Goodman Fielder Wattie Award. Winner of many prizes including PEN Lilian Ida Smith Award for Fiction (1986, 1988) and the American Express Short Story Award; Robert Burns Fellow, University of Otago, 1992.

(A) **Elizabeth Jolley** (1923) novelist and short story writer: eight novels including *The Sugar Mother* (1988), and three collections of short fiction. Winner of the *Age* Book of the Year Award, the NSW Premier's Award and the Miles Franklin Award, and has received an AO for her contribution to literature.

(NZ) **Anthony McCarten** (1961) author of six plays including the internationally acclaimed *Ladies' Night* (with Stephen Sinclair), and short stories (*A Modest Apocalypse*, 1991).

(NZ) **Peter Wells** internationally acclaimed film-maker (*A Death in the Family*, 1986) whose first short story collection *Dangerous Desires* won the 1991 Reed Fiction Award and the New Zealand Book Award for Fiction in 1992.

(NZ) **Debra Daley** (1954) scriptwriter and journalist. 'A Bent Cucumber' is her first published fiction.

(A) **Murray Bail** (1941) novelist and short story writer: *Contemporary Portraits and Other Stories* (1975), *Homesickness* (1980) and *Holden's Performance* (1987). The former novel won the National Book Council Award and was co-winner of the *Age* Book of the Year Award.

(NZ) **Elizabeth Smither** (1941) acclaimed poet, novelist and short story writer: *The Legend of Marcello Mastroianni's Wife* (1981), *A Pattern of Marching* (1989), *Nights at the Embassy* (1991).

(A) **Lily Brett** (1946) migrated to Australia from Germany in 1948. Poet and short story writer: *The Auschwitz Poems* (1986) won the Victorian Premier's Award for poetry; *Things Could Be Worse* (1990), *What God Wants* (1991).

(NZ) **Norman Bilbrough** (1941) short story writer: *Man With Two Arms and Other Stories* (1991).

(A) **Tim Winton** (1960) novelist and short story writer: *An Open Swimmer* (1981), *Shallows* (1984), *Scission* (1985), *That Eye the Sky* (1986). Winner of Miles Franklin Award.

ACKNOWLEDGEMENTS

FOR PERMISSION TO reprint the stories in this collection acknowledgement is gratefully made to the publishers and copyright holders of the following: 'The Woman Who Never Went Home' from *The Woman Who Never Went Home and other stories* by Shonagh Koea, published by Penguin Books (NZ) Ltd; 'Searching for Road Signs on an American Highway' by Lloyd Jones, published by permission of Michael Gifkins & Associates; 'Meeting the Folks' from *Bearded Ladies* by Kate Grenville, University of Queensland Press, published by permission of Australian Literary Management; 'OE' by Fiona Farrell, published by permission of Glenys Bean Literary Agent; 'Fires on the Beach' from *Rim of Blue* by Barry Hill, published in McPhee Gribble by Penguin Books Australia Ltd; 'The Indian Bell Captain' from *Room Service* by Frank Moorhouse, published by Penguin Books Australia Ltd; 'At the Airport' from *Milk* by Beverley Farmer, published in McPhee Gribble by Penguin Books Australia Ltd; 'Kayf' by Michael Wilding, published by permission of the author; 'Stopover' from *Hostages,* Fremantle Arts Centre Press, published by permission of Australian Literary Management; 'Bang Bang' by Nick Hyde, published by permission of Glenys Bean Literary Agent; 'A View of Our Country' from *Tomorrow We Save the Orphans,* published by John McIndoe Ltd — the author acknowledges the use of the setting in V.S. Naipaul's *Finding the Centre: Two Narratives,* Andre Deutsch, 1984, for satirical purposes in his story; 'The Libation' from *Woman in a Lampshade,* Penguin Books Australia Ltd, published by permission of Australian Literary Management; 'The Bachelor' by Anthony McCarten, published by permission of the author; 'The Good Tourist and the Laughing Cadaver' by Peter Wells, published by permission of Michael Gifkins & Associates; 'A Bent Cucumber' by Debra Daley, published by permission of the author; 'From Here to Timbuktu' by Murray Bail, published by permission of the author; 'In the Blue Mountains' by Elizabeth Smither, published by permission of the author; 'Chopin's Piano' from *Things Could be Worse* by Lily Brett, published by University of Queensland Press; 'Eel Dance' by Norman Bilbrough, published by permission of Glenys Bean Literary Agent; 'Business' by Tim Winton, published by permission of Australian Literary Management.